A BUNKER 12 NOVEL

BOOK TWO: CONDEMN
The second installment in the post-apocalyptic saga

Three years have passed since the Flense spread with ruthless speed and stealth across the globe, decimating mankind before it could defend itself. The infected were turned into soulless creatures, Wraiths, which wreaked destruction upon anyone and anything in their path. A few thousand souls have remained safe, hidden away inside ten isolated bunkers . . . until a series of events forces them back out into the world.

After fleeing from the murderer taking refuge inside their shelter, a dozen survivors hope to find a mysterious twelfth bunker, where they believe a clue to Flense's origins may be found . . . and possibly even a cure. But while they risk becoming infected themselves, they soon find that there are far greater dangers than the disease and far worse monsters than Wraiths.

Make sure to look for the companion series
THE FLENSE

Hundreds die in a fiery train crash in northern China. A cargo ship smuggling refugees is lost to calm seas off Libya. Entire villages in Ghana are abandoned overnight.

Contracted by a prepper group to investigate a series of seemingly disconnected global tragedies, a young medical reporter, Angelique d'Enfantine, uncovers a disturbing pattern: each event is preceded by the sudden spread of a mysterious ailment and is followed by the appearance of a man dressed in black and silver who witnesses claim is the devil himself.

Each event is more grisly than the last. As the risk to her life grows, Angel begins to doubt that the tragedies are harbingers of an impending biblical catastrophe, but rather practice runs conducted by a fanatical organization bent on global annihilation. Could her sponsors be using her to advance their own paranoid agenda?

The story begins in China . . . .

ALSO BY SAUL TANPEPPER

GAMELAND
Deep Into the Game (Book 1)
Failsafe (Book 2)
Deadman's Switch (Book 3)
Sunder the Hollow Ones (Book 4)
Prometheus Wept (Book 5)
Kingdom of Players (Book 6)
Tag, You're Dead (Book 7)
Jacker's Code (Book 8)

Golgotha (GAMELAND Prequel)
Infected: Hacked Files from the GAMELAND Archives
Velveteen (a GAMELAND novelette)

Signs of Life (Jessie's Game Book One)
A Dark and Sure Descent (GAMELAND prequel)
Dead Reckoning (Jessie's Game Book Two)

Collections
Insomnia: Paranormal Tales, Science Fiction, & Horror
Shorting the Undead: a Menagerie of Macabre Mini-Fiction

Science Fiction
The Green Gyre
Recode: T.G.C.A.
They Dreamed of Poppies
The Last Zookeeper

Scan for more information:

website: http://www.tanpepperwrites.com
email: authorsaultanpepper@gmail.com

CONDEMN

BOOK 2 OF THE BUNKER 12 SERIES

SAUL TANPEPPER

BRINESTONE PRESS

PUBLISHER'S NOTE

This book is a work of fiction. Names, characters, places, and incidents either are the product of the author's imagination or are used fictitiously, and any resemblance to actual persons, living or dead, business establishments, events, or locales is entirely coincidental.

Published by Brinestone Press
San Martin, CA 95046
http://www.brinestonepress.com

Copyright © Saul Tanpepper, 2015

LICENSE NOTES

Set in Garamond type
Cover credit and interior design K.J. Howe Copyright © 2015
Images licensed from Bigstock.com and Depositphotos.com

ISBN-13: 978-1-51-960111-7
ISBN-10: 1-51-960111-5

There is no salvation

in the Flense

CHAPTER
01

"YOU THINK THERE'D BE MORE CARS ON THE ROAD," muttered Danny Delacroix as he steered the bus past a faded and dusty stop sign canted forty degrees off the perpendicular.

He felt Susan Miller's eyes boring into the back of his skull. She was seated in the first row behind him, leaning forward like she wanted to wrestle the steering wheel away from him at any moment. Like she didn't trust his driving abilities. He wondered what she thought about his coming to a full stop and checking in both directions before proceeding.

Such caution was certainly unwarranted. Theirs was the only vehicle on the road, the only one they'd seen in four hours of driving, and he really had no reason for following the rules at all. In fact, it was quite possible that the bus was the only operating vehicle in the entire world.

Force of habit. Funny how quickly the old behaviors come back.

It had been a long three years since he last sat behind a steering wheel. Three years since he'd even been out on the road. And yet, after only twenty minutes of driving, it felt as if it had been just yesterday. Like nothing had changed.

Except everything had changed. Life as he had known it was gone. Vanished in a touch and a puff of bloody mist. Human civilization had died. And here he was turning on his turn signal and checking the mirrors.

Stupid.

He willed Susan to go away. And yet, at the same time, he was glad for her company, even as uncomfortable as it made him feel. He needed to know he wasn't alone.

"I mean, where on earth are they all?" he wondered aloud.

"We're in the boonies."

"Here we are, yeah. But not back there."

"Home," Susan replied dryly. The sun and rain-rotted plastic crackled as she shifted on her seat, making the skin on the back of his neck prickle. "Dying is a very private matter, you know."

He turned to frown at her. He could have just glanced at her reflection in the mirror, but this particular comment warranted a more personal treatment. In the slanting rays of sunlight, the dirty tracks of her dried tears stood out from the pale skin on her face. He supposed his own appearance was just about the same. They'd all cried back there.

She ignored his stare and kept her eyes glued to the road ahead. They had turned onto a particularly flat stretch of cracked and broken blacktop that had, after years of disuse, faded to a silvery shade of gray. The pavement went on for miles through a barren wasteland of desert scrub, the surface sometimes disappearing beneath untouched drifts of sand or else vanishing into the folds between the silvery ripples of overheated air.

He recalled a memory from his childhood crossing over from Mexico, riding that "ribbon highway" in the back of the coyote's rusted lime green Toyota pickup truck, the tape deck blasting Woody Guthrie. He relived the sensation of the truck diving into the shallow swales and up the other side as they crossed the arroyos.

This landscape was just as bleak and desolate as the one he remembered, despite their being much further north now, closer to America's northern border. It certainly seemed just as hot and arid as he recalled it had been back then.

They had seen few homes since leaving Finn behind, just rock and scrub and a few collapsing structures that might have been warehouses of some sort in the past. Before the Flense.

And a few cars.

Not a lot of them, but certainly less than he expected. They sat along the sides of the road like hollowed out skulls, covered in thick layers of dust and sand. Weeds grew out of the places that trapped the windblown dirt and held water long enough for seeds to germinate. Where the paint showed through, it had faded away like the road signs.

More cars is what he'd expected. And more bodies.

"Death is a very personal matter," Susan explained.

"What's that supposed to mean?" Danny asked. He really didn't want to know.

"It means that when the shit hit the fan three years ago, when it kept right on hitting the fan and people ran out of places to run to for safety, they all just went back and parked their cars in their garages and driveways. They went inside their houses, locked their doors and drew their curtains. No one wants to die in public. No one wants to be seen with their bodies all messed up, rotting away, turning to soup. It's . . . embarrassing."

Embarrassing? he thought, more disturbed by her choice of metaphor than her characterization of behavior. But he realized that she had a point. He remembered coming across a van in the Sonora filled with the bloated fly-infested corpses of a family trying to escape the cartels in Columbia. The runners had run out of fuel. And instead of walking out into the desert to die, they'd shut themselves up inside the van and turned to mummies instead.

"Anyway," she said, "that's what I would've done, if I hadn't bought a spot in the bunker. I would have climbed into bed, probably with a shotgun, a four-pound bag of peanut M&Ms, and a Dean Koontz novel. And when the book was read and the bag empty, I'd stick the—"

"You guys mind changing the subject?" Harry Rollins asked, stepping quickly up to them. There was a look in his eyes, like barely contained sanity. Danny wondered if it was the same look in his own. They were all on that razor's edge, barely holding on. Barely maintaining.

Of course, it had to be worse for Harry. For three years he'd managed to keep his entire family, his wife and boys, safe from the Flense. Alive and uninfected inside the safe haven of the bunker. What were the odds of that? And then, to just set that safety and security aside one day to follow some kid out into the unknown . . . .

You did, too.

"No problem, Harry," Susan said.

"At least keep it down." He tilted his head to where the boys were sitting with their mother. "I think we've had enough of that kind of talk for now. For a lifetime, actually. Don't you think?"

This time, Danny used the mirror to check the people behind him. His gaze fell first on Bren Abramson and

Hannah Mancuso sitting together, the younger girl's head lolling on the older one's shoulder. Hannah's father, Eddie, sat alone a few seats forward of them. Despite his assurances that he wasn't contagious, it seemed that nobody wanted to be near him, not even his own daughter.

Or maybe he chose to separate himself from the rest on purpose.

But it was poor Bren that Danny felt the most pity. She had followed her boyfriend, Finn Bolles, out of the bunker. She'd left her parents behind, mostly because she thought she loved the boy. And then he'd gone and disappointed them all by changing his mind. He betrayed Bren's loyalty by leaving her without so much as a good-bye. He'd just disappeared while she was passed out with exhaustion.

Oh, how she'd fought them all when she woke.

Danny's eyes slipped over to Jonah a couple seats back. The boy, just a year older than Finn, was studying the landscape, drawing on his memories of the day they'd driven this same route from the evac center so he could guide them back there in their search for the mythical twelfth bunker.

He'd taken the brunt of Bren's tirade. She blamed him for letting Finn go, accusing him of driving him away with their petty fighting. She ordered him to turn the bus around.

But rather than try and reason with her or calm her down, Jonah threatened to leave her on the side of the road. He was just like his father, insensitive to other people's feelings, lacking in the tact department.

But it had worked. Bren soon relented and sat back down. Her silence worried Danny more than her protest, and Danny was relieved when Hannah went to comfort her. Hannah was an angel.

Now Bren stared out the window like Jonah. Unlike him, her face was slack and her eyes empty, seeing nothing. Well, there was nothing out there to see anyway. The tears on her cheeks had long since dried and her hair was a knotted mess by the wind coming in through the shattered window.

She's in shock, Danny thought. *We're all in shock, but she more than the rest.*

He couldn't imagine how hard it must have been for her to find out her father had had a hand in bringing about the end of the world, though they were all still unclear exactly how or what the man's specific role had been. Nevertheless, the choice that she'd been forced to make, deciding between staying inside the bunker with a murdering father versus accompanying the boy she loved out into a dead world tore at Danny.

He sighed unhappily and forced his eyes away. They drifted over the rest of the faces in the mirror. The group was down to seventeen now. Waking up that morning safe inside the bunker — or at least with the semblance of safety — they'd numbered nearly twice that many. Twenty of them had fled, leaving a dozen behind. Now, just six or seven hours later, they were already down by three.

How soon before we're cut to half? A quarter? How long before we're all gone, dead or scattered?

He was already regretting leaving.

Staying would have been worse, Danny. That's what Mamá believed. That's what she always said.

His gaze came to rest on Harrison Blakeley. The man sat alone, his head bobbing to an unheard tune as he fingered a song on his guitar without actually picking at the strings. Out of all of the adults, Harrison was the oddest, not showing the least bit of concern for their situation, and that was doubly incredible given the choice his seventeen-year-old son, Bix, had made.

What the hell kind of father would—

"Danny! Look out!"

He'd only been half watching the road ahead. They'd come up over a short rise and were beginning their descent into a shallow dip. Tearing his eyes away from the mirror, he saw too late that the ground at the bottom had eroded away during the rains, collapsing the road from underneath. The hardtop had buckled, throwing up a jagged edge of concrete. There was nothing he could do to avoid it.

The front tires hit, jerking everyone forward in their seats. He nearly lost his grip on the steering wheel. There were startled cries from the back.

And then they were ascending the other side.

The rear tires hit the seam with a loud crunch a half second later and threw everyone out of their seats. There were more cries and more than a few shouted curses. The baby started to cry.

"Anyone hurt?" Danny called out, pulling over to the side of the road. He switched the engine off and got out of his seat to check.

Jonah pushed past him looking worried. Someone shouted not to open the door. "I need to check underneath!" he yelled angrily back.

"Wait! There might be Wraiths out there!"

Jonah made a quick check around them through the windows. Fortunately, Danny had brought the bus to a stop atop the rising edge of the arroyo, and they had a decent view of the surrounding area. Nevertheless, there were still ample hiding places for the things to hide in.

"Has anyone seen any?" Jonah asked, challenging them. "Because I haven't, not since we left the bunker."

"You said there wouldn't be any out here at all," Danny reminded him. "You were wrong about that. Part of the reason we left was because we believed you."

Jonah glared at him for a moment, his eyes narrowed. "Yeah, I was wrong. I admit it. But there weren't any during all the times I spent outside fixing this bus."

"But now we know they're still around," Kari Mueller said. "So we—"

"We need to check that we didn't spring a leak or something," Jonah finished. "Sitting here arguing about it isn't wise. We need to get moving again."

"At least take someone with you."

"I'll be fine. Just keep everyone quiet." He pulled away from Danny and was out through the driver's door before anything more could be said about it.

Danny watched him disappear around the side. "That kid is suicidal," he muttered.

"Aren't we all?" Susan asked.

Danny frowned as he turned his attention to the passengers. "Anyone hurt?"

Most shook their heads. Blood trickled down Kari Mueller's cheek, but she shrugged it off when he passed her on his way to check on Jasmina Cardoza and her baby.

"Is he okay?" he asked the young mother.

Jasmina nodded up at him. "*Es sólo miedo*," she whispered.

"*Estara bien*," he automatically replied, before realizing they were speaking Spanish. "We're all scared, but it'll be okay."

There was fear in everyone's eyes to one extent or another, and he wondered yet again if they'd have been better off staying sealed up inside the dam complex.

Not with that murderer.

He turned to find Bren Abramson staring at him, as if she had heard his thoughts. He quickly averted his eyes. No one had come right out and said it, but he had to guess that others were thinking what he was, that they should have thrown Seth Abramson out instead.

Would have, if not for Bunker Twelve.

Now he wondered if that had been a ruse to get them to come out.

There was a short, shrill whistle. He found Jonah standing beneath a broken window. "One of the dualies popped," he said. "It's shredded, but we still got three more tires on this side, so we should be good for a while."

"Is that all the damage?"

"The rest of the tires are fine. We are leaking oil, though. Not a lot, but steady."

"Dammit," Danny cursed. "I'm really sorry. I didn't see—"

"It's not new. I tracked it back to where we hit. We were already leaking before then." He gestured that they should join him outside. "There's something else."

Danny raised his eyes past Jonah and scanned the surrounding landscape once more. Since leaving Finn behind, the terrain had slowly transitioned, become less flat, dotted by more scrub and scored with more ravines. Anything could be hiding out there. And with the sun so low on the horizon, the shadows were growing longer and deeper. "What is it?"

"Just come."

Harrison Blakeley stood up and strode toward the front of the bus, followed by Harry Rollins and Susan Miller. With a shake of his head, Danny trailed after them and made for the door. "Everyone else stay put," he said, then exited.

The group headed down to where the road had crumpled, perhaps a hundred feet away. Jonah led them. Harry and Susan kept glancing nervously about, just as Danny did, but Harrison's gaze and gait gave no hint of worry. He walked with his hands in the pockets of his threadbare jeans, apparently certain that they would not be attacked.

"What do you see?" Danny asked.

When they reached the bottom of the swale, Danny realized just how lucky they'd been. The surface of the road had cracked all the way across. One edge had risen up while the other folded underneath. Mud and other debris had washed into the gap, partially filling it with fine silt, which had dried into a crumbly clay. Deep ruts had been gouged out of it by the bus tires.

"Tracks," Harrison said. "Not ours."

He stood off the side of the road with Jonah studying a second set of tracks. They'd been dug out of the mud the last time it was wet. Harry bent down and snapped off a piece of the dried earth. "Wonder how old they are."

"Couldn't have been more than a few months."

"That means there are other people out here," Danny said. "And cars." He felt almost justified for his excessively cautious driving.

Harry stood up again and handed the dirt to him. "Question is, are they *nice* people?"

CHAPTER 02

"I SHOULD JUST LEAVE YOU HERE," FINN TOLD BIX.

"And be depraved of the gift that is my company?"

"You're depraved; I'm *deprived*. And gift is not the word I'd use."

Bix's laughter carried across the canyon and echoed back at them. Finn shushed him, stopping to listen. But all they heard was the sound of the wind blowing through the trees.

The river was too far below them for its roar to reach their ears, had been since late the previous afternoon. Finn was glad for it. He'd hated being so close to the rushing water. The noise had made it impossible to hear anything else.

"You need to keep it down," he murmured. "Something tells me once we get back up to the top, there may be trouble."

The two boys continued on in silence after that. Two full days had passed since leaving the bus behind, the wisdom of which had tormented Finn since the moment his feet hit the ground. But what other choice had there been? He couldn't expect the others to follow him. And how could they expect him not to go after Harper?

It had been hard — the hardest thing he'd ever done — leaving without telling Bren. He knew she'd want to come with him, and he couldn't let that happen. So he'd instructed the others to keep going, to find the evacuation center just as they had originally planned. It was their only hope of finding Bunker Twelve, answers to the Flense, and a possible cure.

"No arguments," he'd told them. "This is my choice, my duty, and no one else's. I need to know what happened to my brother. I need to know if he's still alive."

But then, every single step he took away from the bus, away from the safety it represented, had been utter torture for him. Loneliness fell upon his soul even while he was still in the vehicle's shadow, crushing him like a terrible weight. Yet he refused to change his mind. He refused to look up at the faces staring quietly down at him as he passed. He knew that if he did, he'd chicken out and get back on the bus. And he'd never be able to forgive himself for it.

He might even resent Bren.

The only thing that kept him going was knowing that Harper would not have second-guessed the decision at all.

One step at a time, that's how he went, counting silently. One foot in front of the other and his mind filled with hatred for himself for how angry he knew Bren would be when she woke.

He very nearly did turn around when he heard the bus start to pull away. He was blind to the road then, blinded by his tears, feeling as much as hearing the sound of the fading engine as it receded into the distance.

"Bang, you're dead," Bix said, grabbing him from behind and scaring the crap out of him.

"Jesus!" Finn spun around, expecting the bus to have returned. It hadn't. It was gone. "What the hell are you doing here?"

"Watching your back, apparently. I've been, like, three steps behind you for the past ten minutes."

"Does your dad know?"

"Of course, dummy! Everyone knows. Well, everyone except Bren, but she'll find out soon enough." He shuddered. "Glad I won't be there for that scene."

"Thanks for setting my mind at ease."

"Then my work here is done."

"You shouldn't even be here! You need to go back! You're supposed to go to the evac center!"

"Okay, I'll just sit here and wait for the next bus."

Finn gave him a dirty look.

"You're stuck with me, man, so let's move. I don't like being out here on the open road." He began to walk, leaving Finn to stand alone. "I think I saw a cutoff for the river up ahead. We might be able to save a bunch of time if we take it."

Finn turned one last time, in case the bus magically appeared. Then he ran to catch up with his friend.

"I hope you brought sunscreen," Bix said. "You know how easily I burn."

That had been the day before yesterday. They'd made good time, taking Bix's shortcut despite Finn's doubts. And by that first evening, they'd made it all the way back to the top of the gorge, where they made camp without a fire. Neither slept a wink that night.

The next morning, as soon as the sky began to lighten, they descended to the river, reaching it shortly after noon.

They were in desperate need of water by then and greedily refilled their canteens and their stomachs.

They had encountered no Wraiths along the way, though at times it certainly seemed like it wasn't for lack of trying. At least three times they'd forgotten themselves; their voices were loud enough to echo back from the opposite side of the canyon. Twice it was for arguing, one of those times over whose morning breath stunk worse, which really wasn't an argument, since they both agreed that it was Bix. The argument was more about what exactly it stunk like.

The other time, it was because they couldn't figure out how to jump start a car they found on the road. Bix had half of the wires cut and short-circuited beneath the dash before Finn thought to check to see if the battery had any juice left in it. It hadn't, so it didn't matter.

They'd spent the next hour after that arguing over who would've driven had they managed to get the damn thing started.

"I'm older," Finn reasoned.

"Have you ever even driven anything before?" Bix countered.

"Yes."

"Besides a golf cart."

"Then, no."

"Well, I learned how to drive when I was twelve. Dad had me running errands for him when he was doing his gigs. Cars, vans, trucks, motorcycles—"

"You know how to ride a motorcycle?"

"Yup. It's easy."

"Bet your mom loved that."

That comment had brought the conversation to an abrupt and uncomfortable end. Bix grew sullen, which made

Finn feel guilty for mentioning her. She'd left him and his father shortly before the Flense hit, so she was almost certainly dead. Or worse.

The next hour passed in silence.

"How far upriver did that guy say Bunker Two was?"

"I told you, about a hundred and eighty miles," Finn replied. They were getting close to the top of the canyon again, following the road as it wound through the trees. It occasionally drew them away from the river so they lost their view of the other side. He knew they were close to the top because the other rim was nearly at eye level.

"And how far do you think we've gone?" Bix asked.

"Since the bus? Maybe forty miles. But we're probably only about twenty miles upriver from the dam."

"Damn."

"Yeah, about twenty."

"No, damn. As in, 'Damn, that's all?' I'm not sure these shoes'll last another hundred and sixty miles."

"Soon as we find a store or something, we'll stock up on food and water, get us both some good walking shoes. There's bound to be something along the way."

The mention of water made Finn thirsty, and he pulled out his canteen. Despite their thirst the day before, Bix had expressed disgust at the idea of drinking water drawn straight out of the river, at least until Finn pointed out that they'd pretty much been doing that for the past three years anyway. The tap water in the bunker was just the same river water, only passed through metal filters which probably didn't do much more than get rid of the silt. And they both agreed it tasted much better than the stale bottled stuff they'd found in the dead car.

"Some shoes and some decent camping gear, too," Finn added. "Batteries, flashlights—"

"I'd rather just get some good driving gloves for the next car we find, which will be a Maserati, I think. Bright yellow. Oh, and a nice soft bed in a nice secure five-star hotel would be awesome. A hotel with a valet."

"You figure out how to start that Maserati and I'll personally get you the best damn driving gloves money can buy and put you up in a five-star hotel myself."

Bix snorted. "Post-apocalyptic Finn's a big spender—"

"Shh! Quiet!"

They pulled up short and listened.

"What'd you hear?"

Finn cocked his head into the breeze. "I thought—"

"There!"

Finn grabbed Bix by the arm and they made for the trees. The ground was covered in soft pine needles, and yet their footsteps sounded insanely loud to their ears. Dry twigs snapped beneath their feet as they hurried deeper into the forest. They soon found themselves climbing the steep slope to get out of sight of the road.

"Wait!" Finn whispered.

They pulled up behind a wide tree and crouched down.

"Wraiths?" Bix asked.

Finn shook his head and held his finger up to his lips. "We'd have never heard them," he said, keeping his voice as low as possible.

The Wraiths, terrible creatures with dead eyes, hunted their prey in complete silence. They moved with a ghostly stealth and speed that seemed inhuman.

Except that they were human. Or, they had once been.

Three years ago, the Flense had spread with the same stealthy speed that characterized the creatures it infected. Having never seen anything like it before, everyone was caught unawares. The infected didn't appear dangerous to people, they just seemed in a strange sort of daze. They walked right up to their unsuspecting victims, and all it took was a single touch to pass on the disease.

If it hadn't been for his father's quick thinking, Finn would have become one of them.

A lot of the creatures took to walking on all fours, using their hands for stability. It made their movements seem awkward. But when they ran, they ran upright, still jerkily, but with such reckless speed that it was terrifying to behold.

The only time they broke their silence was right before and after they became enraged, when their need to pass on the infection was somehow overcome by their need to kill. In that altered state, they became ravenous creatures, fearsome and merciless. In such a state, they would not stop until they had utterly destroyed their human prey with their teeth and nails. They would devour flesh and bones and hair — sometimes, even, clothing — until nothing was left but a few tattered remains, a large puddle of blood, and fragments of tissue.

When confronted by a Wraith, a person had two choices: submit and become one of them, or resist and be torn to shreds.

"It sounds like—" Finn began.

"*Horses!*" Bix hissed and pointed through the trees. "It's horses! And people!" He stood up and started running down the slope before Finn could stop him.

He caught up to Bix in time to see the lead horseback rider pull back on his reins. The man shouted at them to stop, but their momentum carried them forward, tumbling through the dead litter. The man moved quickly, raising his arm into the air. Finn caught a glimpse of a gun pointed directly at Bix's head.

"No!" he shouted and pushed his friend away. It was all he managed to do before the world exploded. A hot white fog overtook him, searing his skin and eyes with a flash so brilliant that it blinded him.

Pain engulfed his mind, became fire. Then ice.

Then came the darkness.

CHAPTER
03

DANNY WAS BACK BEHIND THE WHEEL AGAIN WHEN they arrived on the outskirts of a small town. The dozen or so former business establishments seemed to huddle together along the main strip, as if in mutual self-preservation. The road was one of two cutting through the town, and where it met the other, a dead street light hung, tugging heavily on fraying wires.

It was late. The sun had gone from being a giant white spider's egg sac to a rotten pumpkin sagging beneath its own weight on the porch of the horizon. Night would soon follow, and they were in need of shelter and food.

Jonah's mood had been sour for two days. It began after Danny bottomed the bus out. They'd had a hard time getting it started again.

Jonah eventually found a blockage in the air intake manifold and the engine started right up after it was cleared. But by then it was nearing dark and they were forced to make camp on top of the bus, as far off of the desert floor as possible.

Thirteen miles. That's all they'd managed to drive since discovering the old tire tracks before the engine quit once more. The next day, they decided to do a thorough systems check, as they didn't want to drain the battery with multiple attempts to restart it. Before they knew it, night was descending once again.

Their diligence had paid off, however, as the bus roared convincingly to life the next day, but their caution also came with a price. Both food and water were depleted, and the oil level was dangerously low. Jonah fretted over the leak like a mother hen.

To make matters worse, the poor baby, Jorge, had come down with a terrible cough that kept them all awake through the long night. They feared that the noise would draw Wraiths to their location.

He had likely caught the bug from Jonathan, one of the guards they had discovered hiding in the tunnel by the dam. In the beginning, they'd simply dismissed Jonathan's cough as a consequence of the horrible conditions under which he had been forced to live. Maybe it was. And maybe the baby suffered from the same condition. But the wet, drowning sound and the ugly green phlegm evoked memories of the terrible flu pandemic which had stricken the world two years before the Flense.

Danny slowed to a stop at the edge of the town and let the bus idle in the middle of the road. "What do you think?" he asked the others.

It was the first real evidence of civilization they'd encountered since leaving Finn and Bix behind at that paltry highway pullout. But if the buildings raised their chances of finding other survivors like themselves, it also raised the threat level. Where there were houses, there had once been people. And where there were once people, there might still be Wraiths.

The closest building was a small single-story home. Its yard had overgrown with weeds that had since choked themselves into a thick brown scab. The white paneled sides were rendered gray with dust and turned brittle from the heat and sunlight. Several of the boards had slipped, exposing the rotting wood underneath. During the rainy season, mold grew on the roof, but it had long since dried, staining the shingles a dark greenish-brown. Fingers of thistle and sage curled over the sides of the rain gutters. Cataracts of dust and cobwebs filmed the windows nearly opaque.

To Danny's alarm, he realized the curtains were all drawn behind them. Recalling Susan's words, he pictured the houses filled with dusty corpses.

Or worse.

They'd have died by now. They're not immortal. They live and breathe and need to eat just like us.

But hadn't that been the very same reasoning Jonah used to convince them they were all gone? He shuddered, as if trying to dispel from his mind the image of those terrible things crawling about inside those decrepit homes, patiently waiting week after week and month after month for someone new to come along to infect or eat.

He turned in his seat and asked again what to do.

Jonah rose. He carried an empty backpack and a heavy metal rod for self-defense, should it be necessary. "We need food, shelter, water," he said. "And motor oil. And gasoline."

"What do I do with the bus?"

"Just pull up next to the intersection and park it there. Don't turn it off. We'll sit a bit and see if anything comes out to welcome us."

"You know, there'll probably be cars here," Kari Mueller said. "We could swap this monstrosity for smaller vehicles, maybe a couple pickup trucks. Or a van or two."

"Bus would still be better," Jonah replied. "It's big enough to hold all of us. And it's higher up off the ground. Easier to defend."

"But the windows are broken," Kari countered. "And if it fails again like it did back there, we'll be completely stranded."

"She's got a point," Harry Rollins said.

Jonah made a face.

"We know you fixed the bus and all, and we're grateful, but—"

"Fine. Kari, you and Harry see what you can find. Cover the right side of the street; we'll cover the left. Gather all the food and water you can. Also look for guns and ammo, weapons. Danny, you'll be with me. We're looking for motor oil. If we're lucky, we'll also find gasoline in sealed tanks."

"What about us?" Nami Thuylan asked, gesturing at the other two ex-guards, Jonathan Nash and Allison Markle. He looked worried, like if they didn't participate, they'd get tossed to the curb. "We said we'd pull our weight."

"Jonathan's in no condition to be out there," Harry said.

They all turned and looked toward the back of the bus where the man lay shivering on the last seat. Another series of muffled coughs rose up from beneath the pile of old coats.

"Medicine, too," Jonah quietly added to their list. "Antibiotics, if possible."

"We'll use them," Nami said, "but I don't know about Jon. Before the Flense he was one of those homeopathic types, never believed in modern medicines. Was always into herbs and natural healing. He told me he lied on his job application, otherwise they never would have let him work."

Jonah scowled. "Time for him to change his tune. If he's contagious, he puts us all at risk. And that baby sounds like he's getting worse, too, so whatever we can find will go toward helping us all."

"You still didn't answer my question," Nami said. "What can Allison and I do?"

Jonah turned to Harry. "You stay here with your family and the rest of the group. Nami'll take your place. Keep an eye out for movement. If you see anything, take the bus and leave. Just go."

"And leave you behind?"

"If we hear the bus going, we'll know something's up and we'll hunker down until things clear enough for you to return. Assuming it's Wraiths—"

"What else would it be?"

"Assuming it's Wraiths," Jonah repeated without answering, "you'll draw them out of town. Hopefully." He pointed to the hatch in the roof of the bus. "If for some reason you can't leave, climb up on top. Shout to let us know you're in trouble. This town is small enough that we should hear you."

He turned to Kari and Nami. "Make sure to stay together. Watch each other's back. Return before it starts getting dark."

Danny hesitated shutting off the bus, then twisted the key. The engine chugged and coughed, then wheezed into silence. Not a one of them didn't utter a silent prayer that it would start up again the next time they needed it.

A few minutes passed, then Jonah gestured to Danny and they stepped off. Each of them gripped a heavy metal pipe in their hands.

Harry watched them go, then turned to Kari. "As much as I thought the boy's father was an arrogant jerk, and even disliked Jonah himself for acting the same way, I have to admit he has some redeeming qualities."

Kari reluctantly nodded. "He's decisive, assertive, capable. I just worry about the choices he makes. That was Jack Resnick's biggest failing— he was reckless when he got emotional. And stubborn."

She plucked a couple sturdy weapons from the stack on the seat by the door and handed one to Nami, who handed over his pistol to Harry.

"Whatever you do," Nami said, "fire that only as a last resort. It seems to trigger the change in them." Then he and Kari followed Jonah and Danny into the town.

Harry nervously fingered the cold metal on the barrel of the gun, feeling the places where rust had begun to etch away at it. Nothing infuriated a Wraith more than the deafening blast of a gunshot. Nothing made them attack with greater violence.

He prayed he wouldn't have to use it.

* * *

Danny would much rather have been anywhere other than where he was, standing on the porch outside the door of an abandoned house. He felt like bolting back to the bus and, indeed, his gaze did flick up the road to where it was parked. Fifty yards, he estimated. He could cover it in about ten or fifteen seconds.

"Hey!" Jonah hissed. "You with me?"

Danny's attention snapped back. "Yeah."

Jonah raised his pipe and nudged Danny back as he tried the knob. It was locked. Nevertheless, the door yielded when he pushed on it. He gave it a good shove and it popped open. The splintering on the jamb around the deadbolt was proof enough that someone had smashed through it before.

Someone, or something.

The air inside smelled musty.

Jonah knocked the pipe loudly against the door frame a few times and waited, cocking his ear and leaning slightly inside.

Danny shook like a leaf. He really, truly did not like this. It was really dark inside the house. Too dark.

"Okay, come on," Jonah whispered. "If anything's in here, it would've come out and attacked us by now. Shut the door behind you."

He stepped confidently into the middle of the room, then disappeared into the next before Danny had taken two steps. Danny cursed under his breath, but Jonah reappeared with a chair in his hands. He wedged it beneath the knob. "So they can't get in," he said.

"And we can't get out."

"Just kick it out of the way if we need to leave in a hurry."

"Easy for you to say." Danny wasn't sure he'd be able to remember under pressure.

"Open the curtains. Let in some light. Come on, Danny, snap to it. We need to hurry."

They went room by room, opening and inspecting cabinets. They spent the bulk of their time in the kitchen and garage, giving the bedrooms a cursory check before moving on.

But the small house had clearly been scavenged already, and there was nothing of any use. Danny was relieved that they hadn't found any bones in any of the beds, but he was also disappointed that there was no car in the garage.

"Guess Susan was wrong."

"About what?" Jonah asked, as they moved onto the next building.

"Nothing."

They checked four more houses and what looked like had been a general store before the sky grew noticeably dimmer. All they'd managed to collect was a few cans of dog food and a two liter bottle of cola that the solids had long since precipitated out of. They decided to take their chances and stuck it in the pack to bring back with them.

Kari and Nami returned to the bus a few minutes after them. They had had better luck, finding more food and water, as well as a few bottles of motor oil in a dusty shed. They had brought it back, though Jonah said it wasn't enough to last them the twelve or so more hours it would take to get to the evac center. Yet despite their relative success, their mood remained solemn.

"Didn't find any cars, just a truck without an engine in the maintenance garage," Nami quietly said. He glanced grimly at Kari, who echoed the look. "Looks like it had been stripped clean of useful parts."

"So much for people going home to die," Danny grumbled to himself. He didn't seem to notice the frowns it brought him.

After the food and drinks had been doled out and the children and some of the adults had returned to their seats,

Mister Blakeley drew the scouting parties together. "Spill it," he quietly told Kari and Nami. "Yes, I noticed. What'd you find?"

"Blood," Kari finally conceded. "In the automotive shop. Lots of it."

"*Old* blood," Nami clarified.

"I think we'd better get used to seeing it," Jonah said. "Or did we forget what it was like at the end?"

Nobody answered right away.

"It was more than just blood," Kari said. "There were chains attached to the walls. It looked like someone had locked people up inside and then—"

"We don't know that," Nami quietly told her. "We don't know what happened in there or why."

But Kari pressed on. "The blood wasn't new, but it wasn't three years old, either. And I don't know if they were Wraiths or uninfected people that had been chained up. I can't imagine why anyone would do that, but it's pretty damn clear that something not . . . not nice happened in there."

Jonah stood up. "I want to see for myself."

"It's almost dark!"

The sun had now slipped completely below the horizon, and shadows covered the land, filling the canyons between buildings with a cold, dead silence. The inside of the bus itself had grown dark enough that the figures sitting just a few seats away were little more than huddled shapes.

"I'd rather check tonight and know better what we're dealing with than to spend the night wondering."

A pair of flashlights was all they had for illumination, but he didn't want to take them from the other passengers. He disconnected the cell phone from the bus's charger and tested the light from the screen. It would do for what he needed. He said he planned to be gone no more than ten minutes.

"You coming, Danny?"

Danny swallowed dryly. "I should have known you'd want company."

CHAPTER

FINN CAME TO WITH A START. AND A POUNDING headache.

And immediately threw up the dried nuts he'd eaten for breakfast into the pine needles beside him.

"Smooth move, bro," Bix said, wiping the splatter off his hand onto his pants. "Blech."

"What happened?"

"Try not to move," someone else replied, a woman. She had a thick southern accent.

Finn attempted to get onto his feet, then decided it was too soon and sat back down again. His head spun. The pain was already receding, though it left his head feeling—

Itchy. Like my brain itches.

"What the hell happened," he asked again.

"We thought y'all was feral," a male voice replied. "Soon's I heard the shout, I knew y'all wasn't, but by then I'd already pulled the trigger."

Finn raised his head from his hands and squinted up at the strangers. The itchy sensation was gone now too, vanished in a flash as if nothing had happened. Even the pain, focused around a growing lump on his forehead, felt more and more distant.

Before him stood a man and a woman. They appeared middle aged, or so he guessed in the evening twilight. Both carried a certain toughness about them, a ruggedness that spoke volumes about how they'd managed to survive the past three years in a world that had gone to hell.

Their clothes — jeans and denim jackets, leather gloves and boots, cowboy hats, bandanas about their necks — were functional without being showy. Both also wore multiple sidearms strapped to their hips.

They stepped forward and kneeled down, giving Finn a better look at them. The man was clean-shaven. The woman had her hair pulled back and braided down to the middle of her back. They both had smile lines at the corners of their mouths and eyes, the latter twinkling with concern in the day's dying light. Concern and not a little amusement.

Finn leaned instinctively away from them.

"It's cool, man," Bix reassured him. "They're cool. They didn't mean to hurt us."

"Y'all hit yer head," the man said, his voice even thicker with accent than hers. The woman raised a hand to touch the knot on his forehead, then withdrew it when Finn flinched away again.

"What the hell did you shoot me with?"

"Stun gun," the man replied. He patted his hip. "Sorry, but I had to do it. Y'all know how it is. Shoot first and ask questions later. Ain't the only way to avoid getting the feral, but it sure is the quietest."

"Feral? What's that?"

The couple gave him a strange look. "The sickness," she said. "Don't tell us y'all don't know about it."

"You mean the Flense?" Bix asked.

The man and woman exchanged glances. "Ain't heard it called that in years," the man quietly said. "Since the televisions and radios stopped reportin. Y'all been hibernatin in a cave all this time? And how come y'all ain't got no weapons sides those measly walkin sticks? Those things ain't no good if'n you get surrounded." He looked at their packs and shook his head. "No food, little water. Where y'all come from?"

"The d—" Bix started to say.

"We had a place," Finn quickly jumped in. He gave Bix's arm a warning squeeze as he struggled to his feet. The throbbing in his head and the sick feeling in his stomach flared, but only momentarily. The others stood with him. "It was safe for a while, secure, but it's not anymore. We had to leave."

"Y'all's alone?"

Finn nodded.

"And just wandering about? Got no place to go?"

Finn didn't answer. He didn't know these people. They looked kind enough, but he didn't trust them. Jonah's warning came back to him about being more afraid of the survivors that had been left behind than of the Wraiths. Of course, that had been when he believed the Wraiths were all dead.

Finn wondered briefly how the other survivors were getting along. He winced at the thought of Bren being alone, but he was heartened to know that they would have reached the evacuation center by now.

"Not talkin, eh?"

"No offense," Finn said. "But . . . ."

"Sure, we get it," the man said, nodding good-naturedly. "Don't we, Jen, dear?" The woman nodded. "It's only natural to be 'spicious in a world such as this one done become. Trustin no one's the best way to stay alive and not taken with the feral. Course, havin friends helps, too." He winked.

"We're looking for his brother," Bix blurted out.

"Bix!"

"Well? Maybe they can help."

Finn shook his head.

"We'd be happy to," Jen said. "We know these parts pretty well. Which way did he go?"

Finn pressed his lips tight. How could he explain what they were doing and where they were going without giving away too much information? "We think he's upriver, maybe a hundred or so miles."

"Y'all are talking about Canada," the man exclaimed. "Or what used to be Canada, anyway. The land gets pretty rugged up that way, and once you start hittin towns and such, y'all are gonna start runnin into real trouble with the ferals."

"We can handle ourselves."

"Not sayin otherwise, son. But like my Jenny said, we know this part of the country. We know where it's safe to wander. Well, safer, anyway. And we know where it's not safe at all."

"You're going north, we can help," Jen said. "Our home's along the way. Y'all could rest up with us, sleep in a real bed instead of on this hard ground, while we figure out a plan and get y'all outfitted proper-like."

"Now, Jen dear, don't go puttin no pressure on the boys." He turned to them and smiled. "She gets the strong motherin instinct, even though she's already gots two of her own at home to look after."

"They're all grown up, Adrian. Wouldn't call them boys no more. But y'all sure look like you could use a decent meal."

The man rolled his eyes. "Here it comes. Y'all better just run away right now, before she gets on a roll. When she does, she'll start talking about cookin and feedin and, fore y'all know it, she's tryin to fatten you up with her deep-fried chicken."

"Fried chicken?" Bix said. He looked over at Finn with hunger in his eyes. His stomach growled.

"Ain't the half of it neither, son. She makes a right sinful apple pie." He patted his ample belly.

"Apple pie? Oh, man. Finn, maybe—"

"Wait," Finn said. A part of him wished where they were going was in the opposite direction so he'd have a reason to say no. But he also longed for what the couple were offering: a place to rest, home cooked food — *fresh* food — a real bed to lie in with real sheets, a house with windows and fresh air. And someone to tell them what to do and how to go about doing it. "It's Adrian, right? How far are we talking about?"

Adrian scratched his chin thoughtfully. "Hmm. What do y'all think, dear? Sixty, seventy miles?"

She shrugged. "Only twenty if'n they take the footbridge."

The man gestured at the horses behind them. Finn noticed that both animals had a pair of leather scabbards, one on either side, and each scabbard held a shotgun. There were also large packs balanced on their rumps. "Cain't take them across. Wouldn't be possible."

"No, but one of us can ride around with one of the boys. The other ones can take the bridge. We'll meet up on the other side. Them boys won't make it walking the whole way round."

"You know I don't like splittin you and me up, Jenny, specially not now with all the recent activity."

"Activity?"

"More ferals lately. Been trying to figure out where they's comin from."

"Well, we can't just let them go by themselves, neither, Adrian. They won't last long."

"More Wraiths?" Bix echoed. He looked worried. "Finn?"

Finn shook his head with indecision. There was no way he was splitting up. And the proposal to do so just felt shifty. Besides, if they did, he feared Bix might end up telling them more than he should. The couple might truly be able to help them, more so if they knew more details, but he just couldn't get the feeling out of his head to be careful around them.

You're just being paranoid.

Maybe so, but if and when they shared their story, Finn wanted it to be on his terms, not theirs.

"We're not splitting up," he told them. "And I don't think it's fair to expect you two to do so, either. Nor is it fair for us to slow you down. Show us where this footbridge is, and we'll take it across. Give us directions and we can meet you two on the other side."

He paused, before adding, "And thank you for the invitation. It's very generous of you to offer to help us, we being complete strangers."

Jennifer nodded. "I think that's best, don't you, Adrian?"

Adrian slapped his knee. "In that case, we'll make camp before it gets dark."

Finn looked around. "Somewhere a little flatter maybe?" He could see himself rolling down the slope toward the road in his sleep.

Adrian patted Finn's shoulder. "Yer a natural born leader. Sharp, adaptable."

He leaned over and placed his other arm around Bix. Speaking in a low voice that they were all obviously meant to hear, he said, "And I do believe you have just made my Jenny the happiest woman this side of the Miss'ippi."

CHAPTER
05

THE FIRST WRAITH FOUND THE BUS SHORTLY AFTER
Jonah and Danny left to check the garage.

The light had failed much more quickly than any of them
had expected, and the passengers had gathered near the front
to watch for their return. They strained their eyes into the
gloom and silently implored them to hurry up. When the
scratching came at the back door, one of the Rollins boys
wondered if that might be Jonah and Danny. He was
reaching for the handle to open it when Hannah started to
scream.

Harrison Blakeley was there, and he pulled her tight
against him, his hand clamped over her mouth. *"Be still!"* he
whispered.

The creature pawed again at the door.

More soon followed, appearing out of the shadows
stretching across the road behind them. Bren let out a stifled
yelp and jumped out of her seat when a hand appeared at the
window beside her. She stumbled across the aisle, pointing
and whimpering. Skeletal fingers, the skin pale and shiny,
curled over the half-pane, leaving greasy streaks on the glass.
The nails clacked against the metal, sounding like rattling
bones.

"What do we do?" Fran Rollins hissed. *"Harry— Oh my god! There's more coming! What do we do?"*

He pushed her and the boys into a seat on the right side of the bus, where the windows were mostly intact, and told them to get down out of sight.

Harrison Blakeley made his way up the aisle at a crouch and urged everyone to keep absolutely silent. "Get down. Don't let them see you. No lights. No noises."

A Wraith scratched at the front door, as if it knew this was where it might get in. Nami sat near the front. He watched it in frozen horror, though he couldn't see it very well because of the shadows. It appeared to have caught the Flense recently. Its skin showed minimal sag, and its arms weren't as emaciated as he'd seen before.

Maybe it's been eating well.

It pressed its cheek against the glass. The skin was a pale shade of gray. It still had most of its hair.

The creature stepped back, giving him a clearer view of its body, and he shuddered. Most of its clothes had fallen or been torn off. Dark brown blood covered it from chin to genitals. Its eyes glistened like obsidian pools.

A second joined it, this one significantly more emaciated. With hands that were more claws than fingers, its nails twisted and yellow, this one was made of the stuff of nightmares. Flayed ribbons of flesh, whatever had been its last meal, clung to its lips.

"Be quiet," Kari whispered to the girls, Hannah and Bren. They'd squeezed into one of the seats and were hugging one another. "Get down on the floor and hush."

She passed them to help with Jasmina and the baby. The poor woman had not let go of Jorge since they'd left the bunker, and the child's silence now troubled her. But she saw him give a weak kick. He seemed to sense the group's need for silence.

"Are you okay?" she asked, kneeling down next to them.

Jasmina nodded. Her body was visibly shaking.

Something scratched the side of the bus just below their window, eliciting a chirrup of fear from the woman. Kari gestured for her to get down onto the floor, urging her to move slowly. Then she got up and went back to check on the girls, keeping as low a profile as possible.

"We need to warn Jonah and Danny," Nami told her, meeting her halfway up the aisle.

"How?"

He shook his head. "I don't know, but there are more coming. There must be seven or eight out there now. And it's dark enough that they might not see them until it's too late."

"No!" Harry said urgently. "We need to go!"

"We can't just leave them out there."

"That's exactly what we need to do, Kari!" He gestured about them, accidentally rapping his knuckles on one of the seat support posts. The sound drew a fearful hiss from several people. "We're endangering ourselves and them by not doing anything. You heard what Jonah said. He told us to leave, to draw them away."

Nami nodded. "If they hear the bus start up, they'll know. They'll find someplace to hide until we can come back."

"We can honk," Kari tried. "Warn them. Then we pick them up as we pass the garage."

"They may no longer be there!" Harry shook his head. "They've had more than enough time to check the place out and come back. Something happened and either they're in trouble, they're holed up, or they know we're in trouble. Either way, we have to leave—"

The silence was suddenly broken by an explosion of coughs. The noise swept through the bus, which shook from the force of Jonathan's fit.

"Dear lord," Fran whimpered. "Someone help him! Make him stop."

But it was too late. Drawn by the noise, the Wraiths at the front door began to move along the side of the bus, at first slowly, then with increasing speed. Their movements went from passive curiosity to a sort of frantic excitement. They patted and scratched at the metal.

Then, all at once, they began to growl.

"It's happening!" Harrison said. He stood up then, not bothering to stay hidden anymore. "We need to leave now!"

"The roof!" Susan said. "We can go up onto the roof!"

"There's no time!" Harry shouted. Both of his boys were moaning in terror, and Fran was crying. Hannah and Bren were babbling on the floor. "They'll climb up there!"

"Give me the keys!" Harrison snapped. "Who has the keys?"

"Danny had them! He drove last!"

"What the fu—"

"No no! I've got them!" Kari yelled, pushing her way past them and diving into the driver's seat. The Wraiths tracked the noise and rushed to the front. They tried to climb onto the hood. From the cries behind her inside the bus, Kari knew that more were trying to climb up into the broken windows.

"Go!" Allison screamed. "*Gooooo!* Oh my god! They're coming in! Help!"

Kari fumbled the keys trying to fit them into the ignition. She wondered why they hadn't just left them in there to begin with. She could hear people running around behind her, could hear them crying out, shouting. Someone screamed. She heard the soft smack of something hard hitting flesh, the distinctive sound of bones splintering, the sound of glass shattering. Someone fell.

"Hurry up! *Hurry uuuuuup!* Oh god, hurry!"

She shoved the key into the ignition, but it twisted in her fingers and fell into the darkness at her feet.

"Oh no! Hannah! Don't touch her! Get away! *Go go GOOOO!*"

Don't touch who? Kari's mind screamed as she swept her hands over the surface of the floor. They hit the keys and knocked them into the step beside her left foot. "I dropped the keys!" she screamed. "I need light!"

"Allison! Oh no! *Allisonnnnn!*"

"Get away from her!"

Something slammed onto the roof of the bus. Everything seemed to stop for a second. Everyone froze and looked up. They all heard the scuttling noises. There was a scream, and Fran Rollins shouted, "They're climbing the telephone poles! They're on the wires!"

"Go! Get out of here!"

Another crash sounded overhead.

"There's more!"

"Get away from the windows! Bren! Hannah!"

"Daddy! Help!"

Kari found the keys and leapt back onto the seat. She almost lost them again, then shoved the damn thing into the slot and turned it. The engine roared to life. She shifted into gear and the bus leapt forward, nearly stalling. "Lights!" she screamed. "Where are the goddamn lights? I can't see—"

The bus slammed into a curb, then hit the light post.

"We're stuck!"

"Get her out! Get her out!"

"How?"

"Hit her! Push her out with the—"

"It's Allison!"

"She's gone! We can't save her! Now! No! Don't touch her! Get back! Don't touch her!"

"You can't!" Allison screamed. "No! Please don't make me go!"

"Oh god. Don't kill her."

"She's gone, Jasmina! No! Get her away. Get away!"

Kari yanked the shift into reverse and gunned the engine. She could hear people falling behind her as she backed up. She twisted the wheel to the right and aimed for the center of the street, toward the paler gray between the darker walls of the buildings. The engine screamed in protest, then bucked and nearly stalled.

She could feel the Wraiths behind her, crawling over the outside of the bus, working their way inside, getting at them. She knew that Allison was already gone, had somehow been touched and had only minutes left before the Flense took hold of her mind and turned her into one of them.

"Get off the bus!" someone shouted. "Allison! Get off!"

"No! I won't! You have to help me!"

"You have to go!"

"Daddy!" Hannah screamed. "Another one's coming in!"

There was an explosion of a gunshot and a flash of light reflecting off the windshield, blinding Kari for half a second. Then another gunshot.

"Alli— Oh my god! *You shot her!*"

"I had to! Go go go!"

The bus roared past the garage, and as they went, Kari thought she saw Jonah's and Eddie's faces. But she couldn't be sure.

The fight wasn't over behind her. She could hear more glass breaking as the metal pipes they had brought with them were used against the creatures. Metal slammed into glass and against more metal. The men shouted, directing each other. Susan shouted. There was a another sickening thud.

Kari wanted to turn around. She *needed* to turn around and see. "What's happening?" she screamed.

"Anymore? " Harrison yelled. "Are there anymore?" He sounded out of breath.

"I don't— No. No!"

"Stay alert. Spread out. Watch the windows! Hannah, get away from there!"

Kari kept driving, caroming from one side of the road to the other. They passed the last structure and the landscape opened up in front of them, glistening in the starlight. The road became a silver vein, straight and unbroken.

Behind them, the inhuman things that had once been human gave chase, loping along on naked feet, somehow running faster than any human — or anything that had once been human — should be able to.

The survivors, men and women and children alike, wept. They wept because they were still alive and untouched. They wept for Allison, whose lifeless body lay folded over the window frame through which the Wraith had reached her. The hole in her skull from the bullet Nami had fired sprayed blood against the side of the bus and onto the road, leaving a trail.

Nami sat beside her, not daring to touch her. He sobbed for the woman he had secretly loved.

Still weeping, he pulled off his belt and wrapped it around her ankles like a lasso. Then he pulled it tight and canted her out the window. Nobody came to help him; nobody came to console him.

He turned his eyes away from the pale lump in the road. He didn't want to see what the Wraiths would do when they reached her.

In his mind, he was already imagining it.

CHAPTER

WHAT JONAH SAW IN THE WAREHOUSE HAD DEEPLY troubled him, but by the time they exited the shop twenty minutes later and headed for the bus, his mood had significantly improved. The search had yielded a better-than-expected outcome. In his arms were two cases of Penzoil SAE 5W-30 weight motor oil. In his estimation, it would be enough to get them to the evac center.

He had to be careful carrying it. The cardboard holding the plastic bottles had gotten wet at some point and was flimsy, threatening to disintegrate at any moment.

Danny followed along behind him with a case of radiator coolant. He had suggested to Jonah that they come back for it in the morning, reasoning that at least one of them should have their hands free in case they encountered trouble. But Jonah didn't want to leave it behind. It was only fifty yards to the bus, and he was pretty sure the town was completely empty, despite what they'd just seen inside the shop.

But the moment they stepped out onto the street, he knew he'd been wrong. Again.

"Shit!" he whispered. *"Go back, Danny!"*

He spun around, nearly losing the oil as the sides of the box began to fail.

"What fo—" But Danny saw the Wraiths converging on the bus. He ducked back, sucking in air in alarm.

"Get back inside!"

As soon as they were in the shop again, Jonah set the cases on the counter, not bothering to chase the loose bottles that avalanched onto the floor. Danny set the coolant beside them.

"What do we do?"

"The warehouse," Jonah said. "Get in the warehouse."

Danny's face went white with fear. He didn't want to go in there, not again.

"We've got no choice. It's the only place we can secure the doors."

Their arrival twenty minutes earlier had been through a smashed front door. The glass was scattered everywhere, and the brick which had done the job lay in the middle of the mess, half buried beneath a season's worth of dead leaves. Evening was rapidly bleeding the sky of light, but there was still enough coming in through the opening and the row of dusty windows in each of the three rolling gates for them to make their way around.

As Kari and Nami had reported, a single vehicle occupied the maintenance section of the building. It was parked in the central repair bay. The ancient heavy-duty pickup truck sat like the empty shell of a giant terrapin, its hood propped open and nothing but a dark, empty space in the engine compartment staring out at them. For some reason, the sight gave Danny a chill.

Jonah aimed the light from the cell phone down through the engine compartment and into the shadows in the pit below. Something moved, either a number of small things or a single large one with multiple appendages capable of reaching into the far corners of the space. He stepped away in fright before letting out a nervous laugh. "Rats," he said. "I can hear the babies."

The animals' claws made dry, ghostly sounds as they scraped against the cement floor.

He reminded Danny to look for oil, then made his way over to the supply shelves. Danny glanced back into the pit, his pulse still pounding in his temples. He knew Jonah was right about the rats, and yet his mind kept conjuring images of other creatures lurking in the darkness. His ankles felt suddenly much more exposed than he wanted.

"Nothing here," Jonah said in frustration. Most of the boxes had been torn open, their contents clearly rifled through by other people in the past. "Brake pads and hoses, filters. Random bits and pieces. Nothing we can really use."

"I think we should come back in the morning, Jonah."

"Don't you think it's strange that there aren't any tools? This place has definitely been picked clean."

"Here's the drum," Danny said. He'd edged his way back toward the front, to where there was more light. He gave the metal barrel an experimental tap. "Might be oil. Sounds like it might be half full."

Jonah joined him, frowning. "No easy way to pump it out without electricity. Keep looking."

He found the doorway to the warehouse behind the supply shelves, propped it open, and went through. A solitary window, high up in the wall, provided almost no light.

Danny stepped up beside him. Air whistled through his teeth. "Let's get the hell out of here."

The room was large and mostly empty. A single wooden chair sat in the middle. It was turned onto its side. Small piles of garbage collected in the corners. Ropes and chains hung from the rafters.

"There's nothing here, Jonah. Come on."

But Jonah was already making his way around the room, peering closely at the dark stains dripping down the walls. He stepped carefully over the dried pools on the floor. He stopped by a set of chains bolted into the wall and rattled them with his pipe. Thick blood caked the links, stiffening them. He could smell it, the rotten coppery tang. Dried blood and clumps of something that might've been flesh or fabric. And clumps of hair.

"Jesus," he whispered.

"Jonah, we need to go."

The splatter pattern reached to chest height, hinting that whoever had been bound there had either been shot or hit hard enough with some object to cause serious damage.

He crossed back to Danny. The look on his face was pale and grim. "You're right. There's nothing here. Come on."

Danny let out a sigh of relief. "Right behind you."

"One last place to check, though." Jonah's voice sounded pinched, and for once he looked scared. He headed back into the shop. "Give me a hand with the truck first."

"The truck? Why? It's useless."

"I want to check out the pit underneath."

"The rat's nest? Come on, Jonah. It's almost dark. We'll come back in the morning."

"We're here now. It'll only take a minute."

"There's nothing under there."

Jonah faced Danny. "When I was in high school, I used to hang out where my older brother worked at a body shop. They would keep supplies down in the pit, although it was against safety regulations. I think I saw something down there. I need to know."

Danny watched him in disbelief, anger rising up inside of his chest as the reckless teenager pulled open the driver's side door. The released emergency brake let out a loud thud that reverberated through the shop. He wanted to smack Jonah.

"Go ahead and give it a push back, Danny. Careful you don't fall in."

Danny did as asked, and the truck began to roll back. After it had gone about eight feet, Jonah then pressed on the brake. The pedal sunk immediately to the floor, but the truck kept rolling.

"You're going to crash!"

Jonah leapt out. He pushed Danny out of the way, then heaved a tire from an old stack under the rear wheel of the truck before it could slam into the metal supply shelves, where it would raise one hell of a racket.

The vehicle hit the tire, bounded forward, and came to rest a few feet away.

"That was close."

"That was stupid!" Jonah hissed. "I should've checked the brakes first. I should've realized they'd be dead!"

"Can we just check the pit and get the hell out of here?"

They found the oil and coolant, along with a half dozen bottles of wiper fluid that had half evaporated away, as well as a full toolbox. But the tools were pneumatic and therefore useless to them.

Rats scurried out of a nest they had built in a ragged tarp dumped there, They ran about the pit floor, squealing in fright, then dissipated into the drainage vent and the sewer beneath the floor.

By the time Jonah and Danny stepped outside with their supplies, the sky had gone from yellow-gray to deep purple and was edging on black. Neither had spoken again about the blood and chains in the warehouse, but it had weighed heavily on their minds. Jonah was excited about the oil, and both were eager to return to the bus for their own separate reasons.

Except that the bus was under attack.

Now they were stuck inside the nightmare warehouse. Daylight was gone, and the only barriers between them and the killer beings outside were a few thin walls and questionable doors. They had no weapons, no food, and no water. And they had limited light.

The bus's motor roared to life in the distance. The gears crunched, then there was the sound of a crash. A moment later, the engine's whine rose as the bus approached the shop.

"We can run for—"

"Sit down, Danny," Jonah hissed. "They'll come back for us."

Afterward, once the silence and darkness swallowed them up again, Danny lowered his face into his hands and quietly sobbed.

* * *

They slept little that night inside the cold, empty warehouse. In fact, other than the hour or two when Jonah managed to doze off while seated against the door to the automotive shop, neither of them spent all that much time doing much of anything but pacing as quietly as they could.

The darkness and silence were infuriating, driving them both to imagine ever worsening fates for the bus and its occupants, each one more grisly than the last. With each hour that passed without their friends returning, their hopes grew dimmer, their nightmares more horrific.

"I can see you."

Jonah had set the chair upright on the floor and was leaning on the back of it. He looked over in the direction where Danny's voice had come. "What?"

"There's light."

Danny materialized out of the shadows, a vague shape taking on the familiar form of the man. He pointed toward the ceiling, where a dull gray rectangle glowed in the wall— the warehouse's only window. "Morning's coming."

"About time."

"I don't know how much more waiting I can take."

"They'll be back once the sun's fully up," Jonah said, but he didn't sound too sure of himself. "Just sit tight."

"Where do you think they came from? The Wraiths, I mean. One minute there were none, and the next they were all over the place."

Jonah had been wondering that same question through the long night. If it were true that they had been in this place all along, hidden away inside the ghost town buildings while he and the others had walked unknowingly among them, then it also had to be true that the Wraiths had waited for nightfall to attack the bus.

He just couldn't accept that.

But neither could he dismiss it outright, and so he struggled with the uncertainty all night. The fear was like a living thing crawling over his skin, scratching at him, trying to find a way inside. He kept trying to push it away, to keep it from entering. He knew that once the fear entered, it would take hold on his mind, and then take over. He couldn't let it.

The Wraiths had to have come from somewhere else. Perhaps they'd been drawn across the desert by smell or sound. Or perhaps simply by coincidence.

It was no coincidence.

Where had they come from?

The only logical explanation was that the Wraiths had followed the bus all the way from the dam.

No, not possible. How could they travel all those miles in just a few days? Those things are still human, after all.

Except they weren't human. Not anymore. He'd seen what they were capable of, both in the days before arriving at the bunker and the day they had escaped from it. The Flense turned people into something else, something both superhuman and inhuman at the same time. People became creatures with abnormal strength and resilience. They lost all constraints. They consumed with a hunger that seemed insatiable, yet at the same time they seemed not to require food or water at all. They ran like animals, covering ground faster than any human being possibly could. They jumped higher and climbed better. They could suffer more injury, seemingly without pain.

So maybe it really was possible that they had tracked them all the way from the dam, maybe even following the strong scent of the burning oil.

Running nonstop at six miles per hour, they'd need only forty or fifty hours to cover the hundreds of miles the bus had traveled.

It would be a grueling pace for any human, but maybe not for a Wraith. And the numbers worked out with uncanny precision.

If that were so, then it could also explain where they had come from to begin with and why he hadn't seen them in the weeks he had spent outside the bunker fixing the bus.

They followed Micheal Williams down the river. They're the infected from Bunker Two.

And if all that were true, and they had followed the bus, then they would have met up with Finn and Bix on the road.

And there was no way the boys would survive an encounter like that.

CHAPTER
07

"OH MY GOD!" BIX EXCLAIMED. "ARE YOU FREAKING nuts? No way am I crossing this!"

Finn frowned. "I'm supposed to be the one afraid of heights, remember?"

He reached forward and slapped one of the metal cables on the bridge. It barely moved, proving that the structure was solidly anchored, as if the thick aluminum posts embedded in concrete weren't enough to convince them.

Three years of neglect had had no noticeable effect on its integrity at all.

"We're not going to fall, Bix."

"Well, ain't gonna lie," Adrian said, and gave the boys a wide grin at the irony. "It's possible y'all could fall."

Full introductions had been made the day before, which is when they discovered Adrian was really *Father* Adrian Bowman. Despite knowing he was a religious man, the boys were reluctant to entrust more to him than their names.

The woman's name was Jennifer McCoy.

Father Adrian pointed at a metal cable running eight feet above their heads. "Used to hook people up to that in case they slipped. But we ain't got no harnesses."

"It's not the fall I'm worried about," Bix said, peering over the edge. "It's the landing. That's a long way down."

Adrian handed his reins over to Jennifer and got off his horse to join the boys. "I done crossed this bridge dozens of times myself. It's perfectly safe. Nothin to be skeered of." He gave the boys a mischievous wink. "Long as y'all don't look down."

"Adrian!" Jennifer scolded. "Don't go scarin them like that. You boys don't listen to him. He likes to tease."

"It's all right, Miss McCoy," Bix said. "Like I said, I ain't crossing it."

"Ain't?" Finn said. He was beginning to lose his patience with him. "Fine, I guess we'll be walking an extra forty or fifty miles out of our way then."

"The reverend will cross over with you, won't you?" Bix said. "I'll go with Miss McCoy. We'll be fine."

"It's Jennifer, please. Or Jenny."

Since rising that morning, it had seemed to Finn that Bix was paying her an inordinate amount of attention, feeding her an unending stream of flattery that bordered on blatant flirtation. Finn kept waiting for Father Bowman to get angry, but the man seemed as amused with Bix's hapless attempts to curry Jennifer's favor as she appeared to relish in the attention. "I think yer partner there's tryin to sweet talk his way into the lady's heart," Adrian confided to Finn along the way.

"More like trying to sweet talk himself into a permanent seat at her kitchen table."

The man had laughed heartily, though quietly. It was a wheezing sound, nearly silent. Both he and Jennifer were always careful to keep their voices down. They never dropped their guard.

As they rode along on the horses or walked alongside so the boys could rest, they always kept a hand on the stun guns in their hip holsters and their eyes constantly on the trees about them. They listened intently both before and after speaking.

They had made their night's camp soon after Finn felt steady enough to walk. There was still ample daylight left but, as Adrian said, it was better to settle in with light to spare than to enter the darkness ill-equipped.

Both boys found their preparations fascinating. The couple picked out their spot with utmost care, quietly weighing the strategic advantages and weaknesses of the location. They then established a wide perimeter around a central point, which would be their campfire, and they strung bare wires about them using the trees as posts. One was at shin height, the other two feet higher. To these, they added motion sensors.

"The alarm is a siren," Adrian explained. They had learned that the noise confused the Wraiths — ferals, as they called them. Simultaneously, flashing spotlights would be triggered, which had a similar effect on their senses. Then, around the outside on all sides, they carefully placed claymore mines.

The setup was powered by a pair of twelve volt batteries, which they unloaded from the packs balanced on the horses' rumps.

"Don't touch the wires," Adrian warned. "Not unless y'all enjoy gettin a little juiced." he clutched his sides as he laughed, as if the image were hilarious. The boys exchanged uncertain glances before chuckling. "And don't step outside the wires, neither."

"Don't pee on the wires, either," Bix whispered to Finn. Jennifer snorted in amusement, bringing a grin to Bix's face.

"You shouldn't encourage him," Finn told her.

The couple took turns keeping watch; not a minute passed when one of them wasn't prowling the edge of the campfire. Bix slept like a baby, but Finn couldn't seem to settle down. And despite his offers to take a turn guarding the camp, neither Jennifer nor Adrian would hear of it.

They had set out early the next morning after disassembling the alarms and traps, and it was then that the boys learned how the pair had settled in at a sprawling ranch on a small lake about a day's hike north of where they were.

The ranch had been a hunting lodge before the Flense, probably owned by some television celebrity. It was empty when they found it, free of Wraiths because of its remoteness and the ten-foot rock wall surrounding the compound.

"You live there alone?"

"Us and the boys, Billy and Luke," Jennifer told them. "But people come and go all the time. Father Adrian ministers to them as needed."

They had installed electrical wires along the wall as an extra precaution after moving in. There were additional measures for security, which Adrian promised to tell them about later.

To Finn, the place sounded like an impenetrable fortress, and once more the specter of worry raised its uninvited head. He hated that he was being so paranoid.

"With that kind of protection, why leave?" he asked. He was curious what they were doing so far away.

"Tryin to figure out why there are more ferals lately," Father Adrian reminded them.

"And we have to gather food and supplies, of course," Jennifer said. "But then there's also our work."

"Work?"

"Figurin out how to rid the world of the sickness," she explained. "What else? That sometimes means leavin the safety of home behind."

"A scientist and a minister? How does that work?"

She smiled. "First, I ain't no scientist, though I do take a more logical approach." She shrugged. "Adrian's way is more . . . ."

"Spiritual," he said.

"He believes the ferals can be saved."

"Y'all make the best of what yer given," Adrian said. "I am the good Lord's instrument."

Finn turned to Jennifer. "Have you had any luck?"

"Some," they replied together.

"We were trying to figure it out, too," Bix said. "Inside the dam—"

"Cabin," Finn quickly interjected. "The dam cabin we were in. In the woods. But we're not scientists either, and we never got very far. Do you have any idea how the Flense, you know, how it works?"

He hoped Bix picked up on his caution. The last thing he wanted to share was what Seth Abramson had told them a few days before.

"Well, like I said, I ain't got no formal scientific schooling," Jennifer said. "I know about medicines, bein as I worked in a pharmacy. But there's school learnin and there's life learnin, and I've lived a lot of life these past three years. We know, for example, that these stun guns can do more than just slow them down. The shock seems to block their ability to infect."

"Really?" Finn asked, surprised.

Both Adrian and Jennifer nodded. "That tells us something, right? Once we figure out how to completely stop them from spreadin the disease," she went on, "then maybe we can cure the poor souls."

"Physically *and* spiritually," Adrian added.

"That'd be truly awesome," Bix remarked, sounding more and more like he was possessed with the spirit of Scarlett O'Hara. The fake accent had initially amused Finn, but by the time they reached the footbridge, it was really starting to grate on him.

The sun was fully up, though a chill still lingered in the air. The cloudless day promised to be a hot one.

"We're sticking together," Finn said, putting the subject to rest. "No splitting up."

He stepped out onto the narrow metal grate that formed the base of the bridge and bounced on it. It felt as solid as the ground.

"Either we both cross here, or all four of us go all the way around. I don't know about you, Bix, but I'm tired of sleeping on the ground." He stretched, and his back gave an audible pop.

"I slept just fine," Bix countered, though Finn could tell his resolve was weakening.

"Course y'all did," Jennifer said, winking at Finn. "Nothin like fresh air and sleepin out neath the stars. But I bet a real bed sounds real nice, don't it?"

Bix gave the gorge a wary look.

"We get back early enough, I might even have time to cook us up a decent meal."

"Fried chicken?"

"Maybe tomorrow. How does fresh bacon and eggs sound?"

"Oh my god. Bacon? Seriously? You guys promise to meet us on the other side? You won't ditch us?"

Finn rolled his eyes.

"Truth be told," Adrian said, "we're actually real fortunate runnin into y'all. We're in the middle of a project at the ranch and could use some strong hands fer a day or two. That sound like we're gone ditch y'all?"

"What kind of help?" Finn asked, suspiciously. "And what do you mean by a couple days?"

"Two days at the most," Mister Bowman assured him. "We're in the middle of raisin a new barn."

"His church," Jennifer said, drawing air quotes with her fingers.

"The last one collapsed. We really could use some strapping boys in gettin the sides up."

"And the fence needs repairin," Jennifer reminded him.

"Fence always needs repairin. But I cain't ask fer yer help on that. Not unless y'all decide to stay a bit longer."

"I don't know . . ." Finn began. They hadn't discussed spending more than a single night.

"Y'all are eager to be movin on. We get that. But give us a couple days, three at the most, and we'd be much obliged to return the favor."

He turned and addressed Finn directly. "Y'all must see how ill prepared you are for the challenges ahead."

Finn hesitated before nodding. Seeing the precautions the couple took to protect themselves told him that he and Bix had been lucky that their first encounter had been with nice people instead of Wraiths.

"Then it's agreed? We meet up again on the other side. Tonight we dine in style!"

They told the boys which roads to follow after crossing, and provided them each with a stun gun and a rifle to share between them. "Doubt you'll be needin either. We done cleared out the other side of the river a while back, but those things do move about. And with the activity lately, it's better to be safe than sorry."

Finn watched them go, then turned toward the cable bridge. He expected to have to pull Bix onto the structure by force, but his friend was already twenty feet out and moving steadily toward the other side.

"Guess I know what to bribe you with from now on," Finn called over to him, and set a foot onto the walkway. "Bacon."

"Bacon or Scooby snacks. Or Cheetos."

Finn's stomach growled. He grabbed the metal cable rail and began to follow. "Least you could do is wait for me."

CHAPTER

"I'M OUT OF BULLETS!" NAMI SHOUTED, KICKING THE dead Wraith off the roof of the bus and onto the hood. It hit with a sickening crunch, bounced, then slid off onto the ground.

Another shot rang out, this time from the rear of the bus. Nami looked back in time to see the Wraith, a shallow, bloody notch carved out of its skull, reaching out for Kari. It almost looked like it was pleading with her not to shoot it again.

But then it bared it teeth and began to pull itself higher.

Kari drew a foot back to kick it, but the creature suddenly disappeared, pulled down by another climbing up to get at them.

The children huddled in the middle of the roof of the bus, near the hatch they had used to climb up top. Eddie Mancuso stood between them and Nami, guarding the group from any Wraiths that might scale the sides, while Harrison Blakeley and Kari protected the back.

"You out?" Nami called.

"One more!" Kari shouted back. She held Jonathan's pistol with both hands, waiting for another Wraith to breach the top.

"Make it count!" Nami said, and turned back. Susan stood with him, stomping and kicking at the skeletal fingers as they searched for something to grab onto.

Kari had driven them five miles out of town before stopping to see if the Wraiths would follow. They had, appearing in the distance on the moonlit road just over twenty minutes later.

What had happened back in the town shocked them all, and they were still unable to process that Allison was dead. Or that they had left Jonah and Danny behind. They had no idea where to go or what to do.

"Go back," Susan told her. "We need to get Jonah and Danny."

Kari started the bus up again and shifted it into gear, but instead of turning around, she drove on, putting more distance between them and the town.

"Did you hear me?"

"We need distance," Eddie said, drawing Susan away. "Thirty, forty miles."

"Why the hell for?"

"Because we don't know what's happened to the guys. We may have to search for them, and that'll take time. Plus, we're in seriously bad shape." He pointed at the oil pressure gauge. "Engine's heating up. We need that oil Kari and Nami found, and that'll take time, too."

"We *think* we found," Kari clarified. She didn't sound so sure anymore.

They arrived at another crossroads about twenty-five miles outside of town, and there ensued another argument. Kari preferred to avoid another encounter with the creatures, whereas Susan was all for running them down.

In the end, they decided to take the side road and return from a different direction rather than risk heading back the same way.

They waited for three hours at the intersection, keeping the engine in idle as they didn't dare to shut it off again, before the first ones showed up or the horizon.

"Don't those things ever give up?" Hannah asked.

Nobody answered or challenged Eddie when he turned onto the side road.

They had less than five miles to go when the bus hit a deep sand drift and became mired.

Eddie, Harry, Susan and Kari got off to dig them out, while Nami, the two teenage girls and both Rollins boys climbed up onto the roof to keep watch.

The desert shone with an eerie silver light beneath the nearly full moon, but eventually clouds began to form, erasing what features they could discern.

"Hurry up guys," Nami hissed down at them.

Three times they returned to the bus. Three times they tried to drive out of the drift. Three times they failed.

Nami and the others had just climbed back topside when Bren detected movement a hundred yards away. "Oh my god! They're here! They're coming!"

All but Jonathan managed to make it onto the roof. He was too sick, too weak to move, despite the others pleading for him to hurry. They held the hatch open, but then his coughing abruptly stopped, and they knew the Wraiths had made it inside the bus.

Their only consolation was that the sky was beginning to lighten by then. Blessed morning was creeping across the desert. If it hadn't been for the advantage the light afforded them, the Wraiths would surely have taken them within minutes.

"We can't hold them off forever!" Kari yelled.

"How many are there?"

"I count seven," Eddie said, hurrying over to kick another one loose. The bus rocked as the creature lost its grip and fell off.

The shift caused Nami to lose his footing. His legs were already weak with fatigue, weaker than the others because of his three years hiding inside a dank cave and perpetual near-starvation conditions. He simply had no stamina. He fell to his knees and found that he simply had no more strength to stand up again.

"Behind you!" Kari shouted. "Get up!"

Something grabbed Nami's boot and pulled. There was a *snap!* and a bolt of pain tore up his leg. "Help me!" he screamed.

Without thinking, Susan grabbed his arms to keep him from sliding off. There was nothing to plant her feet onto. She leaned back but began to slip as another Wraith climbed up, using its companion as a bridge.

"Let go of him!" Harry yelled. He jabbed at a Wraith pulling itself up from one of the bus's windows. It snarled at him and slapped the weapon away, sending it flying to the ground nine feet below. "Jesus Christ, Susan, let go of him! He's going to bring the rest of them up! Let go!"

"No!" Nami shrieked. "Oh, god. No! I'm not infected!"

His knee hyper-extended, twisted the wrong way. One of his hands slipped out of Susan's grip, and he began to slide over the side.

"I'm sorry," Susan said. She shook her head. "I can't hold you."

"Noooo!"

With a roar of defiance, Eddie leaped over the huddled children and landed hard on the roof beside Susan. He grabbed Nami's flailing hand and pulled. Susan fell back, letting go to catch herself from tumbling over the other side of the bus.

Eddie lifted Nami by the arm, drawing the two Wraiths up with him, and lashed out at them with his foot. One fell immediately, slamming into the dirt. The second emitted a vicious growl and lunged at him.

Nami's body twisted as he tried to avoid being touched. He screamed in pain and grabbed at his dislocated shoulder.

The Wraith let go and scrambled onto the slick surface of the bus. A half second later, it regained its feet and charged. Eddie let Nami fall from his grip. The man crumpled to the roof, writhing in agony. Susan screamed in terror. The creature was too fast.

But Eddie was even faster. He stepped aside at the last possible moment, just as the Wraith leapt. The snarling creature flew past him, its arms and legs a blur, and disappeared over the other side.

"We are not losing anyone!" Eddie shouted.

"They've stopped," Kari said. "They're leaving!"

Eddie turned to look. The Wraiths had indeed retreated.

"What are they doing?"

Six were all that remained. They seemed to have given up. But then they regrouped.

"They're heading to the front!"

The survivors knew that they couldn't defend against a concentrated attack, not when those things could sustain a seemingly endless assault. Even with Eddie's help, the risk of being touched was too great.

"We're not going to last like this," said Harrison, moving around to help.

"What are you doing? Get back there!" Eddie shouted at him.

"But you won't be able to—"

"Guys!" Kari yelled, and pointed up the road. Something new was coming through the scrub, traveling fast enough to kick up dust.

"Oh no."

The Wraiths, as if sensing the survivors' desperation, attacked with renewed vigor. They poured onto the hood of the bus, growling and hissing as they came.

"Get Nami back!" Eddie cried, and pulled Susan out of the way so he could take up a position along the front. He kicked the first Wraith away, snapping its neck and sending it flying to the dirt. It did not get back up.

The next one ducked beneath his foot, as if expecting the kick. It grabbed Eddie's plant foot and leaned forward to bite him. A shot rang out and its head disappeared in a cloud of red spray. The hand let go; the body slid onto the hood.

"My last bullet!"

The next two came together, one on either side of the bus, followed by the last two straight up the middle.

"I can't hold them off!"

"I'm out of ammo!"

Eddie kicked at one, missed, tried again. The other was up, preparing to leap.

A shot rang out, and the thing collapsed and tumbled off.

"Where the hell—"

With another blast, the first one arched its back. It, too, fell dead to the ground.

Motorcycles roared toward the bus, circling them. Men in dusty gray and brown garb quickly dismounted and dispatched the last two Wraiths. Several other men formed a quick perimeter. They occupied themselves for several minutes securing the area. The survivors could only watch in numb relief.

A thick-necked man with graying scruff on his cheeks stepped to the front. "I'm coming up!" he shouted. He stepped easily from the bus's bumper to the hood, and from there to the windshield. He reached up with a gloved hand, waiting for a lift. Eddie gave it to him.

"Grantham Cheever," he said, by way of introduction. He held a pistol in his free hand and quickly scanned the rest of the group. "Anyone touched?"

Eddie turned. "Nami?"

The former guard was moaning in pain. His leg was still bent the wrong way at the knee, and his arm dangled uselessly beside him. Susan stood helplessly nearby. She looked like she wanted to help, but she didn't want to touch him.

Cheever aimed the pistol for his head.

"No!" Hannah cried. She jumped up and onto Nami before anyone could move.

"Hannah!" Eddie yelled.

"Don't shoot him! Daddy, he's not infected!"

"I'm not . . . . Please," Nami panted. "It didn't touch skin. But . . . my shoulder . . . knee." He cried out. "Oh, god! I think they're broken."

"Dislocated," Cheever stated. He turned back to Eddie and something like revulsion flashed across his chiseled face. Or maybe just wariness.

Eddie's visage was still a bit of a shock, even though his skin had returned to its normal hue in the three days since they'd escaped the bunker. The veins on his face, neck, and arms, however, pulsed like dark, wriggling worms. And his muscles bulged and rippled like a snake's.

Or perhaps it was the complete absence of hair that startled the stranger.

"Anyone checked on Jonathan?" Eddie asked, disregarding the man's stare. "Is he . . . infected?"

No one replied.

Another motorcycle rider pulled up to the bus. He switched off his bike and dismounted. "All clear, Captain! Ramsey and Bolton found another straggler in the bushes. Took it out. Nothing else nearby."

Captain Cheever nodded. "Keep watch. Private Singh, report!"

Another man stepped out of the bus. He spun around as soon as his feet hit the dirt. "All clear inside, sir. "He shielded his hand from the morning sun. "But you'll want to see this."

"What is it, Private Singh?"

The man pointed toward the back of the vehicle. "I think we got ourselves a ghost."

CHAPTER 09

"COME ON, YOU CAN DO IT. WE'RE MORE THAN halfway there."

"All right, Colonel Sanders," Finn growled.

He slid a foot ahead and shifted his center of mass forward to meet it, then brought his back foot up. His palms were raw from rubbing against the twisted metal and his fingers were cramped. His hands were nearly black from the dirt caked between the twined steel threads.

"Stop telling me I can do it. You were the one who needed convincing to begin with, remember?"

The river rushed along thousands of feet below them. He knew it wasn't that far — probably no more than three hundred feet — but it sure felt a lot farther. And he hadn't expected the wind to be so strong. It hadn't looked windy at all standing on the rim.

Another gust slammed into them, knocking him against a cable. His knees threatened to buckle. The wind whistled angrily through the perforations in the foot-wide grating beneath their feet. It had seemed amply wide at the beginning. Now it felt like he was walking a tightrope.

"Colonel Sanders," Bix said, chuckling humorlessly. "That's a good one. Finger-lickin' good."

"Last time I ever let you talk me into anything for a piece of fried chicken."

"Not just chicken. Bacon," Bix muttered to himself as he inched along. "Soft bed. Warm shower. Fried chicken. And bacon."

Slowly, they made their way across the gorge. With his concentration stretched to the breaking point, Finn began to wonder what would happen if a Wraith suddenly appeared behind them. Would he be able to run?

What if one shows up ahead? Or on both ends?

He decided not to share these concerns with Bix. They just needed to get across, and the sooner, the better.

"This totally sucks," Bix groused as the bridge shook, canting them a couple inches to one side. It felt as if the movement displaced them by a dozen feet. "Can I just say that? Who the hell's idea was it to put a goddamn footbridge over the goddamn canyon here? I ain't a freaking mountain goat!"

"Adrenaline junkies."

"Screw them."

Finn wanted to tell Bix to shut up, but he had to admit that his griping was amusing enough to distract him from the vertiginous height.

"I feel like a freaking spider."

"I don't think spiders get elevation sickness, Bix."

"That's it, Finn. Next time we take the bus."

"As I recall, I told everyone to stay on the bus and get to the evac center."

"And let you have all the bacon to yourself? No way, man."

"Yeah, because you knew we'd meet—"

Another gust battered them, and they both kneeled. A shudder passed through the cables, threatening to flip them off. "I think I just peed," Bix announced. "I don't want to look down to see."

"I think I'm going to be sick," Finn replied.

"If you spew, just keep it on the downwind side."

"That goes for you, too."

Bix started to laugh.

"Glad you find it funny."

"It's not funny. I'm scared shitless. This is my terrified laugh. Can't you tell? My hilarious laugh sounds like this: *'Hee hee hee!'* "

Finn nudged him in the back. "Just get going already."

They traveled another thirty feet. "You don't trust them, do you, Finn?"

Finn didn't answer right away. He sighed and said, "They seem nice enough. But . . . . I just don't think it's wise to tell people where we were and where we're going and why. Right now, telling people stuff makes us even more vulnerable than we already are. And, to be honest, I think Jonah was right about there being other dangers than Wraiths. We just need to be more . . . circumspect."

"I'm not Jewish."

"Circumspect, not circumcised."

They inched along a few more minutes before Bix muttered Jonah's name with a sour note in his voice. "That guy is truly messed up in the head. His parents are messed up— *were* messed up. And what the hell was Bren's father talking about that was Jonah's big secret?"

He edged forward experimentally, and when the bridge and wind didn't immediately conspire to throw him over the side, he straightened up again and stepped forward with growing confidence.

Finn kept quiet. He had an idea what the secret might be, but he wasn't sure. Some of the hints the girls had dropped, both before and after their escape from the bunker, had opened up his mind about the boy. *People aren't always what they appear.* And that seemed to describe Jonah perfectly.

If his guess was correct, then this big secret about Jonah proved deeply insightful. It especially explained a lot about their interactions with each other over the past few years.

"You know what I think?"

Finn grunted noncommittally. The bridge was feeling considerably more stable again, now that the middle was behind them. They moved along at a faster clip, rising up toward the end. He honestly didn't want to break his focus to have a discussion about Jonah with Bix.

"I think he might be in love with Bren, that's what I think. Or maybe even Bren's mom. I don't know, it's just a feeling I get."

This brought Finn to a stop. He stared at Bix's back and shook his head. "No, I don't think it's either of those things."

"Well, that's because you ain't the master of *loooove*, bro. I have the sight."

"Speaking of love, how's that flirting thing going with Jennifer?"

He expected Bix to blow him off, but he didn't respond. He didn't even seem to be listening anymore. He was kneeling with his head down and breathing funny, making strange little noises with his throat.

"Downwind, remember," Finn said.

"Shh!"

"What?"

"Down there."

"Are you serious? I'm not looking—"

Bix let go of one of the cables and pointed past his left foot. *"It's him!"*

"Who? Jonah?"

It took a moment for Finn to quell the vertigo that swept over him as he looked down, another moment to see what Bix was pointing at. Far below, like a tiny ant moving beside the silver and white thread of the river, was a person.

"It's that guy," Bix whispered, "Micheal Williams, from Bunker Two. I recognize the clothes."

"But that's impossible. He threw himself over the side of the dam. No person could survive that fall."

"No human being maybe. But he was infected."

Finn realized that Bix was right. It was the same man, his clothes torn and bloodied.

The boys watched as the creature picked its way over the stones, moving in that creepy way that brought shivers to their spines.

When it was nearly beneath them, the Wraith stopped. It suddenly looked up. Both boys sucked in a sharp breath. A second or two later, a long, faint howl reached their ears.

They ran the rest of the way across the bridge.

CHAPTER

"GHOST?" EDDIE ASKED. "WHAT DO YOU MEAN? What's that?"

"Why don't we get down off this roof first," the captain said.

Using metal hooks, the other men had already begun pulling the dead Wraiths into a heap twenty yards away. They were careful not to let any part of their skin come into contact with the things.

The survivors watched as they sprinkled gasoline over the bodies and then flung a lit match onto them. The smell of the burning corpses made Kari sick, and she dropped to her knees and vomited over the side of the bus. Harrison had to hold onto her to keep her from taking a header.

"What's a ghost?" Eddie asked again. He didn't move.

"Are you in charge of this group?"

Eddie looked around at the others. "We don't have—"

"Yes," Susan said, stepping forward. She gave him a pointed look. "Eddie's our leader."

Once again, the captain gestured for them to climb down first. It took them several minutes to get Nami off the roof. He cried out in agony half a dozen times. Once they were all safely on the ground, one of the men came over to attend to him, a medic by the name of Carter.

"A ghost," Captain Cheever said at last, "is someone the infected don't seem to bother with. For some reason, they don't seem to notice them."

Eddie frowned. "What do you mean?"

He waved at the door of the bus. "May I?"

Eddie nodded.

The captain climbed the steps with Eddie, followed by the other adults in their group. He stepped quickly toward the back, where another of his men stood beside the seat where Jonathan had been lying before the attack. The former guard was still there, still very ill, but clearly not infected with the Flense, despite the Wraiths getting inside.

Kari pushed her way past them. After Allison's death, she'd taken over caring for him, keeping him comfortable, applying damp washcloths to his forehead to keep his fever down.

"They didn't touch him," she whispered. "They were in here with him, and they didn't touch him. Why not?"

Eddie shook his head. In all the attacks he had ever witnessed, the Wraiths spared no one. He'd seen people lie down and pretend to be dead. The Wraiths always stopped for them. They didn't for the people who really were dead. Somehow, they knew corpses wouldn't make suitable hosts to the contagion they carried.

"A small percentage of people just seem invisible to them," the captain said again. "It's very rare, and we don't understand how or why."

"Could it be because he's sick?"

The captain's eyes narrowed. "Sick how?"

"We don't know. It's some kind of lung infection, maybe pneumonia."

Cheever's face tightened, and he swiveled to each of them in turn. "Anyone else?"

They all shook their heads. "Just the baby," Susan said.

Outside, as if on cue, the baby cried out, a wet, gurgling sniffle that became a cough. The captain leaned down and stared at him through the window. No one spoke for several heartbeats.

Finally he straightened up again. He looked like he'd seen a real ghost. "Off," he said. "Outside. Now."

"Why?"

"Flu."

He pushed his way past them, and they all followed, all except Kari, who remained behind with Jonathan.

The moment he exited the bus, the captain let out a huge breath. His face had gone pale. "Carter!" he shouted. "Specialist Carter!"

A man ran over. "Yes, sir?"

"You have the first aid kit? Go fetch it."

Carter nodded and ran to one of the bikes.

"I want antibiotics!" Cheever shouted after him.

"You think it's the flu?" Eddie asked.

A global epidemic of influenza had swept across the globe two years before the Flense, wiping out a third of the population before it could be brought under control again. The infection persisted through the next winter, but its devastation had been greatly diminished through careful management and a massive global immunization program. Millions still died, but those numbers were significantly smaller than the billion who had succumbed to the disease a year before.

But as devastating as the flu had been, it had been nothing like the Flense.

"Maybe," Cheever replied.

"Some of our people suffer from severe malnutrition. Their immune systems are likely compromised. It's just a cough."

The captain spun around to face Eddie. "I need to know where you people came from, what you've been exposed to, where you're going."

Eddie shook his head. "We appreciate your help, we really do. We would have been in dire straits had you not shown up when you did."

"Dead or infected is more like it."

Eddie shrugged. "Point is, we don't know you. How can we trust you? No offense."

"Understood, and none taken, but it's a two-way street." He sighed and gestured at his men. "You already know my name. I was a supply officer at a small military outpost called Westerton Army Depot before the fall. The base is about eighty, ninety miles south of here. One of our sentries reported seeing your vehicle lights in the desert last night."

"Sentry? Army Depot? You're with the army?"

"Not the army you're thinking of. That one doesn't exist anymore. We're a group of survivors. We run the base in a military fashion, but we're more of a sanctuary now. It's just one of about twenty or so safe refuges that formed after the fall. Refuges that we know about, anyway."

His last words felt like he was fishing for information.

"You're able to keep out the Wraiths?"

"Wraiths?" The captain's eyes narrowed. "Yes. But they aren't the only things you need to watch out for out here. There are some unsavory characters living in the world.

Roamers, we call them. They're lawless people. If the creatures don't get you, a roamer might. Inside our gates, we offer sanctuary to those who need it. Outside, there are no guarantees."

"And in exchange?"

"Everyone contributes in one way or another in our community."

"How many people?"

"About three hundred. We're under the command of Colonel Wainwright."

"Colonel?" Eddie looked dubiously over at the men. "Sounds a lot like the old military to me. Your men don't look like soldiers."

"Listen to me, Eddie. The old military is gone. So is the government, has been since the fall. But that doesn't mean we haven't tried to keep some of the structure and order of the past as we try and rebuild the future."

Eddie realized how much he'd just given away. The captain now knew that they had been living in isolation for a while, perhaps as long as the fall, as he put it. This insight was bound to elicit even more questions about him and the others, questions he simply wasn't comfortable answering. He shuddered to think what these men might do with knowledge of the bunker if they didn't have good intentions.

The captain lowered his voice. "I understand your reluctance. No pressure. But once we get you back to Westerton—"

"Whoa, wait a minute," Eddie said. "We're not going with you."

Cheever spun around. "It's for your own good."

Eddie glanced at the men around them. They seemed to have taken on a hostile posture all of a sudden.

"Are you going to force us?"

The captain turned around. "Your vehicle runs, does it not?"

"It's damaged. It needs oil."

"Oil and repairs we can provide."

"But, Daddy," Hannah cried. She pulled Eddie aside and whispered, "What about Jonah and Danny? We can't just leave them."

"Listen, Eddie," Cheever said. "We need to move quick. There's too much cover here, and every minute we spend is another minute those things have to find us."

Eddie walked back over to him. "We need to go back to that town."

"Why?"

Eddie pursed his lips. "Because we left a couple people behind there. They were scouting for supplies when we were attacked. We had to run."

Captain Cheever's jaw tightened. "How many?"

"Two men."

"You left them overnight? I can almost guarantee they're dead. Or infected. We can't afford—"

"Almost is a long way from a guarantee."

Cheever pointed at the burning pyre. "Those things attacked you in town last night? They followed you there, didn't they? Your people are gone. You only put yourselves at further risk by going back. And you put my men at risk—"

"Nobody's asking you or your men to do it, Captain. But I have a responsibility to my people just like you do to yours. We're going back."

Cheever surveyed his men. "Private Ramsay," he called. "Singh! You two drive into town. Check in the shop for a couple people, two men. They were left there last night. Thorough search, but no dawdling."

"The auto shop?" one of them asked. He looked troubled, his eyes flicking from the captain to Eddie. "They won't be alive, sir. Not overnight."

"Did I ask for your opinion, Ramsay? Just find them."

"And if they're alive, then what?"

"Bring them back. Do I need to spell everything out to you?"

Ramsay's face burned with anger.

"Here, sir?" Private Singh asked. "Bring them here?"

"Straight back to base, Vinnie. We're clearing this scene as soon as we get this tub dug out."

"Yes, sir."

"Well? What are you waiting for?"

Cheever turned back to Eddie. "They're good men. They will find them, one way or another."

Eddie swallowed his frustration. By telling his men to take Jonah and Danny back to the base, the captain had just made it impossible for him to refuse going there, too.

CHAPTER
11

"IS THIS THE ROAD?" BIX ASKED, GLANCING AT THE sign. "I don't remember what the reverend said the name was."

Because you were too busy ingratiating yourself with Jennifer, Finn thought, then felt bad for thinking it, especially since his own mouth was watering at the thought of bacon and fresh eggs. Truth be told, though, he'd be just as happy with a can of congealed stew and the security of the dam.

He suddenly felt homesick— oddly, not for his home before the Flense, but for the bunker. He missed his food storage room — his own private refuge — and now regretted that they hadn't thought to pack more of those supplies before busting out. Of course, they hadn't figured on it taking so long to get anywhere, or that it would be so hard to find stuff along the way.

They had passed several houses and even a general store on the road, but the buildings had clearly been ransacked, leaving nothing to eat or of any use as a weapon against anything which might attack them.

Some of the buildings had been burned down. One house, standing alone at the end of a long dusty driveway, had some dark brown spatter marks on the walls of the entryway, and the carpeting just inside the door was shredded into pieces. They left the place in a hurry, not bothering to search it.

As a result, all they'd had to eat in the hours since leaving the gorge behind was some stale homemade granola bars Jennifer had made and a half dozen small apples that the couple had given them to tide them over until they met back up again.

As bruised as the apples were, both boys had eaten them nearly to completion, nibbling away until nothing more remained than the seeds and the bottom, which Bix called the "fuzzy butt" in an attempt to gross Finn out enough that he'd give his part to him. Which he did not.

It was the first fresh fruit they'd eaten in over three years, and it was almost too much for their stomachs to handle. Bix had twice needed to excuse himself. Thankfully, they'd reached a forest by then, which provided him with privacy, though not enough that Finn couldn't hear his groans of misery. He couldn't be sure if Bix was exaggerating them for comic effect.

The cover also made him nervous, and he began to wish they were back out in the open again, despite the blistering sunlight. Bix kept emphasizing that they were safe now, since Adrian and Jennifer had cleared the area of Wraiths. Finn seriously doubted that two people could do such a big job as that on their own.

"Well? Is this, or is this not, the right road?"

"It is," Finn said. He looked around them nervously, half expecting to see something following them. "About a mile up the road, he said, we'll reach a gate. We wait there."

"Finally. My feet are killing me."

They walked along the semi-shaded path, kicking at the thick carpet of alder and birch leaves, thrilling at the novelty of it. There were also cottonwood and maple trees, though in lesser abundance.

The surface of the road was visible only in spots, and had it not been for the overgrown signs and metal rails, they might have easily wandered off track.

Birds happily chirped in the trees all around them. Leaves rustled in the breeze. A twig snapped.

Finn stopped and turned to stare at the spot where the sound had come from. The road behind them was clear, as was the road ahead. But the woods seemed to have grown gloomier, hiding dangers that had not been there a moment before.

Bix stepped closer to Finn's side. *"What was that?"*

They both stared into the trees and waited. Something rustled, perhaps thirty or forty feet away.

"I can't see—"

Another twig snapped.

Finn nudged Bix in the arm. *"Go,"* he whispered. *"Quietly."*

They began walking again, Finn's hand on Bix's back, Bix with a fistful of Finn's shirt.

Suddenly, the forest around them was completely silent. The only sound was the rustle of the leaves beneath their feet. Their walk became a jog; the jog turned into a run.

Something trampled through the bracken off to their right, keeping pace. To the left, birds exploded from the trees with their raucous cries, blackening the sky.

They were separated now, Bix ahead by several feet, running at an all out sprint. Finn stumbled, slipped, and they switched positions. Behind them, to the left, something howled. Bix cursed. His face had gone white with terror. Off to their right, something else answered.

"I can't . . . keep it up!" Bix cried, no longer bothering to be quiet.

"Keep running!"

"They're getting closer!"

"Don't stop!"

"And what do we do when we get to the gate and can't go any further?"

Shit! Finn realized. He tried to think as he ran. What should they do? Should they turn around?

They rounded a curve and a hint of a shape off to his right caught his eye, a shadow moving quickly, dark and low to the ground. Branches snapped. The noise grew louder. Whatever it was, it was getting closer.

"There's something there!" Bix squeaked. "Finn! It's going to get us!" He was running awkwardly, trying to shed his backpack.

Something shrieked behind them, raising the hair on Finn's neck. The creature was on the road.

Bix flung the pack away, nearly knocking Finn down with it. "Shoot them!" he screamed.

Finn's hands were full. In his right, he carried the rifle. In the left was his stun gun. He tried to aim the latter, but there was nothing to shoot it at.

Don't pull the trigger until you see the whites of its eyes, the reverend had warned. *You get only one chance to zap em.*

Finn had wanted to remind him that their eyes were black, not white, but he figured that was just being a little too literal.

"Take this!" he shouted at Bix, and tried to pass him the stun gun. Bix reached out and grabbed it. For a split second, the weapon floated in mid air between them, then it simply fell away on its own. It slid into the leaves. Neither boy stopped to retrieve it.

Finn tried to raise the rifle to eye level. The pack on his back jounced up and down, throwing off his ability to aim.

"There!" Bix cried, pointing to the right. Finn pulled the trigger and the air exploded with the blast of the shot.

"You missed!"

Of course I missed, you idiot! Finn wanted to shout back. *How the hell am I supposed to aim when I'm running?*

The forest rang with laughter. Finn's blood froze in his veins.

"Stop shooting, assholes!" rang out a man's voice. "Jesus Christ, don't be stupid!"

Bix and Finn kept running. By the time their minds had parsed the words and what they meant, they'd reached the gate.

"Don't touch the wire!" another voice warned.

Finn pulled Bix back by the collar, and they slid to a stop. The electrified chain link rose up less than two feet away.

"Billy, you okay?" came a shout from behind them. The boys spun around, but no one was there.

Once again, laughter pealed through the trees off to their right.

"Billy?"

"I'm good, Luke!"

"Boys!" Jennifer McCoy appeared on the other side of the gate astride her horse. "Quit scarin our guests, boys!"

Bix and Finn scrambled to their feet. They were both shaking, gasping for air. Feet pounded the road behind them, and then a figure appeared around the bend, slowing to a walk. He wore dirty jeans and a long-sleeved shirt, and his long brown hair was tangled with leaves. In his hands was a military-style assault rifle. He'd slung Bix's discarded backpack over one shoulder.

"You boys should be ashamed of yourselves!"

"Aw, come on, mutha!" cried the second one, emerging out of the woods. He was even more disheveled than the first. "We were just havin fun."

Finn and Bix stood gaping at the "boys." They weren't young at all. In fact, they looked to be in their thirties.

Jennifer flipped a switch, then drew the wire gate to the side. "Well, y'all coulda gotten yer damn heads blasted off!" she snapped. She took the rifle from Finn.

"I, uh, dropped the other one," Finn panted. "The stun gun. It's back there on the road somewhere."

"You hear that, Luke? Go back and find it."

"Aw!"

"I don't want to hear another word! Billy, go with him." She turned to Finn and Bix. "They ain't the smartest tools in the shed, those boys. Coupla no good fools." She shrugged. "But they're family, and we take care of family, don't we?"

Bix nodded. He'd forgotten to shut his mouth.

"Good. Now, come on inside before y'all trip over those chins of yers."

* * *

"We arrived about twenty minutes ago," she explained, riding her horse beside them as they walked. "Wanted to get here before y'all to avoid the boys shooting first n'askin questions later. Shoulda known they was goin to try and scare ya." She shook her head. "Their mother shoulda whupped them more when they was growin up."

"They're not yours?"

Jennifer laughed. "Do I look old enough to have children that age?"

Bix's face flushed bright red.

They abruptly exited the woods and found themselves in a broad, flat clearing that had been disked up to prevent last season's grass seed from growing. Finn guessed that the deeply rutted ground would also slow anyone and anything that might try to cross it to get at the house, which was a massive, beautiful log cabin. It stood several hundred yards away on a short spit of land jutting out over a pristine lake.

"Oh man," Bix murmured. "Please tell me there's a Jacuzzi inside."

"There is, but it ain't workin."

"The lake?"

She shook her head.

"What are the markers for?" Finn asked, pointing at the several dozen golf flags fluttering in the field to their left.

"Land mines," Jennifer replied. She turned to Bix. "They're in the water, too, so no swimming."

"Mines?"

"It's a different world than the one y'all remember. Best get used to it."

Later, long after they'd both enjoyed hot showers and a wonderful home-cooked meal of sliced smoked ham steaks and scrambled eggs and real potato hash browns — thankfully without the company of Billy and Luke — after they'd all gone to bed that night, Finn would recall that comment and wonder, *How could anyone get used to it?* The more he thought about it, the more he worried.

The comment seemed to have been made offhand, a throwaway remark. But in the darkness and silence of the giant guest room in the giant house, as his ears longed for the sound of the old comforting turbines, it would feel more and more like a veiled threat than advice. And he'd drift off to sleep with her words echoing hollowly and ominously in his mind.

Of course, the next morning the smell of cooking bacon would smack him in the nose and make him forget his trepidation.

"Before we get you settled," Jennifer said, steering them away from the house, "we should take care of the horses. Y'all can help Adrian and the boys feed and water while I rustle us up some dinner."

She shielded her eyes from the setting sun and peered out over the turned-up field in the direction of the dark trees and pointed at a new path, which they took.

After a bit, they came to a large barn adjacent to a number of animal pens. The strong smell of manure wafted over to them. Bix took a deep breath, as if relishing it.

Several smaller plots were marked out with string. They appeared to contain vegetables.

"Just four of you living here?" Finn asked, incredulous at the amount of work that had clearly been done.

"That's right," Jennifer said, chuckling. "We once had more, but life is tough and it sometimes takes the ones we love before their time. Wish it wasn't so, but it is. We take wanderers, too. They stay for a bit, but they always end up leavin sooner or later."

They'd reached the barn by then and the whinny of several horses inside mingled with the mournful low of a cow and the agitated squawks of chickens. Jennifer lowered herself from the saddle and stepped over to the door.

"Now, before we go in, I want y'all to remember what we said before about findin an end to the plague. That's always been our main objective."

Finn nodded, but the hairs on his neck were starting to prickle again.

She pulled the door open and led them in. It took a moment for their eyes to adjust.

"What the—?" Bix said. "Jesus Christ!"

A wire cage occupied the pen just to the left of the door, and inside were two naked figures. Dried blood covered their ashen skin, staining their chins. Their wrists and ankles were manacled to the floor.

"Wraiths?" Finn cried.

The creatures looked up and snarled. Then they launched themselves off the ground at the trio.

CHAPTER

IT WAS **D**ANNY WHO FIRST HEARD THE MOTORCYCLES, confusing them for the sound of the bus returning. He was out of the room he and Jonah were searching, running down the stairs before Jonah could stop him.

"Wait, Danny!"

But Danny wasn't listening. He was shouting for the bus. He slammed through the front door just as the two bikers disappeared around the corner.

Jonah grabbed his arm and drew him back up onto the porch with a hiss. "It's not them!"

"It's people, though! And they might know something about the bus!"

"Except they came into town from a different direction. Did you notice that?"

"They did?"

"Did you also notice the semi-automatic rifles?"

Danny slowly shook his head.

"Slung over their backs, and another in their saddlebags. We need to know who they are or at least their intentions before introducing ourselves to anyone that heavily armed."

"So they have guns. That doesn't mean they're hostile. You saw what happened last night, Jonah. We should be carrying that kind of fire power, too. If we'd had guns, we wouldn't be trapped here now."

You may be right," Jonah calmly answered, "but it doesn't mean we go running after the first uninfected people we see. Friendly or not, they're liable to shoot you dead before they realize you're not a Wraith."

Danny winced, but he nodded. "You're right."

"Look," Jonah continued, "I hope as much as you do that they can help us, but let's be careful, okay? Even if they are good people and want to help, it doesn't mean we stop helping ourselves. Besides, the noise those motorbikes make is loud enough to draw whatever Wraiths in the area straight to them. I'd rather not walk into the middle of that scene."

He pulled Danny back inside the house, where they had gathered the few useful items they'd managed to scrounge up in town since sunrise. It wasn't much— a couple kitchen knives, a cracked baseball bat, a rusted hatchet, a few cans of dog food, and some expired bottles of aspirin and veterinary antibiotics.

There were a few more buildings that they hadn't yet searched, including the small brick bank on the corner, and the church opposite it. What they had seen so far convinced them that others had come through town before them with the same intention, probably many others at many different times. The pickings were slim indeed.

Jonah began to fill his pack and instructed Danny do likewise. Keeping one of the kitchen knives out, he hoisted the heavy bundle onto his back. "Keep close. I want to find out as much about these guys as we can before we show ourselves. We'll circle around."

They stepped back out onto the porch, making sure to keep in the shadows. "House-to-house," he said. "Try to stay out of sight. When we reach the corner—"

"What if they didn't stop?" Danny suddenly asked, looking afraid. "What if they just kept on going? I don't hear the bikes anymore."

Jonah didn't answer. He frowned and shrugged. He knew it was a possibility. If the men had left, then it would be all on him for keeping Danny from stopping them. But it didn't mean they'd been abandoned. He had faith the bus would return.

Assuming anyone on it is still alive.

They slipped down the steps, then sidled over to the corner of the house. Jonah checked around the corner, shook his head, and ran for the next. In this fashion, they made their way down the street, and when they reached the end of the block, Jonah held Danny back. "They're parked in front of the auto shop. No Wraiths in sight."

Danny's eyes widened. "The shop? Seems like too much of a coincidence. Do you suppose they knew we were there?"

"Maybe. If so, it could mean they found the bus and were told where to find us."

Danny's mood brightened. "I knew it!"

"So where's the bus? It could also be that they have something to do with that mess we found inside. We can't assume anything."

He took another look. The shop was across the street, past the light that the bus had knocked over onto the sidewalk last night. He shrugged off the pack and laid it onto the ground at Danny's feet. "Stay here with the stuff. Don't let them see you."

"Where are you going?"

"To get a closer look."

"But what about me?"

"Just trust me on this, Danny. I can get over there faster and stay hidden better than the two of us together. No offense."

"What do I do if they start to leave?"

Jonah pursed his lips. "If it looks like they're leaving town and I'm not back, then I guess we have no choice. Stop them. Just, please, don't get yourself shot." He saw the look of alarm on the older man's face and tried to reassure him. "Be smart, and it won't be a problem."

Before Danny could say anything else, he sprinted out into the street, keeping a low profile. He made it to the bank and slid to a stop around the corner of the building, then turned and gestured at Danny to sit tight. When Danny nodded that he understood, Jonah continued along the side and around the back.

The town had been built with most of the businesses lining the main road and a few more extending along the intersecting street. There was a lot of concrete, but thankfully little fencing separating the properties. Businesses immediately gave way to residential homes.

Many of the houses had low pickets or decorative wire fences in front, which we easy to step over, and the property lines separating neighbors appeared to have been marked with simple shrubs. The plants had since shriveled into lifeless skeletons from neglect.

He climbed over an elevated ramped between the bank and the next building over, which had once been some kind of office, then skirted that structure and hurried over to the next. A sign on the side advertised BAB'S BBQ &

NOTARY PUBLIC. He wondered idly what had become of Bab. The memory of barbecued steaks and hamburgers reminded him of how empty his stomach was.

Each of the businesses had a small apron of concrete in back for parking. At the rear edge of the bank's lot was a cinderblock wall, and beyond that were either empty fields or more houses.

A large rusted barbecue grill sat near the restaurant's back door. Next to it was a dumpster, one of its two lids propped slightly open with what appeared to be an old plastic dairy crate.

The repair shop was the next building over, but to get to it, he'd have to climb over a six-foot wooden fence or go around it.

He hurried over to the dumpster and leaned down beside it. With the butt of the knife, he quietly rapped on the side. No sound came from within. Carefully, he pushed the lid open and set it against the side of the restaurant.

The plastic crate was wedged inside the nearly full dumpster, half buried beneath piles of dusty, faded black plastic trash bags. A foul odor of decay rose out, surprising him, and he gagged into his elbow. After three years, how could there still be anything left to rot?

Rain got in, he thought. *That's all. Then an animal crawled in and drowned. Maybe lots of rats. Or a raccoon.*

He tugged on the crate, grunting quietly, and whatever was keeping it in place finally began to yield. He gave it a stronger tug while twisting, and it broke free with a snap, throwing him backward to the ground. The crate flew out of his hand and clattered to the cement behind him.

"Shit!"

A moment later, the side door of the shop creaked open "—heard something outside," a man said, speaking with a slight accent. "I'm going to check, Wayne."

Jonah scrambled to a crouch. He was ready to run if necessary.

"Dammit, Vin, I keep telling you, there ain't nothing here. And if there was, it's gone now. Now, we've come and looked. It's time to go back."

"We just got here. The captain will know we barely looked anywhere."

"Cheever's going to be stuck for a while back there. Besides, he won't care if we come back empty-handed. I could see it on his face— he knows this is a waste of time. Ain't no one here."

"They said those two would be in the shop—"

"And they ain't. You know as well as I they're dead or infected, and I don't intend to stick around to verify it, neither. We done our duty. Besides, ain't you the one who always says this place gives you the creeps."

"It does."

"And now we know why Cheever picked you for this job. That's why he always picks you for the crap jobs, Vin, because you ain't got balls."

"Then why does he pick you?"

"Because he knows I'm smarter than he is."

"It's because everyone else has more seniority."

"No, he thinks we ain't shit. That, and he wants to save the best for himself."

"Best of what?"

"How many you count back there? How many women? How many *girls?*"

Vinnie didn't answer right away. When he finally did, he sounded uncertain. "You're wrong, Wayne."

"What? Don't tell me you ain't thought about it. We're all human? We all got needs."

"No."

"Hell, even Wainwright ain't a saint. You don't think he doesn't—"

"You're going to get us into trouble talking like that."

"And who's going to tell him? You?"

"It's not right."

"Here's what's going to happen, Vin. Cheever and his pals, first thing they plan to do when they get back to base is separate the newcomers, don't let them talk to one another."

"That's for quarantine. Colonel Wainwright—"

"It's so they can pick and choose who stays and who goes. And who gets to be whoever's private girl toy."

Jonah frowned. They hadn't come right out and said they'd found the bus, but it seemed obvious enough that they had. What was also obvious was that the others were in danger, especially the women.

Especially Bren and Hannah.

Wayne's next words were much more private, spoken in a conspiratorial tone of voice. Jonah missed half of it, but the part he did hear chilled his blood to ice.

"There's two girls on that bus, Vin. Pretty little girls with pretty little faces. One for you, one for me. Now, let's get the hell back."

The door slammed shut on his last words, leaving Jonah frozen with horror.

CHAPTER

DANNY WASN'T WAITING WHERE JONAH HAD LEFT HIM.
The packs were still there on the ground, but Danny was nowhere to be seen.

"Dammit," Jonah muttered, and looked around at the
ghost houses along the street with their blind windows and
their dead, overgrown lawns. Everything lacked color.
Everything was some variation on dirt. Even the business
signs. "Where the hell did you go?"

He peeked around the corner to check on the bikes.
They were still parked where the two men had left them.
Despite their eagerness to leave, they seemed to be taking
their time.

Get their bikes!

He couldn't be sure, but he guessed the keys would be in
the ignition for a fast getaway. The men probably thought
someone stealing them was about as likely as them sprouting
wings and flying away.

Can't leave without Danny, he thought. And he didn't even
know where to begin looking for the bus. Or this military
base the two men talked about. *"Danny!"* he whispered, as
loudly as he dared.

His eye caught the door to the bank across the street. Had it been open before? Is that where Danny had gone?

Why would he leave the packs here?

Checking that the street was empty, Jonah sprinted across and slipped inside. The floor was littered with debris. Leaves and old trash had blown in. Weeds grew in the cracks around the threshold. In the center of the large room, the business counter rose up like a barricade. The teller windows had been smashed. Large curtains of dusty cobwebs hung from the ceiling like moth-eaten tapestries. The place smelled of must and mold.

He stepped further inside, past a melamine coffee table whose laminate had been warped by dripping water. A glass bowl of lollipops sat in the middle of it, the partially gnawed candy shared space with petrified mouse droppings.

"Danny?"

Outside, the motorcycle engines roared to life. Jonah spun around, banging his shin on the table. He ran limping to the door in time to see the men pass, returning in the direction they had come.

Danny appeared out of the house on the opposite corner, running down the porch steps waving his arms. The bikers screeched to a stop thirty feet away and drew their guns, which they pointed at Danny.

Jonah was out the door and running before he realized it. "Wait! " he screamed. "Don't shoot!"

The guns shifted toward him. He stopped in the middle of the intersection, hands held out. "I'm not armed! Don't shoot!"

One of the rifles jerked, directing him to join Danny on the sidewalk. After he complied, the two men turned off their bikes and dismounted.

"You two with the people on the bus?" one of them asked, a hint of a southern accent.

That must be Wayne, Jonah thought. His eyes flicked to the other, who had caramel-colored skin. *And that's Vinnie.*

Wayne stared at Jonah for a long time. He seemed to be making some sort of calculation in his head, perhaps measuring the distance between the bank and the shop. He caught sight of the backpacks on the ground, and another calculation was made. The man's gray eyes were deeply etched with distrust.

He knows, Jonah thought. *Or he suspects.*

"What are you doing in there?" Wayne asked suspiciously.

"We're not armed," he called out to them. "You can put those down."

Vinnie lowered his rifle. "You said they wouldn't be here."

"Shut up, Vin!" He turned to Danny. "Who are you? Are there more?"

"Just us two," Danny replied. "I'm Danny Delacroix. We were with others but got stranded when our bus was overrun by Wraiths."

Wayne lowered his rifle and sheathed it in the bike's saddlebag. Vinnie followed suit. "Well, Danny. Is that short for Daniel?"

Danny nodded.

"Your people are fine," he said. "They were stuck in the sand a few miles from here. Sent us to find you."

Danny laughed with relief. "God, are we glad to see you!"

"So glad that it took you nearly twenty minutes to find us? What've you been doing, spying on us?"

"We were inside a house," Jonah quickly answered. "Didn't hear the engines at first."

Wayne turned back to Jonah, once again studying his face. He glanced pointedly at the bank door, then at the auto shop a couple buildings away. He knew there was no way for Jonah to have missed the bikes parked there.

"Well, lucky thing you found us then, ain't it? We was just about to leave for good."

Danny stepped forward, smiling, extending his hand. The man took it into his own gloved hand and shook it. "Name's Wayne Ramsay. This here's Vinnie Singh. Or Vin, which is short for Vinay, which I'm told is short for Vinay-lama-dama-ding-dong or something like that." He snorted. "You two realize how damn lucky you are to even be alive?"

Jonah returned the man's unwelcoming smile as best as he could. He had to suppress an urge to take the man's gun and slam the stock into his face.

"Your people are on their way to our base about seventy miles south of here," Vinnie said.

"Why didn't they come back for us themselves?"

"That bus is in pretty bad shape," Ramsay said. "It's a deathtrap. And it needs repairs. That's why."

Danny frowned. "So how are we supposed to get back?"

Ramsay pointed at the bikes. "Well, Danny-boy, we ride double."

* * *

"Yo, Vin!" Wayne shouted over the roar of the bikes. "Let's stop at the truck and refuel."

Vinnie looked down at his gauge. "I'm good!"

"So am I, but I gotta take a piss anyway. And your guy's looking a little dehydrated."

Jonah glanced over at Danny on the back of Vinnie's bike. The wind had brought tears to his eyes, streaking the road dirt over his face. Danny looked over, smiled, and gave him a thumbs up.

They pulled off the road a few miles later and onto a dirt track that wound down into an arroyo. Jonah noticed that there were recent tire tracks in the dust.

After a mile or so, he spied a refueller tank truck parked in the shade beneath a cut, its shiny aluminum surface dulled beneath a thick coating of dirt. The tracks led up to it, but not beyond. It was clearly a common refueling stop for the bikers.

They pulled up beside the tank and shut off their engines. Everyone dismounted. Jonah noticed that Wayne removed the keys from his ignition and slipped them into his pocket.

"Hey, Vinnie, whyn't you take our guests over to the piss spot while I fill us up?" he said.

"I don't have to go," Vinnie said.

"Go anyway and make sure they stay safe. We don't wanna lose anyone."

When they returned, Wayne was just finishing up filling Vinnie's tank. He replaced the nozzle to the truck and secured the padlock holding it in place.

"Might as well fill up the old stomachs too, while we're at it." He dug out a metal canteen from his saddlebag and offered it to Jonah, who shook his head.

"Thanks. I got my own," he said.

"Suit yourself." He unscrewed the cap and took a big swig, sighed contentedly, then wiped his mouth on his sleeve.

Vinnie and Danny shared Vinnie's water. Jonah stepped out of the shade.

"Don't wander off now," Wayne warned.

"Wraiths?" Danny asked.

"Funny that you call them that. But, no. Rattlesnakes, coyotes. And mountain lions."

Jonah ignored him. His mind was going a mile a minute. He had hoped for a moment alone with Danny so he could tell him what he'd heard back in town, but it hadn't happened. And they had to be getting close to wherever this base was. He had a feeling that once they got inside, it wasn't going to be easy to get back out again.

He could hear Danny having a conversation with the two men, asking how much fuel the tanker held and how they had managed to get it down there.

Vinnie hadn't been able to answer, but Wayne was more than happy to share what he knew. "Eleven thousand gallons," he said. "Might be a thousand left. Have to hide it, else roamers'll come and steal it."

"Are there a lot of people still alive?"

"Not as much as there were before, that's for sure." He sat against the rear wheel of the truck, leaning on an elbow. He used his keys to draw shapes in the dirt. "Hey, cowboy! Whyn't you join us, instead of standing out there in the hot sun?"

Jonah remained where he was. "Tell me about this base camp," he said.

"Used to be an army supply depot or something. Colonel Wainwright can tell you more about it. He was in charge there when all hell broke loose. Captain Cheever's in charge of the scouts, of which you have the pleasure of knowing two."

"How many people?"

"Few hundred. Stragglers, mostly. They come in over time. Some stay, some don't. Most of the soldiers stationed there died in the first few days defending the place, so it's mostly civilians and volunteer soldiers nowadays."

Danny whistled appreciatively. "Women and children? Families?"

"Women? Yeah." He seemed to study Jonah's face as he said this. "A few children. Not enough in my opinion. Could always use more."

Jonah thought he felt his face redden, though he tried to remain as stoic as possible. "What do you mean by that?" he asked.

"Just saying," Wayne coolly replied. "The whole damn human race got knocked to the mat. Without children, how're we supposed to rebuild it?"

Vinnie seemed to be picking up on the tension between the two. He stood up and replaced the canteen into his pack. "Come on, Wayne." He glanced nervously at his partner. "Let's get back before dinnertime."

"You know, everyone's got a job to do on base," Wayne said, not moving. "The men scout and guard, build, repair. It's hard work, dangerous work. The women, well . . . ." He smiled at himself. "They take care of the men."

Something inside of Jonah was close to snapping. He could feel it.

He's testing you. Don't let him get to you. Don't lose your cool.

"Sounds positively feudal," he muttered. "I'm sure the women just love that arrangement."

Wayne chuckled humorlessly. "They're more than grateful to do their part. Ain't they, Vin? They know we might never return from a mission. Lots of men die out here in the wilderness. Lots. We could, too. All it takes is one screw up and *BAM!* You're dead meat."

An image of his father came to Jonah, standing over him in the middle of the night, waking him up. He'd been fourteen at the time.

John's not coming home anymore, Jonah. He screwed up and now he's gone away for good. So you need to grow up and do your part now.

That's all he'd said, before leaving again, and Jonah had lain awake the rest of the night, too afraid to sleep, wondering how his brother had died. Had it been in a shoot-out with police or the brutal people he worked for?

Wayne Ramsay stood up and brushed himself off. "Guess we better get going then, eh?"

"I thought you had to piss," Jonah said.

"Guess I don't after all." He pointed at Danny. "Why don't we switch for a while. You can ride with me."

Vinnie actually seemed to be relieved. But although the tension was thick, Danny hadn't seemed to clue in on it. He shrugged and climbed on behind Ramsay.

The bike sprayed dirt as Wayne tore off up the path. Vinnie cried out for his partner to wait, then he motioned for Jonah to get on.

By the time they rose up out of the ditch to the desert floor, Wayne's bike was a cloud of dust in the distance. Vinnie tried to catch up, but it was clear he wasn't as comfortable as his partner driving with a passenger over such questionable terrain.

"Don't worry about them," he tried to assure Jonah. "They'll wait for us when we hit the road."

But a half mile later the engine began to struggle. Jonah felt it hesitate and immediately knew something was wrong. A hundred feet later the bike stalled. Vinnie tried to restart it, but it just wouldn't run. "I don't understand," he told Jonah.

"I think I do." He asked for the keys and removed the gas cap. He expected to find it empty, perhaps as some kind of cruel prank. But there was gas in it.

It was also full of sand.

CHAPTER

14

"IT'S CRAZY," FINN WHISPERED FROM THE BOTTOM bunk. "I mean, how easy would it be to become infected? All it takes is the slightest—"

"Touch. I know," Bix said, yawning loudly.

"Seems to me like an unnecessary risk. These people don't know what they're dealing with. They have no idea what they're doing."

"How else are they going to figure out how to cure the Flense?" Bix countered. "I mean, think about how helpless we were inside the bunker. After three years, we knew absolutely nothing about it. Isolation doesn't work, maybe this will."

Helpless, maybe, Finn thought, *but also safe.*

The scene in the barn had deeply troubled him, and once more he sensed his adolescent anxieties returning.

He wanted to find someplace isolated and away from people, someplace he could go and just shut down. The need was so strong that he began to resent the horrific circumstances that had forced him to make the decisions he had over the past few days.

He shoved the feelings angrily away. Hiding wasn't the solution. He couldn't just crawl into a hole anymore and hope tomorrow would magically fix everything. The world had changed. And he had to accept that so had he.

"I'm just—" he started to say, but stopped, unsure what he was trying to convey. "It's just that I—"

"It's okay, bro."

"No, it's not." He sighed. "I just wish I were more like Harper."

"I doubt he would've done much better."

"Don't say that!"

"Finn, can we talk about this in the morning? It's time for sleeping now."

Finn frowned up at the sagging mattress above him. Bix had called dibs on the top bunk the instant Adrian showed them the guest room, like they were at summer camp or something. Finn was just as happy with the bottom one, but for some reason it still irritated him.

You're just jealous that everything seems to roll off of him so easily.

He lay in the darkness for a long time listening to his friend's breathing slow down, and he wished that he could just turn it off as easily as Bix seemed able to do.

But he couldn't. The sight of the Wraiths chained inside that cage in the barn had shocked him to the core, and that shock had remained with him all through dinner. Lying there, he now regretted not having pushed the couple harder for answers while he had the chance.

He had wanted to, but after the humbling grace Adrian had delivered before the meal, he felt it would be incredibly rude, especially when the reverend asked the Lord forgiveness of their trespasses, including the boys', and begged for His mercy on those who needed salvation.

Even when the topic inevitably gravitated to what they had seen in the barn, Finn couldn't bring himself to be critical. As Jennifer tried to explain, chaining the Wraiths up was actually more humanitarian than letting them run around in the wild, killing and infecting.

"They don't last long out there," she said. "It's because of their violent and delicate nature. They just don't last very long."

Of course, this didn't seem consistent with Finn's understanding of the creatures. But then again, he'd spent the last three years isolated from the real world. He had no relevant experience with Wraiths other than the few minutes they'd spent trying to get away from them back at the dam.

"But I don't understand," Bix had asked between bites. "You said you wanted to rid the world of the Flense. Why keep them? Why not just kill them on sight?"

"They are the Lord's creatures," Father Adrian said. "They may have been taken by the devil's germ, but that don't mean they cain't be saved. It is our job to exorcise them of their disease."

"Just seems like an awful risk," Finn commented. He was terribly uncomfortable with those things so close, even with the safeguards in place, the alarms and mines and sensors and such. What if the industrial scale diesel-burning generators failed?

"The Lord challenges us," Adrian said. "The path to righteousness must be filled with the cleansing fire of hardship. How else can our souls be purified?"

Jennifer nodded. "We try, but we can't eliminate all risk, of course. We do take precautions, especially when it comes to direct physical contact."

"How?"

"Well, first of all, we make sure we're properly covered."

"The gloves," Bix said. "Bandanas."

She nodded. "We also discovered that there are ways to control them using a special electronic device. It sorta works like the stun gun, except it don't knock them out like one. Instead, it makes them more like they're sleepwalking."

This had raised Finn's curiosity, and he had wanted to know more about the nature of the device, but by then it was getting late, and the adults insisted on continuing the discussion in the morning.

"Y'all are dead on yer feet," Adrian said. "And if'n we kept y'all up much longer, yer chins'll leave permanent indents in yer chests."

Bix yawned, and that triggered a wave of yawns from the rest of them, even Finn.

After four days of walking, of constant vigilance and lack of a regular diet, with his stomach full for the first time in as long as he could remember and the road dirt washed off and replaced with soft, clean, fresh clothes, all he wanted to do was sleep.

Except, now he was wide awake. Or, he thought he was.

Before he knew it, it was morning, sunlight was streaming in through the windows, and the delicious smell of bacon filled the house.

* * *

"Now, I know y'all are still tryin to process what you seen last night," Father Bowman told them at breakfast the next morning. "I can see it in yer eyes. It kept y'all up into the wee hours."

"Not me," Bix said, mumbling past a mouthful of pancakes and maple syrup. "I slept like a baby."

"Babies wake up a lot," Finn pointed out. "You snored like an old man."

"Did I keep you up?"

"Actually, no. I slept pretty good, too. I guess I was more tired than I realized."

"From all that runnin," Billy joked. He elbowed Luke and snorted. The two men had already finished their breakfast when Finn and Bix walked in. It did not, however, stop them from stealing the bacon off the boys' plates as soon as Jennifer put it there.

Finn frowned at the two men and wondered if they suffered from some kind of developmental deficiency. They both acted like twelve-year-olds at times.

Jennifer scraped the last of the hash browns onto Bix's plate and told the troublemakers to get on out of the kitchen. "Finish up your chores. We'll meet you at the new barn later and get those walls in place."

"I guess I'm just trying to wrap my head around the idea of bringing Wraiths here inside your compound," Finn said. "Why would you take such a risk?"

"Our duty," Adrian told them, leaning in. "The Lord has called us to be soldiers in His army to fight this evil scourge."

"Fight it by inviting the enemy inside?"

"They ain't the enemy, Finn. They're just human, like y'all and me. For too long, the devil was allowed to sow his germ in the world. This is a time of judgment. To prove our worthiness, we must cleanse ourselves of it. *All* of us."

"Judgment?" Bix asked. "Are you talking, like, the Rapture? Or extinction?"

Finn shifted uncomfortably. It all sounded like a bunch of religious mysticism to him.

"Both," Jennifer answered. "Or neither. Maybe this plague is biblical, or maybe it's manmade. I don't know. All I know is that it nearly destroyed mankind. Most were infected; many were killed. Precious few are left behind to rebuild. But to do so, we have to figure out what caused the Flense— to stop it, to cure those infected, and to rebuild."

"Just as Noah did," Father Adrian said.

"Seems to me that didn't turn out as planned."

"The Lord's will is not for man to understand, Finn."

Jennifer set her plate and a steaming cup of coffee down and sat between the boys. "I think that's enough of this for now, Adrian."

He shrugged.

But Bix wasn't finished. He wanted to know more about the world right after the Flense. He wanted to know how they'd survived. "You said most people were infected. How did you escape?"

"A fair amount of luck," Jennifer said.

Something dark clouded Adrian's face for a moment. He looked over at Jennifer and took her hand and held it. "The faithful see luck as providence. The good Lord guides us."

"I worked in a pharmacy at Walmart," she said. "It was late one night, and Father Adrian was in for his yearly flu shot when the police ran in and told the managers to lock the doors. There were shootins in the parkin lot. The store went straight into lockdown. We waited for hours. By then, we could see how bad it was through the storefront windows. It just kept getting worse and worse."

Adrian nodded.

"We survived for nearly a year inside that buildin, always holdin out hope that someone would come and tell us it was safe. But that never happened."

"A year in a Walmart?" Bix exclaimed. "How many of you were there?"

"Thirty or so to start, but we lost nearly half in the first few days. When people—" Father Adrian choked up. "When people lose their faith, they stop thinkin clearly. Some drunk themselves into comas on the free liquor. Many others tried to leave when it was clearly not prudent."

"They just wanted to get back to their families," Jennifer quietly countered.

"I don't blame them for that."

"After about six months, we were down to a half dozen, includin Billy and Luke."

"God's children," Adrian said. "They're a bit slow upstairs, in case you ain't noticed. But they's good boys, sometimes a little childish, but harmless nonetheless."

Jennifer gave them both a wide grin. "Which is why it's so refreshin to find a coupla smart young lads such as yourselves."

Bix coughed uncomfortably. His face turned bright red.

"Anyway, we ran outta food and water and had to move on," she continued. "After a year, the world had become unrecognizable. No power, no government. And no longer so full of ferals runnin around wanting to eat everyone."

"What happened to them all?"

"Died, I suppose. Humans are fragile creatures to begin with," Jennifer said. "Poorly adapted to survivin out in the elements. Same with the ferals. I guess most of them died of exposure or starvation."

Finn frowned. Once again, her claims didn't mesh well with his own observations. The creatures were a lot tougher than she gave them credit.

"Or ate each other," Bix said.

"We packed up a coupla cars and drove straight north until we found this place."

"Not straight," Adrian corrected. "Cars kept breakin down. Took us weeks to get here."

"That's why he doesn't like cars. He doesn't trust them."

Finn wanted to ask them where they'd found the land mines, but decided it wasn't that important.

"We resolved then to dedicate our lives to fixin what had been broken. We caught our first feral about a year ago, thinkin we could cure it. Each time, we get just a little bit closer."

Both boys' stomachs were full by then and they were growing drowsy. The conversation strayed to the subject of family. Finn was surprised when Bix opened up about his mother leaving shortly before the Flense.

"I know she's . . . dead, but sometimes I imagine her out there somewhere."

The couple seemed very sympathetic, which only encouraged him to talk about his father's freewheeling lifestyle before the Flense. Finn's thoughts drifted away, but when he heard Bix mention looking for the mine up north he snapped back.

"We're going to look for Harper there, right Finn? Family's important."

Finn wanted to choke him. After reminding him this morning not to divulge any details about where they'd been or where they were going, Bix was spilling everything.

"I think know which mine yer talkin about," Father Bowman said. "There was an old molybdenum operation years ago up along the river."

"You know where it is?" Finn asked, hopeful despite his anger.

"Sure do, son. It's a good ten-day walk from here by foot, three or four on horseback."

Finn was crushed. He hadn't realized it would take so long.

"Listen," Adrian said, patting Finn's arm, "I know y'all are eager to find yer family, but there's a lot of ground between here and there and too many chances for somethin to go wrong. But properly outfitted, y'all stand a much better chance of succeedin. Give us a coupla days to get y'all ready. In the mean time, help us erect the new church. When it's finished, we'll put y'all on a coupla horses. It'll sure beat walking. Y'all will still git there ahead a schedule."

Finn was torn. He hated to wait, especially now that Adrian knew exactly where this mine was located. Plus, he worried about inertia setting in, which would make it harder for them to get moving again after a few days of being pampered. He exchanged glances with Bix.

"It's your choice, bro," Bix said.

After a moment, Finn nodded.

"Yahoo!" Bix shouted. He broke out into a huge grin and asked if there were anymore pancakes.

"As much as you want," Jennifer replied, beaming.

CHAPTER

15

EDDIE WAS AWAKE BEFORE DAWN. HE SLIPPED OUT OF his military style bunk bed as quietly as he could, hoping the creaking metal frame wouldn't wake his bunkmate.

He padded over toward the bathroom in his bare feet, frowning as he passed the word LATRINE stenciled into the painted cinderblock beside the door, and relieved himself into one of the sparkling urinals.

"You really are one ugly sonofabitch," he told his reflection in the mirror over the sink. It's what he had told himself every day since Doc Cavanaugh's death. "That's a face only a mother could love."

Or a daughter.

He thanked his lucky stars for Hannah. Without her, he might not have had the will to carry on.

In truth, his appearance wasn't as grisly as it had been just after the accident, when he had begun to heal. It had terrified Hannah at first, but she quickly overcame her fright and accepted that it was what her father had become.

Just in the few days since leaving the bunker, the horrific visage he had once presented was mostly gone, faded away like the ink on an old newspaper left out in the sun. He still had no hair, and his skin was an odd shade of pink with a grayish sheen. His eyes were darker than they had been before. He was still a bit startling to look upon, but no one would mistake him for a freak anymore. Not automatically.

He welcomed the return to normality, but with it came a new fear, a sense of becoming somehow . . . less.

The gruesome superficial changes he had suffered had been accompanied by a startling change in his physical abilities: a heightening of his senses — everything from improved sight and hearing, to touch and taste and smell — and the development of incredible speed and strength. If his appearance was returning to normal, would his abilities do so as well?

Last night after arriving at the base, Captain Cheever had insisted on separating the group by gender and age into quarantine barracks. He claimed that it was only temporary and for their own protection, as well as for the protection of the other residents. The segregation would only be enforced until they could all be thoroughly examined by the base medic, after which they would be assigned regular quarters.

Of course, they'd all protested the arrangement— not only the separation, but the more permanent assignments. They made it explicitly clear that they didn't plan on staying.

However, Cheever would not be budged. It was standard procedure, he explained, the directive coming down from the man in charge himself, Colonel Lyle Wainwright. Civilians and soldiers alike were expected to abide by the same set of rules, and no exceptions would be made, no break from protocol tolerated.

"It's best to just comply until you're ready to leave," he told them.

In his frustration, Eddie had nearly torn out the railing to the men's barracks from its concrete base. The metal made a squealing sound, drawing Cheever's attention. Eddie feigned surprise and gave the railing an experimental shake while mumbling something about the cement failing. The captain grunted and continued on without further comment.

The others in their group knew about Eddie's abilities, though he'd conscientiously tried not to flaunt them. Nevertheless, he didn't want the strangers to know about them. It was partially because he didn't want them to fear him, but also because he knew it gave them an advantage against strangers, one he didn't want to lose.

Mostly, however, he kept his abnormal strengths secret because he lived in constant fear that he would wake up one morning and find that they had forsaken him, and that he had returned to being just as ordinary as everyone else.

From where he stood inside the bathroom, he could still hear the snores of the other three men in their beds down the hall— Harry Rollins, Harrison Blakeley, and Danny Delacroix. He sniffed the air and was relieved to find that he could detect each of their individual scents; only Jonah's was missing.

You also smell hot vegetable oil coming from the cafeteria. Big deal.

He knew that none of this proved he'd retained his full abilities. Those were strong scents. And they said nothing about his other powers.

Above his head, pipes and electrical conduits crisscrossed the open ceiling. He reached up with one hand, hopped slightly, and grabbed onto one. Then, with his free hand tucked against his stomach and very little effort, he pulled himself up until his chin met the bar. It creaked from the weight of his body.

He held the position for a count of a hundred before finally letting go with a satisfied grunt and dropping silently to the floor.

For now, at least, everything seemed to be working just fine.

* * *

The question on everyone's mind when they gathered to meet with Cheever a few hours after breakfast was whether Jonah had been found. Most vocal among them was Danny.

"A couple of hours ago, at daybreak this morning," Cheever reported to them, "I sent out a couple bikes to search the road between here and the refuelling truck. Private Ramsay went along with them. As you know, Private Vinay Singh is also missing. They plan to return to the point where they became separated if necessary. I expect them back at any moment."

"How could your man possibly think it was okay to just leave them behind?" Fran Rollins demanded. She turned to her husband. "This is exactly why we shouldn't have split up!"

Eddie watched her carefully. He knew she wasn't just talking about yesterday. She hadn't been happy with Jonah and Danny going out a second time in town and had made her displeasure known then, as well as afterward. She'd also been one of the more vocal dissenters last night during Cheever's announcement of the sleeping arrangements.

But Eddie also suspected that she was referring to their decision to leave people behind in the bunker. He needed to talk to Harry to make sure she kept such thoughts to herself. He didn't need her further fracturing the group by sowing seeds of doubt. And he didn't want them talking at all about the bunker or their plan to get to the evacuation center. He didn't know what these people might do with such knowledge.

"I spoke with Ramsay last night after he came in," Cheever said. "He told me that Private Singh was behind him and assumed he still was when they reached the gate. By then, of course, it was too late to send anyone out to look for them. But Singh is a good man, and I have faith in his ability to make good decisions. He understands the desert and its perils, as well as how to survive in it. He spent a year on his own before arriving here, so I'm sure your man is just fine with him."

He removed a clipboard from beneath his arm and referred to it. "In the mean time, we have a few other things to deal with."

They were all sitting or standing inside an unused motor pool maintenance bay. Food had been delivered earlier, in keeping with their quarantine from the rest of the community. Jonathan, Nami, Jasmina and the baby, Jorge, were not in attendance. They'd been taken directly to the infirmary upon arrival and remained there under observation.

They all suffered from severe malnutrition and were being given intravenous fluids. Jonathan and the baby were also being given IV antibiotics for their lung infections. Despite Jonathan's objections, he was too weak to fight them. He did, however, refuse to take anything orally for his fever.

The dislocations Nami incurred to both his knee and shoulder during the Wraith attack were also being treated. Both had been splinted.

"Let's begin with an overview of base operations," Cheever said.

"Not until you promise us better arrangements now," Fran declared. "I refuse to spend another night separated from my family."

"Me, too," Hannah said, clinging to her father.

"As I said, strict adherence to procedure is essential for survival. Once you're cleared, we'll find permanent residence. Also, we'll need to assign each of you to your duties, which you will assume once you have been medically cleared."

"Screw this!" Harry cried, among a chorus of protest. "We didn't ask to be brought here!"

"We're fixing your bus," Cheever calmly replied. "We're feeding you, outfitting you, and giving you medical treatment. Nothing is free. Everyone carries their weight around here."

Harrison stepped forward. "Look, we appreciate the assistance, Captain. And we don't mind working to pay off our dues— No, wait, guys!" he said, quickly turning when the others started to gripe. "Just hold on a sec. We owe the captain and his men a debt of gratitude for rescuing our butts out there yesterday, let's not forget that."

He turned back to the captain. "But we do need some assurance from you that we'll be allowed to leave at the time of our choosing. Assuming, of course, that all reasonable reimbursement has been made."

Cheever lowered the clipboard and stepped up to face Harrison. "This is a refugee camp, Mister . . . ."

"Blakeley."

He checked his clipboard. "Yes, Mister Harrison Blakeley. We may run this place like a military compound, but it works well precisely because of the discipline and the commitment of its members. Every resident, whether soldier or not, is a vital contributor. What this place is not is a charity. Nor is it a prison. Each and every member of this community is free the leave at his or her will, as long as we deem that it doesn't create a new threat. Is that assurance enough?"

The door at the far end of the bay opened, letting in a flash of daylight and a man dressed in a white lab coat. The door slammed shut with a reverberating clang that echoed through the large space.

"And here is our medic," Cheever said. "He'll be asking you to answer some questions. He'll also be drawing your blood and checking your lungs, temperature, and blood pressure. Please give him your every consideration."

"Um, sir?" the medic said. He had stopped a good twenty feet away from the group. Cheever went over and the two exchanged a few words.

After a moment, the captain looked over at the group and told them to do as the medic instructed. "Mister Delacroix?" he called. "Will you come with me please?"

"Why?" Eddie said, stepping forward. He held a hand out, stopping anyone from leaving. "What do you want with Danny?"

"I just have a few questions to ask him in private." He stopped, seeing the grave looks on their faces. "One of my men is missing, as well as one of yours. I need information about what happened. It'll be easier to interview him separately, without distractions."

"It's okay," Danny told them. "I'll be fine."

There was a low rumble of displeasure from the group when the two men left. "What was that all about?" Harry demanded of the medic.

The man wouldn't say. He just began the examination by passing out forms and pencils.

But Eddie had heard their exchange perfectly well. A member of the scout team looking for Private Singh and Jonah had returned. He reported that they had gone to the refueling spot, and while there was no sign of either man, they did find the motorbike, as well as a massive patch of blood.

CHAPTER

BILLY AND LUKE TURNED OUT TO BE SURPRISINGLY good workers, toiling away without complaint in the hot sun, their shirts off and their backs burning as all six of them struggled to get the framing up for the new structure.

They were all business when they needed to be, but as soon as a break was called, their antics resumed right back where they'd left off. Finn and Bix learned soon enough to just play along, and the jokers eventually lost interest in teasing them.

There seemed to be some disagreement about what to call the building and its precise function. Billy insisted on calling it a barn, which caused Adrian to roll his eyes and shake his head. "That boy is as simple as they come."

"I thought it was to be a church," Finn said.

"It is. Billy just calls it a barn because that's what it looks like," Luke said.

"Because that's the only kind of buildin Adrian knows how to build," Jennifer told them. "Four walls and a big slidin door. Slap on a coupla sloped roofs and call it a church, but it's still a barn."

"Jesus may have been a skilled carpenter," Adrian said, "but the holy Father did not see fit to endow this son with the same abilities."

Everyone laughed.

The frames had already been assembled, and except for a quick break when a stack of sawed boards collapsed and left a gash on Adrian's forehead, which Jennifer quickly bandaged, they went up very quickly.

By lunchtime, the walls were all secured in place. The horses had been employed to help tilt them up. When they weren't being used, the animals simply grazed on the grass nearby.

Bix and Finn sat beneath the shade of a lone maple tree and looked out over the lake as they ate lunch. Bix lamented that they couldn't go swimming. Luke guffawed. "Not unless you wanna be fish food!"

"Itty bitty fish food pieces!" Billy added.

They started chasing each other, disturbing the horses and making Adrian shout at them to stay on the trails or in the clearing or else they'd end up being itty bitty fertilizer.

"We've buried mines in the forest, too," he told the boys.

"Why are you building this all the way out here?" Finn asked.

The clearing was nearly a half mile away from the house, along a well-marked path running through the wood parallel to the shore. Both the house and the animal barn were well out of sight and earshot.

"The noise," Jennifer replied. She glanced meaningfully over at Adrian, and he shrugged.

"My sermons have been known to raise the roof."

Finn had been watching Billy and Luke sprinting through the woods. They seemed exceptionally nimble for their age. A sudden suspicion came over him. "You said you're trying to cure the Wraiths. Have you ever succeeded?"

As if sensing his thoughts, Adrian turned his own gaze to the boys. "Not entirely," he replied enigmatically. "We think we've come close."

A chill passed through Finn's body. He suddenly didn't want to be there.

Troubled, he stood up. The apple he'd been eating felt like a rock in his stomach. "Mind if I feed the rest of this to the horses?" he asked.

"Go right ahead."

After finishing their meal, the older adults excused themselves. "Regular chores ain't gonna do themselves," they said, urging the boys to rest a bit longer. "Not good fer the digestion to work so soon after eatin."

Bix chuckled from his seat at the base of the maple tree as he watched Father Adrian and Jennifer leave. "They make a cute couple," he said.

"Just a feeling I get, but I'm not so sure they are," Finn answered.

He gathered up the loose wrappers and uneaten food. It was a strange thing for him to see leftovers. Nothing had ever gone to waste in the bunker.

"You know, I think I could live here forever," Bix said, sighing. He patted his stomach and yawned.

"You've already forgotten about your father?"

"I'll send for him. They can all come here. This place is large enough, don't you think? And no silly rules. It'd be like one of those hippy communes."

"My father made those rules. Remember?"

"Not what I meant."

"So we'll all just sleep in tents and sing kumbaya."

"Chillax, bro. Just enjoy the moment."

Finn shook his head. He didn't agree at all with Bix, but he kept his mouth shut. On the surface, the ranch did seem like an improvement over the bunker. They were outdoors again, protected, eating fresh food. But they were still trapped, still living in fear. The lake and the fields were mined, the barrier surrounding the compound was electrified.

And unlike the bunker, there were Wraiths inside the walls.

How many?

Billy and Luke eventually ceased their adolescent antics and resumed work. They seemed to know instinctively what needed to be done, as if they'd done it all before. They showed the boys how to apply plywood over the studs, then they worked on framing the roof.

Once more, they used the horses to help lift the materials to the tops of the walls using a series of pulleys and booms that Billy rigged up. The men were quite adept with the tools, and their muscles rippled with the exertion and glistened with sweat. Their faces contorted in concentration.

It struck Finn as odd how both Billy and Luke seemed to have two polar opposite modes, like they had switches inside their heads.

By late that afternoon, the building began to resemble something functional.

They were all beyond tired when Luke abruptly announced that it was time to stop, as if the switch in his head had been flipped off. They were right in the middle of nailing the last set of roof supports into place. They balanced precariously on the walls, and the possibility that it might fall didn't seem to have crossed his mind.

He and Billy climbed down a hastily-constructed wooden ladder, then challenged the boys to a race back to the house.

"Last ones back hasta clean the pig pen!" Billy shouted, and they took off running.

Finn rolled his eyes. "Those two make me feel like an old man."

"You are an old man," Bix replied. "Compared to me, anyway."

"Gee, thanks."

"Do you think we're supposed to bring the horses back?"

Finn looked over. "I don't know."

The animals had wandered over by the water's edge, where an old dock jutted out over the still lake. The sun was still hovering above the horizon, silhouetting the animals' heads. Crane flies and gnats swarmed over the reeds. Dragonflies buzzed the water, dipping their tails in to lay their eggs and creating the illusion of a light rain.

Bix flashed him a mischievous grin. "Come on."

"We're not going in the water!"

"No, dummy. You want to be mucking out the pig pen? We'll ride those horses back to the house and beat those losers."

"But they're not saddled!"

"They got reins!"

Bix helped him up onto the back of one of the horses, then used a paint bucket to mount the other. "Clamp your legs onto the horse's sides. Hold onto the mane. Let's go."

"This is just one big game to you, isn't it?" Finn said.

"Less yakking and more riding. I'm not slopping pig crap!"

The horses seemed to know exactly where to go. They immediately turned down the path, picking up their pace, as if they were eager to get back to the barn. Pretty soon, they were trotting along at a decent clip.

Finn tried to tell Bix that the others were probably already back, but he bit his tongue on an especially hard jolt and tasted blood.

"Hold on!" Bix shouted, and leaned over, digging his heels into his horse's sides. In a flash, he was gone. Not wanting to be left behind, Finn's horse followed suit.

The trees flashed past. Finn gritted his teeth, afraid of being thrown off, and held on for dear life.

The horses raced up the path until it forked. Bix expected to turn left and leaned into the curve. With a shout of surprise, the horse went right.

"I'm slipping!" Finn cried.

"Hold on!"

"This is the wrong way!"

"I know! I'm trying to steer, but this damn horse is stubborn!"

The trees ended abruptly, and they entered a new clearing. In the center of it was another barn, although its walls were crumbling.

"Whoa!" Bix said, pulling back on his reins. The horse trotted over to the structure and stopped.

Finn's kept on going around the corner, where he finally fell off. Thankfully, the ground was covered in grass.

"Told you this place is huge," Bix said, lowering himself off his horse. "You could build a whole other house on this clearing big enough for three families."

"Wonder if this is Adrian's old church."

This side of the barn had crumpled into itself, and the roof had partially fallen. Finn made his way over the rotting timber, drawn by a low buzzing sound.

"What'd you find?" Bix asked.

Finn turned back, covering his mouth. He wanted to run away, but Bix pushed past him.

"What's that noise— Oh, crap!"

Three of the walls were still standing, and the insides were splashed with blood. More stained the straw strewn on the ground. Chains dangled from the rafters over a large metal cage made of chain link.

The humming came from a dark mound at the far end of the barn, partially buried beneath the collapsed fourth wall.

"Jesus Christ," Bix whispered, throwing his hand over his mouth. "What the fu—"

"You boys shouldn't be here," Jennifer said. She emerged from the darkness inside the barn carrying a small blue box. "You shouldn't be wanderin about."

"The h-horses," Finn stammered. "We couldn't stop them. They brought us here."

"What happened to this place?" Bix asked.

"The roof collapsed during an experiment." She shook her head. "All but two ferals died."

"You worked on them here?"

She nodded. "Kept them and treated them."

"And what's all that equipment?"

Jennifer flicked on a flashlight and swung the beam into the depths of the barn. It came to rest on a portable generator. The bright yellow of its diesel tank shone in the gloom. Thick cables extended out of it, branching like giant veins. Some reached up into the rafters, where several lights had been strung, while others snaked across the ground toward a cart piled high with electrical devices of one sort or another.

"This is where we're trying to find a cure." She shut off the flashlight and turned back to the boys. "Now take them horses back to the other barn and get yourselves ready for dinner. Supper's gettin cold."

CHAPTER
17

BᴵX wᴬs ᴄonsidᴇrably qᴜiᴇter ᴛhᴀt ᴇvᴇning ᴀt dinner than he had been all day, and his mood did not improve by the next morning. But if any of the others besides Finn noticed his gloominess, they did not remark on it, despite ample opportunities to do so.

The rest of the next day passed without much conversation. The boys finished nailing on the plywood panels, then spread dry straw onto the ground so it wouldn't get muddy.

Luke and Billy continued bracing the roof, although they left it open for light. Not once did any of them bring up the ruined barn or the corpses the boys had found within it the night before.

Finn tried a few times to get Bix to talk, when he could get his friend alone, but he wasn't very responsive. Finn couldn't tell if he was merely distracted or if he was feeling somehow betrayed.

A few hours after lunch, Finn noticed that Billy and Luke were gone with the horses. They reappeared twenty minutes later with the cart piled high with the equipment from the ruined barn, as well as several rolls of unused eight-foot chain link fencing. They circled the clearing, finishing with the cart situated just outside the opening that would become the new barn's door.

Adrian clapped his hands in excitement, though to the boys it felt forced. "I hadn't dared to hope to get this much done so soon," he exclaimed. "Figured it'd take another week before we even got the roof on. You two boys did the work of four! Ain't that right, darlin?"

Jennifer nodded.

He pulled the tarp away and began to unload. "I ain't got no idea what half this stuff was meant for before the Flense. Some we picked up along the way. Some was brought to us by others to test. But these here devices have a definite effect on the ferals, so maybe it was meant fer us to find, like us runnin into y'all out there on the road, somethin of a blessin, like the good Lord was lookin out fer us."

They unloaded the equipment, and Jennifer began to arrange it on a bench they had previously installed along the back wall. With Finn's and Luke's help, Adrian erected the chain link inside the building, employing the four center posts as corner braces and installing a heavy locking gate.

The cage — for that's clearly what it was — occupied more than half of the barn's floor space, an area roughly twenty feet on a side. Not only would the so-called "church" look nothing like a real one, but it would also apparently function nothing like the boys imagined.

The vague sense of dread that Finn had been feeling sharpened.

As soon as the cart was empty, Billy and Luke left with it. They returned after a half hour with the generator and hauled it around to the back, where they lowered it to a platform of wood.

When Finn went to check on it later, he was amazed to see that they had already built an enclosure to protect it against the weather.

Adrian showed Bix how to string the flood lamps across the rafters. It was a race against the dying light, as the sun dipped into the trees and the shadows grew darker. When they were finished, it was almost too dark to continue.

He threw the end of the electrical cable toward the back wall and shouted for Jennifer. Then he and Bix climbed down to the ground.

Outside, the gennie started up with a loud metallic rattle before settling into a steady drone. Jennifer threaded the cable through a hole in the wall, and soon the bulbs blinked on, flooding the barn with light.

"Need more lamps there and there," Adrian said, pointing to a couple places still in shadow. He immediately started unspooling more wire through the center of the cage. "Bury this neath the ground," he told Luke and Billy. "Connect it like we did in the other. We'll ground it all tomorrow."

Despite the strangeness of it all, Finn couldn't help but feel a sense of accomplishment in the work they had done. He'd never built anything with his hands before, much less a structure of such scale. The blisters on his hands stung, and the muscles in his arms and back ached, but it all felt good in a way.

He glanced over at Bix and saw that he was smiling, too. "Look what we did," he said.

Bix's brow furrowed, and the smile thinned, like he hadn't intended to be caught with it on his face. "Yeah."

"Y'all did some fine work here," Jennifer agreed. "But it's getting late, and I ain't even started supper."

"There's still time," Adrian said.

"Time for what?" Bix asked. It was the longest sentence he'd spoken in hours.

"After what y'all seen the past coupla days, I know y'all have questions, perhaps even serious doubts. I don't deny it would've been a shock to anyone. So bear with me a few minutes. Y'all will see that what we done here was worth it."

"Not tonight, Adrian. The boys are tired. I'm tired."

"Luke and Billy's already gone to fetch one, Jenny."

"But it ain't got no roof on it."

"It's safe."

"Safe for what?" Finn asked. He shot Bix a worried glance.

But Adrian gestured at the opening in the wall, where the sound of horses' hooves could be heard growing louder.

Luke soon emerged from the trees, astride one of the animals. As he passed them in the clearing, Bix and Finn yelped in alarm. At the end of a rope, tied to the saddle horn, was a Wraith. Another rope passed from its neck to the second horse which carried Billy. In his arms was one of the blue boxes Finn had seen Jennifer holding the night before.

"Jesus Christ!" Bix whispered. Finn was already backing away. He raised the hammer in his hand, ready to defend himself.

"Don't worry. It ain't gonna hurt no one."

The creature shambled along, its movements restrained by the ropes. Its head sagged forward. Drool dripped from its swollen lip. It showed no desire to touch or attack. In fact, it did not seem to be aware of any of them.

"What did you do to it?" Finn asked.

"We calmed it," Jennifer said in a normal tone of voice. Any displeasure she had expressed earlier for Adrian's decision was gone, replaced instead with a hint of eagerness.

"Stand back," Luke said. "It's still contagious. Y'all don't want it touchin you just yet."

"What do you mean by 'just yet'?" Finn asked.

But Adrian guided the boys to one side as Luke dismounted and pulled the Wraith into the barn. Billy had also dismounted. They kept the ropes taut so the creature couldn't go anywhere except where they wanted it to. Together, they maneuvered it to the cage opening, then swung the gate shut.

"What if it climbs out?"

"It won't," Adrian assured them. "We'll finish the top tomorrow, but fer now, we don't need one."

The men gave the ropes a skilled flick, and the lassoes slipped off the Wraith's neck. Despite being free to move about, it just stood there mindlessly staring at the ground.

"Now," Adrian said, "do we all agree what will happen if it touches us?"

Both Finn and Bix looked up in alarm.

Adrian walked over to the bench where the equipment had been arranged. He selected what appeared to be a cattle prod, an eight-foot long metal rod with two knobs at the end. Extending from the handle was a cable, and the cable was plugged into an electrical power strip.

Sparks flew when he touched the tip to the chain link.

Before they could stop him, he carefully threaded the prod through an opening in the gate. For a moment, Finn flashed to a childhood memory of him and Harper playing the game *Operation*. His brother had steadier hands and almost always won.

Any moment now, he's going to touch the wire and a buzzer'll go off, and then it'll be Jennifer's turn.

But the man's hands were rock steady.

"Don't," Bix whispered. He gripped Finn's arm. "It's not right."

But Finn was fascinated. He wanted to see what would happen.

The tips touched the skin of the Wraith, and a loud *bang!* rang out. The lights dimmed at the same moment that sparks exploded off the creature's body. It flew half the length of the cage before rolling in a tangled heap on the ground.

"You killed it," Bix cried.

"It's a Wraith," Finn said, his eyes glued to the motionless figure. The sharp tang of burning flesh pinched his nose.

Adrian pulled the prod out and set it back on the bench. "Forty-five seconds," he said, holding up a stopwatch. "That's how long they're harmless."

He nodded to Billy, who went inside the cage. The look on his face as he reached out a hand at the creature was one of kindness.

"What are you doing?" Bix cried. "Stop!"

Billy laid his palm on the Wraith's scalp.

"No!" Finn yelled, but of course it was already too late.

"It's okay," Billy said. He showed his hand to the group, as if the absence of any change was proof he hadn't been infected. He walked back over, a big smile on his face.

"Twenty seconds," Adrian said, and let him out.

Finn peered into Billy's eyes. He saw no trace of the Flense.

"You've figured out how to make them not infectious!" he gasped. "That's incredible!"

"It's only temporary," Jennifer said. Excitement danced in her eyes. "Even so, it's a start."

"The first step to salvation is always the hardest," Adrian said.

"And what is that?"

"Forgiveness."

Finn turned to Bix, his thoughts whirling. He didn't know what to say.

But Bix did. "This is wrong," he whispered. "It's not salvation. I don't know what it is, but I do know it's wrong."

CHAPTER
18

"FINN. HEY MAN, WAKE UP!"

Finn's eyes popped open. Bix's disembodied face hovered over him, a dimmer shade of night than the ocean of darkness it swam in.

For a moment, he thought he was back in the bunker, and Bix was getting him up to stir up some form of mischief. Wasn't it time to rearrange Jonah's food supplies in the upstairs pantry? He couldn't remember if they'd already done that this week. He almost told him to keep it down or else he'd wake his father.

"What? What's happening?"

"They're gone."

Finn blinked into the darkness. He felt stupid for not understanding. "What's gone?"

"Not what, who. Everyone. Adrian and Jennifer, Billy and Luke. The house is empty."

Finn sat up, pushing Bix away. "What the hell are you talking about?"

"I couldn't sleep. I was thirsty, so I got up to get something to drink. I didn't think anything of it at first, but when I passed Billy's bedroom, I didn't hear anything."

"So?"

"So? That guy snores louder than a hive of bumble bees stuck inside a tin can.

"Bumblebees don't snore."

"Not relevant. The point is, I went down to the kitchen to get some water, and I was standing there looking out the window, and I see this glowing through the trees. Scared the crap out of me at first, because I thought it was moving, like one of those willow wisps."

"Will-o'-the-wisp," Finn corrected.

"That's what I said, like a ghost or something. But it wasn't a ghost. It was just the wind blowing the trees and making it look like it was moving, which made me think about—"

"Bumblebees? Ghostly fireballs? Get to the point, Bix." He resented being woken up. He'd been dreaming about Bren, and to have her taken away from him, especially *right* at that particular moment, had not put him in a good frame of mind.

"I knocked on everyone's door to alert them about the light. You know, because it might be a fire or something. But no one answered. Everyone's gone."

They got dressed and slipped out of the house. The grass on the front lawn was wet with dew. Above them, a nearly full moon sat high in the sky, making everything look like it had been plated in liquid silver.

Navigating was difficult, as there were no lamps yet along this part of the trail. And the moonlight didn't penetrate through the forest canopy that well, so they found themselves stumbling off the path once or twice.

"Glad thing those mines aren't right off the trail," Bix whispered.

139

Finn was beginning to wonder if there were any at all, or at least as many as Adrian made it sound like. He recalled how Billy and Luke had raced through the trees that first day. Maybe they knew exactly where the mines had been set, but that didn't explain the horses venturing into the wood on a couple of occasions. He didn't think the animals would know exactly where to avoid.

Billy and Luke were running outside *the wall.*

That was another thing that didn't sit right with him. Wouldn't it make sense to lay the mines there, rather than inside, stop Wraiths before they had a chance to get in?

They're already inside.

The boys were still a ways off when they determined the light Bix saw was coming from Adrian's new church. "Maybe they're working on it," Finn suggested.

"At night?"

"You saw how eager he was to get it up and working again. Jennifer, too. And if they're really close to—"

An odd sound reached their ears, both familiar and unexpected. Neither boy could place it at first.

"Cheering?" Bix whispered. "It sounds like cheering."

And by more than just a few people, too.

"One of Father Adrian's roof-raising sermons?"

"Good thing there's no roof."

The man's voice boomed out from inside the church as they arrived at the clearing. His words were muffled by the walls and distorted by the wind. Light rose into the sky.

"Sounds like a freaking carnival barker," Finn said.

Bix nodded grimly. "Or a religious revival."

"For just the four of them? In the middle of the night?"

Keeping in the shadows, they skirted along the edge of the clearing, circling around until the barn door opening came into sight. Each step revealed a little more of the scene inside . . . and swept away any doubt the boys harbored about the couples' intentions.

There were perhaps a dozen people crowded just inside. They were shouting and waving their arms in excitement. Adrian stood in back on the cart and shouted through his cupped hands. His words were clear enough now for the boys to understand. He called out numbers, pointing to various individuals in the crowd. It sounded like an auction. Each cry elicited more cheers.

He soon stopped, and the hubbub died away, and the strangers milled restlessly about, as if waiting for something to happen.

Through the bodies, the boys caught a glimpse of the cage. The Wraith they had seen earlier was still inside of it, except that it was now completely naked. The creature was chained to a long, thick post hammered deep into the ground in the center of the cage, so it couldn't climb out the open top. It attacked the fence, eliciting excited shouts from the onlookers.

Skeletal arms reached through the openings, trying to get to them. Trying to touch or tear.

Billy and Luke stood just outside of its reach. They poked at the creature with the cattle prods, but the electrical pops were considerably smaller than before. They must have dialed down the current. Each shock didn't incapacitate the Wraith, only infuriated it all the more.

"What the hell are they doing to it?" Bix whispered.

"I don't know."

"I told you it was wrong."

The boys watched in disbelief for several minutes. "Maybe this is part of the rehabilitation," Finn wondered aloud.

Bix didn't answer.

The sound of scuffling feet and muffled grunts forced the boys deeper into the shadows. *"Look,"* Bix whispered, and pointed toward the lake.

Several rowboats were tied up at the end of the dock, gently knocking against one another. A man stepped out of one. He reached down and heaved something large out from the bottom of the craft. It landed on the dock with a thump and an audible cry.

"That's a person!"

"Or maybe another Wraith," Bix said.

"Those men aren't wearing gloves."

"It's wrapped up."

A second body was thrown to the dock. It took several men to wrestle each one to its feet and then along the dock toward the barn. "Clear the way!" they shouted, and shoved the packages through the doorway. Both fell to the dirt.

"Stand them up," Adrian cried.

They were pulled upright.

"Let's see them!"

The hoods were yanked off.

"Shit!" Bix cried, before clamping a hand over his mouth.

"Not Wraiths."

"What the hell are they going to do?"

"Which one begs forgiveness?" Adrian demanded.

A man stepped out of the crowd and studied the two bound men. After a moment, he pointed to one. The men cheered.

"Finn?" Bix moaned. "Please tell me—"

There was a sharp *crack!* and a flash of light, and the cage-bound Wraith fell to the ground and didn't move.

"No! Please!" the man who had been selected cried out. "Please, no! I won't do it again! I'm sorry! Pleeeeease!"

His bindings were removed, then he was quickly stripped down naked except for his underwear. He struggled against the men holding him, trying to escape, but they were ruthless.

"Thirty seconds by my count!" Adrian shouted.

The crowd started to chant: "Twenty-nine! Twenty-eight! Twenty-seven . . . ."

"No! NOOOOO!" the prisoner screamed.

"Finn! What are they doing?"

"Shhh! I don't know, Bix."

"Twenty five! Open the gate!"

"Twenty-three! Twenty-two!"

"Positions!"

"You can't do this to me! Reverend! You know me! Don't do this!"

"Twenty! Shove him in!"

The men threw the victim inside the cage and immediately swung the reinforced cage door shut. The man flew across the dirt and landed with a pained cry. He immediately tried to climb the chain link. Luke touched the cattle prod to the wire and the man fell off.

On the other side of the cage, the Wraith began to stir.

"Seventeen!" Adrian shouted. "Sixteen!"

"Fifteen!" the crowd chanted in turn. "Fourteen!"

"Holy shit!" Bix cried. He grabbed Finn and shook him. "What the fu—"

143

"Do it," Finn growled, pushing Bix away. His eyes were glued to the scene inside the barn. "Do it, man! Get up!"

"Eleven!"

The man stood up. He spun around to face the recovering Wraith.

"Ten!"

"Do it!" Finn yelled, no longer caring to keep his voice down.

"Nine!"

The man ran at the Wraith just as it lifted its head. The crowd screamed "Seven!" The creature stood unsteadily. The naked bodies slapped against each other. The Wraith flew into the wire and fell to the ground.

"Six!"

"Do it!" Finn screamed. Bix tugged on him, pleading with him to run. But Finn didn't seem to notice. "Goddamn it, kill the Wraith!"

"FOUR!"

The man grabbed the creature by its head and dragged it into the center of the cage. He wrapped his legs around its body for leverage and tried to twist. The Wraith was fighting back now, its strength returning.

"TWO!"

They wrestled. Then, just as the crowd cried out "ONE!" the Wraith's body went limp. The man was underneath. He heaved the dead creature off with a desperate cry.

"ZERO!" the crowd screamed.

The man stumbled away from the corpse. He fell against the wire, but managed to hold on. "Let me out," he panted. "LET ME OUT OF THIS CAGE!"

The crowd stilled and went silent.

"Goddamn it, Adrian! I did it, okay? I killed it. Am I forgiven? Please, let me out."

"No. You took too long."

The man stumbled back, collapsed. He threw his hands up to clutch at his head.

"Finn!" Bix whispered into his friend's ear. *"We have to go. Now!"*

"No, wait!"

A high, keening cry escaped from the prisoner's throat, rising until it shattered like glass, leaving nothing but a thin, dry whistle in its wake.

"Sorry," Adrian said. "But you are not worthy of salvation."

A gleeful cheer rose from the crowd.

"Finn? We—"

"Yeah, I know. Let's get the hell outta here."

He stood up and turned around, only to find Bix having some kind of seizure. A moment later, his friend collapsed unconscious to the ground.

CHAPTER 19

BIX SAT UP, GROANED IN AGONY, AND FELL BACK ONTO the cushion. "Where am I?"

"The house. Try not to move, sweetie," Jennifer quietly told him. She rewet the washcloth in the bowl on the floor and reapplied it to his forehead. "I'm afraid you got a double zappin before I realized it was you two and not a couple of ferals."

Bix shot her a surprised look, then glanced over at Finn, who was pacing across the worn carpeting between the couch and the doorway. He looked like a caged lion.

All the lights in the room were ablaze. Jennifer had turned them on after arriving ahead of Finn, who had carried Bix's slumped form over his shoulder the entire way back. Adrenaline had given him the strength, but now his body shook from the exertion.

"Goddamn it," he growled at Jennifer. He opened his fists and shook out his cramped fingers for the hundredth time. "You need to tell us what the hell is going on here."

Jennifer sighed unhappily. "I knew we shoulda told y'all the whole truth, but Adrian believed the demonstration would be more than enough to process for now. He planned on tellin y'all in the mornin."

"Telling us what?" Finn demanded. "What truth? Huh? That you're using the Wraiths to murder innocent people? That truth?" He pointed at the woods. "That it's all some sick game? We believed you! Instead, you turned out to be some kind of . . . depraved . . . ." He sputtered, unable to find the right words.

"I know what it looks like, Finn, but we ain't depraved. We're tryin to save those poor creatures, rehabilitate them."

"Infecting others sure as hell doesn't look like rehabilitation! It looks like you're making more of them. And how does inciting someone to break a Wraith's neck help save it?"

"Justice, Finn. That man sinned. And that feral was already too far gone to be saved. The only humane thing left to do was to put it out of its misery."

"You could just shoot it in the head! It's faster and cleaner. People should not be getting their kicks watching an execution!"

Jennifer stood up and crossed the room. For the first time, she looked exasperated. "Shootin is too easy," she said, her voice thick with emotion. "It's heartless and it's cruel exactly because of how fast and clean it is. There ain't no personal commitment to it, no thinkin, just doin and movin on."

Finn stepped back in stunned disbelief. "What the hell are you talking about?" he cried. "Those things are animals! You call them that yourself. You call them ferals! Like rabid dogs, and you shoot rabid dogs to put them down."

"Sit down, Finn," she snapped, finally reaching the end of her patience. "Sit down and listen for a moment."

"No!" he roared. "I need you to explain what we just saw back there! Tell us why a bunch of people cheered on while

Father Adrian — I can't believe he thinks it's God's work — while he threw an uninfected man inside a cage with a Wraith. How is forcing someone to choose between becoming one of them or being torn apart by it saving anyone? It's not God's work! It's horrible!"

"That man we put inside that cage wasn't innocent. He betrayed his neighbor, stole his food. And for that he needed to be punished. It's about doing right."

"Right? What do you know about right?"

"Y'all may think this is the wild west again, that there ain't no laws, but that ain't true. Without laws, we'd all be animals, no more different than the ferals out there."

"So that was punishment?" Finn collapsed into a chair, squeezing his head in his arms. "Why?" he cried. "Why make him do something like that?"

"Because that's how we keep order, Finn. Everyone understands it. Everyone knows that if'n you break the law, then you'll be punished. It's a deterrent. You get a chance to redeem yerself. Ten seconds is more than enough time. Everyone gets at least fifteen. Only the truly repentant will be saved."

Finn shook his head. "You sound like Adrian. It's sickening."

Bix groaned. "How did I get here?"

"I carried you," Finn answered. He stood up and went to sit beside his friend, flicking Jennifer away with his hand and a hateful glare.

"I feel like shit."

"Here, honey," Jennifer said, offering a glass. "Sip some water."

Finn slapped the glass out of the woman's hand. He wanted to scream at her not to touch him.

She patiently went over and picked up the glass, refilled it, then gently helped Bix sit up and drink. When he was finished, she set the glass back on the table.

"It's a new world, Finn," she quietly said, "with new rules and new ways of doin things. And before y'all get to judgin, y'all need to know that some good comes out of our work. But nothin is free, and in a world that ain't got no use for money, sometimes we have to pay in other ways."

"Pay for what?"

"Goods that we need to do our work. Supplies. Wood fer buildin. Till the world is rid of the Flense, it's how we have to do things."

Finn rocked where he sat. The buzzing in his head threatened to blow him apart.

"What's going to happen to that man now?" Bix asked, his voice weak. He gagged and sounded like he was going to throw up.

Jennifer moved a large plastic bowl closer to the side of the couch.

"The one being punished," Bix clarified. "He's a Wraith now, isn't he?"

"Yes, he is infected."

"What's going to happen to him?"

"We'll try to cure him."

"And if you can't?"

Jennifer looked kindly down on the boy and gave him a gentle smile. "You think we're heartless, but we ain't. We ain't cruel."

"Quit defending your sick actions and just answer the damn question," Finn growled.

"Father Adrian will—"

"Stop calling him that! He's no holy man!"

"I will try to save him usin my methods. Me and him, we have different ideas about salvation, different paths to take. That man failed to save himself last night. Now it's my turn to try."

CHAPTER

20

"I DON'T BELIEVE IT FOR A SECOND," HARRY TOLD Eddie at breakfast. "Danny wouldn't just up and leave without saying anything to the rest of us. And why? Did he think he could just go back to the bunker on his own? By foot?"

"Keep it down," Eddie warned. "No talking about that place in public."

He glanced suspiciously over at a group of men who had just entered the dining hall, their clothes dusty, fully automatic rifles slung over their shoulders. Their faces were black with road grime, except for the patches covered by their goggles.

Someone at another table said something that elicited a roar of laughter from the others, and they looked unabashedly over at the new people seated at Eddie's table. There was open curiosity in their eyes, but they made no attempt to interact.

The previous day, once the medical examinations were completed and the survivors were cleared, each individual was assigned a task. A couple of women came in to explain the process. "Everyone has to work for their keep here," they told the group. "Yes, even those just passing through."

"You get a lot of people just passing through?"

"A few."

"Anyone change their mind after leaving and come back?"

"Usually when people leave here like that, it's permanent."

"And why is that?"

The woman gave them a perplexed look. "Because it's dangerous outside the fence. And it's not just roamers and infected. There's wild animals. People die out there."

They talked a while about the various jobs that needed to be done. Most of it sounded like busy work, but some of it was clearly necessary. Three hundred people living in a small space produced a lot of waste and required a lot of food, water, and supplies.

They were assured that the assignments were on a rotating basis for most residents, so if they didn't like the job they got, it wouldn't be long before they would move on to another. "But seniority plays a role, too. If you choose to stay on here—"

"Which we won't," Eddie declared. "Once our bus is fixed and we have all our people together again, we'll be moving on."

They gave him looks that suggested they knew better, but didn't argue.

Danny had been assigned to sanitation detail, but no one saw him for the rest of that day. And when he failed to show up that night in their quarantine barracks, some began to suspect that something bad had happened to him.

"Now, we don't know," Harrison told them. "It's possible he got assigned to regular quarters, like Harry and his family."

But other than the Rollinses, no one else had been reassigned.

Then, just that morning, their second at the base, Eddie overheard one of the two guards talking about how Danny had demanded to leave in the middle of the night with nothing more than a backpack and some water. Eddie was in complete disbelief. He hid around the side of a small storage shed about eighty feet away to eavesdrop on the rest of their conversation. Though they spoke in normal tones, he had no problem hearing them.

He saw Captain Cheever emerge from the administrative building, where he shared an office with Colonel Wainwright, and wander over to the guards. He acted surprised by the news of Danny's departure. "And you just let him walk out?"

"You informed the newcomers they could leave whenever they wanted to."

"Dammit, Sergeant Bolton! Not in the middle of the night! It's suicide! You should always advise with me first before letting anyone go."

"I wasn't at the gate," the sergeant insisted. "Private Ramsay was! Do you want me to discipline him?"

"Ramsay? Dammit. No, I'll deal with him myself." The captain spun around to leave.

"Um, sir?" Bolton asked. "I heard the search team found Private Singh's bike yesterday."

Cheever stopped. He took a moment to allow a couple people to pass out of earshot before stepping back over. "They found it abandoned by the side of the road about a half mile from the fuel truck. It was covered in blood. The tank was full, but the men couldn't get it to start." He sighed and shook his head. "It sounds like a mechanical failure. They were attacked."

"By infected?"

"Them or mountain lions."

"Jesus," Bolton said. "I'm sorry to hear that. Singh was a good man."

"Yes, he was," Cheever snapped. "We're not telling anyone just yet what happened, understood?"

"Yes, sir."

The captain nodded and walked away. He didn't see the smirk on Bolton's face, but Eddie had.

He couldn't decide if he should tell any of the others what he had seen and overheard. They already guessed that Jonah might be dead, but now he wondered if there might be more to the story. There had been something sinister in Bolton's smirk, and the convenient explanation of Danny leaving in the middle of the night didn't sit well with him.

Which is why he decided to wait for Harry to show up at breakfast. He needed to talk it through with someone, and he didn't want it to be Harrison— not that he didn't trust the man, but because he seemed too blasé about things sometimes, too willing to accept the status quo and not expect something more. He was too accommodating. After all, he'd let his only son run off on what was almost certainly a suicide mission.

Harry had echoed his own alarm. "This stinks," he said, when Eddie finished telling him what he knew. "Danny had no reason to leave. He didn't want to."

"So, what do we do about it?"

"It's that Cheever guy. He's as crooked as a dog's hind leg."

Eddie frowned. Until that morning, he'd have agreed, but now he wasn't so sure.

"I'm telling you," Harry went on, "that man is trying to break us apart. First, it was separating the men and women."

"You and Fran and the boys are together."

"Because I went straight to Cheever's boss, that Wainwright guy, and demanded it. You should do that, too. It's wrong that you and Hannah are separated."

Eddie nodded in the direction of the girls at the other end of their table. "At the moment, Hannah and Bren need each other more than she needs me."

Harry's forehead furrowed. "That's not the Eddie I know. You used to be a lot more protective of her."

"I still am. But I know exactly where she is, and I know she's safe with Kari and Susan. I'm also confident enough in my own . . . abilities that I'll be able to protect her if I need to."

"Hey, what are you two talking about?" Fran Rollins asked, shifting closer to her husband. "Making secret plans to blow up the latrines so you don't have to dig them out?"

Harry gave her a dirty look, then shook his head. "Eddie says Danny's gone. He heard the guards say he decided to leave in the middle of the night."

Fran shook her head. "That doesn't sound like Danny. In fact, I know it's not true."

Eddie leaned in and asked, "What do you know, Fran?"

"I saw him yesterday, right after lunch. He was coming from talking to the captain."

"What did he say?"

"Nothing really. He was in a hurry and couldn't talk because he was supposed to go report to some guy about work. He said he'd see us at dinner."

Harry shook his head. "He was assigned with my team on latrine duty, but he never showed up. I just assumed he was still with the captain."

"If the captain was finished with him, and he didn't show up for work, then what happened to him?" Eddie asked. "And why are they saying he decided to leave last night if he didn't? He had no reason to. He had no place to go." He shook his head. "It doesn't add up."

"Do you think it has something to do with Jonah?"

Eddie grimaced. Should he tell them what he'd overheard? They had a right to know that Jonah was dead. But how would they react?

"Looks like you're the one who knows something and isn't telling," Fran said, studying his face.

"Is it that obvious?"

She nodded.

"We don't know for sure what happened," Eddie said. "They haven't told us anything. And I don't want anyone to worry unnecessarily. Let me gather some more information."

He stood up from his uneaten breakfast, then bent back down again. "Regardless of what is happening, everyone needs to watch each other's back."

He glanced over at the group that had come in earlier. The man who had brought Danny back on the motorbike was with them, but he had moved over to where Sergeant Bolton was seated in the opposite corner of the hall. They were in the middle of a heated discussion, though the background noise was too loud for Eddie to hear what it was about.

He turned back to Harry and Fran. "Don't get too comfortable. We should all be ready to leave at a moment's notice."

CHAPTER
21

FINN WOKE THE NEXT MORNING WITH THE SUNLIGHT streaming into the room and memories of the night before filling his head like a bitter hangover. His entire body ached from carrying Bix, and his stomach wanted to revolt. But as badly as he felt, he knew that Bix must be hurting even more.

He lay in bed for a while with his arms tucked under his head, staring up at the sag in the mattress just a few feet away from his nose, and listened to the sounds of his friend's restless sleep.

They hadn't gotten to bed until nearly four by the clock on the bedside stand, after Adrian had returned and the argument they'd had with Jennifer repeated itself in a somewhat abbreviated form. The explanations had done little other than baffle and frustrate Finn, and Bix had remained mostly silent, likely because he hurt too much to move.

The worst part was that he had been terrified that Adrian would do something to them for sneaking around. After all, as Jennifer said, it was a different world with different rules, and he was still trying to understand exactly what they were.

But Adrian had looked sympathetically down at them and said, "Y'all are just babes lost in the wilderness." He told them to go to bed, that things would look differently the next day. It bothered Finn because it made him doubt whether he was right to be so self-righteous. After all, the world had indeed changed, and maybe it was wrong of him to judge others based on ideas that might no longer be relevant.

The clock now read nearly noon. That he'd actually slept at all was surprising enough, but to have slept so soundly was a shock.

"Bix?" He nudged the mattress with the tips of his fingers. "Hey, man, you awake?"

"Yeah."

"You okay?"

"Surprisingly . . . yeah. But I'd recommend keeping your distance for a while. I think I may have absorbed some of that electricity, because I've got some wicked lightning farts going on up here."

Finn wrinkled his nose. The room did smell stale. "What're we going to do?"

"Do? Well, first, I'm going to eat breakfast. Then I think I'll take a giant poop. Or maybe I'll poop first. Just hope I don't electrocute myself sitting on the toilet."

Finn frowned. "Be serious."

"I know. It's just . . . ." He sighed. "I guess it's time for us to leave, bro. This place is seriously whacked."

"Yeah, that's pretty clear. I mean, do we tell them we're leaving? Or do we just sneak away? Do we ask for horses?"

"We owe them enough to tell them. Whether they want to give us horses . . . that's up to them."

"It's a hundred and fifty miles to Bunker Two. That's a hell of a long way to walk, especially through territory infested with Wraiths."

"Yeah." Bix was quiet for a while. "You know, I still can't get over what they did to that man last night."

"Me, neither. It was crazy."

"Insane in the membrane crazy."

"Do you think they can be rehabilitated?"

"The infected or us?"

"Either."

Bix didn't answer for a long time. Finally, he said, "Not them. But I do believe Jennifer and Adrian believe they can be, in their own twisted minds."

"I don't believe they do," Finn said. "I think they know it's all lies. They're just crazy."

"Well, they did prove that they can make a Wraith uninfectious, at least temporarily. If they managed to figure out that much, why don't you believe they're trying to figure out the rest?"

"I don't know that they did, actually. I'm not convinced they proved anything."

"You saw it. You watched Billy touch that Wraith. Nothing happened to him."

"I know. I believed it right after, but then . . . . I mean, I guess after last night, after them trying to explain it to us, I just don't buy any of it. I've been working on a theory of the Flense, and so there may be other explanations for what we saw."

"Like what?"

But Finn avoided the question. He didn't want to get Bix's hopes up. Or worse, make him believe that it was possible for some people to be immune.

"I just don't understand," he said instead. "They seem to genuinely care about the Wraiths, but then they're profiting from them at the same time."

"You heard what Jennifer said. That's how they get the things they need to do their experiments."

Bix sighed. "You and me, bro? We've been living under a rock for the past three years. Literally. Maybe we just have to see things the way they do." He shifted, shaking the entire bed.

"It just seems unnecessarily cruel for people who claim to be merciful."

"So, we're sympathizing with Wraiths now?"

"Those things used to be people, Bix."

"But they aren't anymore. They don't deserve mercy. They certainly don't show it to us. All they know is spreading the Flense. That, and killing in the bloodiest way possible."

"I guess you really don't believe they can be rehabilitated."

"Hell no. People, maybe. But not them."

"Well, it's a moot point anyway," Finn said, sitting up and placing his bare feet onto the floor.

He remembered crashing fully dressed, complete with shoes on, but he must have gotten hot in the middle of the night and taken them and his socks off. The wooden floor was cold to the touch, even though the air in the room was warm from the sunlight coming in through the window.

"It's not our fight. I say we tell them we'll be on our way to find Harper. Horses or no horses, it's time for us to leave."

"After breakfast."

"It's noon, so, technically, I think you have to call it lunch. But, fine."

"And one more poop on a real flushing toilet with real toilet paper."

"Fine. If you must."

Bix let a loud one rip under the covers. "Oh, I really must."

CHAPTER

22

"TOMORROW," ADRIAN TOLD THEM. HE GLANCED UP at the gathering clouds. "Smells like rain. It'll be better if y'all wait till tomorrow."

Finn glanced over at Bix. He was frankly surprised at how easy it had been to convince them to allow them to leave. Although, now that they'd gotten the couple's blessing, he was disappointed that their departure would be delayed by another day.

They had found cold scrambled eggs, ham, and coffee in the kitchen with a note instructing them to meet up at the new church. The two ate in a tense silence, feeling strange at how normal it all seemed, yet on edge, as if they expected the crowd from last night to burst in on them at any moment to drag them away in chains.

By the time they arrived at the new building — not without a considerable amount of dread — they found the four hard at work. The roof was nearly completed, and Adrian was working on the inside, finishing the cage and installing permanent wiring for all of the electrical equipment.

"Ah, good. I trust y'all had a good rest after yer busy night," Adrian said. "Yer just in time for the detail work."

Finn helped install a circuit breaker and they grounded all the wiring in case of a lightning strike. "Don't want it all to go up in flames next time we have a thunderstorm." Once more he checked the sky. "Looks like we're just in time, too."

"A little rain's not going to bother us," Finn said, pressing the issue of their departure. "We'll have to deal with it eventually."

Adrian shut the cover on the breaker box and turned to address the boys. "Today's more'n half gone already. By the time y'all get outfitted proper-like and we've saddled up the horses and mapped out yer route, it'll be evenin. Trust me, y'all don't wanna be travelin at night."

So they worked for the balance of the afternoon without bringing it up again. Bix helped Luke build a sliding door, which took all four of them to install onto the rolling track. Afterward, Billy and Adrian returned to reinforcing the cage. Finn buried the underground cables with fresh dirt and smoothed it out. They brought in fresh hay and spread it around.

Jennifer came and went, sometimes bringing them drinks and snacks, sometimes to critique their work, and once to rebandage a cut on Billy's leg that he'd received several days before. "Dang thing's takin its own damn time to heal," she remarked, and squeezed out a ribbon of antibiotic ointment from a tube that had expired the year before. While she was at it, she rechecked the wound on Adrian's forehead and dabbed the medicine on the multitude of scrapes Finn and Bix had sustained during their labors.

"Don't know what it is about them boys," she said. "They're always getting nasty scrapes that take forever to heal."

No one spoke directly of the night before, although Finn wondered aloud where the people they'd seen had come from.

"They's other houses scattered elsewhere along the shore," Adrian told them. "Huntin and fishin lodges. Most of them properties is walled in like ours. Makes fer a safe little community. Some others live elsewhere. They's a large group some couple-three hundred miles south of here. We trade with them sometimes. Other folks's roamers, livin off the land with no real social structure."

"And you pay them to bring you Wraiths?" Bix asked.

"Ayup. Them and other things, such as food, supplies."

They finished up with the day's work and headed back to the house, discussing what exactly they would need to depart the next morning.

"I'd come with y'all if I could," Adrian told them. "But I'm expectin some new ferals in, so I cain't afford to leave here."

Finn glanced at Bix. Tomorrow couldn't arrive soon enough for him.

They returned the horses to the barn, fed and watered them and the other animals, then made their way to the house. Despite their discomfort, the boys looked forward to their last real meal for a while. They'd been assured that Jennifer was preparing a surprise meal to celebrate, and indeed, the most delicious aromas hit their noses even before they walked in the front door.

"Sure you don't want to stay just one extra day?" Bix teased Finn.

"Don't tempt me."

"You boys wash up before you come inside," Jennifer called from the kitchen.

"We're already in!" Adrian yelled back. He grinned at Bix and winked.

Jennifer came out, wiping her hands on her apron, and ushered them away. "Shoo! Use the outside spigot. I got laundry hangin in the washroom."

"Delicates," Billy said, and made girlie sounds.

"You boys, show them the way. Adrian, when you're done out there, I need help with the roast."

"Hot damn!" Bix exclaimed. "Did you hear that? She made a roast."

"Come on," Billy said, pushing them toward the back door.

"Keep your pants on, bro," said Bix. "We're all hungry."

The outside spigot was a manual pump situated next to a small wooden structure the size of an outhouse. They'd been told it was the woodshed. Bix reached for the pump handle, but Luke grabbed his arm and twisted it away.

"Dude, you'll get a turn!"

He tried to free himself, but Luke refused to let go. Instead, he slammed Bix into the side of the shed and wrenched his other hand behind him as well.

"Hey!" Finn cried. "What are you—"

But Billy jumped on him, wrestling him to the ground. Finn gasped, unable to catch his breath. Billy dropped a bony knee into his back and leaned his weight onto it. His breath was a hot stink on the side of Finn's face when he spoke. "Did you really think you could break the rules?"

"What rules?"

But Billy didn't answer.

Out of the corner of his eye, Finn saw Adrian unlock the shed door and swing it open and enter. Luke wrestled Bix in after him, and Adrian shut the door behind them. There was a click, like a latch had been secured inside.

"Hey! What are they doing to Bix?"

The knee in his back pressed down, driving the air from his lungs. "Shut yer trap!" Billy said.

The others were gone only a few seconds when a bloodcurdling scream came through the wooden walls. It cut off abruptly.

A moment later, the latch released and Adrian and Luke reappeared.

"What'd you do to Bix?" Finn cried. He struggled against Billy, but without any leverage he found it impossible to move. "What'd you do with him? Where is he?"

Adrian kneeled down beside him and shook his head. "The good Lord may forgive, but I am only a man and cannot so easily." He looked genuinely remorseful, and in that moment, what Finn had suspected deep down became indisputably clear.

"Should have trusted my instincts about you from the beginning," he muttered.

"Pardon me?"

"You're a psychopath!"

"And the devil is whisperin in yer ear."

"You're crazy!"

Adrian tilted his head toward the shack, and before Finn could react, he was lifted bodily up into the air. With a yelp of pain, he landed hard on his foot, twisting his ankle. Then he was half-dragged, half-carried toward the door.

"Stop!" he screamed. He tried to twist around and saw Jennifer standing on the porch watching them. "Liar!" he screamed at her. "Murderers!" Her face was white, but otherwise showed no emotion.

Billy shoved him through the door into the shed, then pressed him hard into a wall. Finn tried to see, but he couldn't turn his head. Behind them, the door shut and the lock caught.

"Where's Bix?"

A single naked light bulb swung from a thin wire attached to the ceiling, causing the shadows to sway. The room was empty.

"What have you done with Bix?"

Luke stepped past them to the back wall. He jangled the keys in his hand, found one, and inserted it into a hole. The wall, flat and gray, swung inward, revealing nothing but darkness.

"We worked for you," Finn grunted. "We helped you!"

"Y'all betrayed our trust."

Finn twisted, wrenching his shoulder against Billy's grip. He brought his foot up and kicked at Billy's leg, aiming for the place he'd seen Jennifer bandaging. Billy let out a scream and let go. But Luke grabbed him and shoved him into the opening. "Get in there!"

Finn tried to catch himself, but there was no floor. He flailed as he fell, and barely had time to brace himself before he landed in the darkness below.

With a loud bang, the door slammed shut behind him. With it went the last of their light. They'd been locked inside some kind of underground room. And by the sounds coming to his ears over the rasp of his and Bix's breathing, he knew they weren't alone.

CHAPTER
23

FLOOD LAMPS ILLUMINATED EVERY INCH OF THE BASE perimeter, but many of the lights along the inner streets and several of those mounted on various buildings deeper inside the camp had either blown out or been shut off to conserve what little remained of the depot's precious diesel. Colonel Wainwright clearly did not expect an attack to come from within.

He had been the depot's executive officer prior to the outbreak, and so he'd inherited its command by virtue of being the most senior officer to survive the Flense. But he was poorly prepared and had squandered fuel during the first two years, as he'd always expected relief to come sooner rather than later.

Then, as local supplies ran thin, he had to send his patrols out further afield, increasing the risk to life and limb. Too many casualties forced him to reduce the base's power consumption, which included banning all nonessential electrical items, such as video games. He also placed curfews on lighting.

Now, after more than a year of those restrictions, diesel supplies were nearly gone. The base's residents lived in constant fear that the generators would soon go silent, that the perimeter lights would fade to black, and the fence be left without its high-voltage protection.

Of course, Eddie didn't know about any of this, nor would he have cared if he had. All he knew was that the extra darkness between buildings made it easier for him to slip from one shadow to the next without being seen by the ever-present foot patrols.

Getting past the desk sergeant for the infirmary and evading the on-duty staff was another story, however. Fortunately, there were very few patients inside, and the medicos were mostly gathered in the lounge playing cards to while away the hours.

He checked every bed, and what he found — and didn't find — deeply worried him.

Earlier that evening, he had asked Colonel Wainwright if he could visit his people being treated there, and he'd been told in no uncertain terms that it wouldn't be possible. The infirmary was strictly off limits to non-medical personnel, always had been, always would be. "I can assure you, however, that they are doing fine," the colonel said.

He received several updates each day from Captain Cheever, who had told him that both Jonathan and the baby seemed to be improving, that Nami's dislocations were healing, and that all four, including Jorge and his mother, were responding well to intravenous fluid replacement. They would be ready for discharge in a few more days.

Eddie couldn't tell if the man was speaking the truth or not. Either way, it felt like he was stalling for time, perhaps hoping to wear them down. The man had repeatedly asked him and the other Bunker Eight survivors where they'd come from and where they were planning on going.

They'd all steadfastly refused to divulge any information. As far as Eddie knew, the man hadn't yet pressed them very hard, but he knew that Wainwright's — and Cheever's — patience had limits. He feared what methods they might resort to once it ran out.

His mind took him to some very unsavory places as he scaled the wall outside the female barracks where the single women in his group were still being housed, and climbed in through an open second-story window. Both of the beds in the room he entered were occupied, but neither woman knew he was there, even though one of them had not yet fallen fully asleep.

Stepping silently into the hallway, he raised his face, sniffed the air, then turned left.

"Hannah," he whispered, gently jostling the girl in the top bunk. The room was nearly pitch black, but he didn't need much light to see by. He knew his daughter by her scent.

It broke his heart to detect the smell of her tears mingling with it, tears for Jonah. Cheever had finally broken the news to them all, and Hannah had taken it especially hard.

"Hannah, honey, it's me."

"Daddy? What are you doing in here? Is something wrong?"

"Shh. Listen, we need to talk."

"Now?" She sat up, shaking the bunk.

Bren stirred in the bed below. "Hannah!" she cried in alarm. "Who's there?"

Eddie ducked quickly down, shushing her as best he could. "It's me, Bren, Hannah's dad. Please, be quiet."

The barracks were arranged so that each bay contained several alcoves, each with a pair of beds, and a central latrine and showers. The cinderblock barriers between them helped keep some of the noise from traveling, but not all.

Kari and Susan were in the adjacent alcove, but strangers occupied others in the same bay, women he didn't know and therefore couldn't trust.

"Eddie?" Bren asked, and the litany of questions started anew: "How did you get in here? What's wrong? Why are you here? What time is it?"

He answered the last one to cut her off. "Listen to me, you two. We need to talk."

"Why now?"

"Just come with me."

Hand in hand, the three slipped out into the bay, where light from one of the distant flood lamps spilled in from a single window at the opposite end of the building. They entered Kari and Susan's room, where the girls gently roused them.

"Eddie's here," they whispered.

"We're in danger," he told them. "They're lying to us, Cheever and Wainwright and the others. Something bad is happening, and unless we leave soon, we may not be able to go at all."

"Lying about what?" Kari asked.

"How Jonah died, for one thing. About Danny's disappearance for another."

"Danny left on his own," Bren said. "He told me he wished he'd never left the bunker. He wanted to go back."

Eddie turned to her in the darkness. He saw her face clearly enough, though he knew none of the others could. To them, they were all little more than vague shapes. "Do you really believe he'd leave, Bren? In the middle of the night?"

She didn't answer.

Eddie knew that she had grown terribly depressed and was questioning her own decision to leave the bunker. Hannah had told him as much. He worried that Bren's resolve was starting to crumble, and that it'd soon affect them all if they didn't manage her expectations.

Now he wondered if Bren had already spoken to anyone outside of their group about her concerns. He had noticed a couple people, especially Private Ramsay and Sergeant Bolton, starting to take an inordinate amount of interest in the girls, going out of their way to endear themselves, almost flirting. He'd given Hannah a knife to carry underneath her shirt and told her to be wary of men and their intentions. But he didn't feel right giving Bren the same precautions. The tiniest thing might send her over the edge.

But he couldn't afford to be so cautious anymore.

"Danny may have told you he wanted to go back," he whispered, "but he wouldn't have left in the middle of the night, on foot, and without letting one of us know he was going first. Besides, he knows how dangerous it is out there. He knows it would have been suicide."

The others were silent. "So, what do you think happened?" Susan asked.

"I don't know. I just know the story they gave us is a lie."

"And Jonah?" asked Hannah, hopefully. "Do you think he was attacked by Wraiths?"

"Something about that story doesn't jive, either, honey. But I don't think Jonah is alive. I'm sorry."

Kari shook her head. "You snuck in here in the middle of the night and woke us up because of a suspicion?"

172

"I asked Colonel Wainwright today if I could visit our people in the infirmary. He told me no."

"Medical personnel only," Susan said. "I know. I asked, too. I feel bad for Jasmina and the baby all alone in there."

"She's fine. So's the baby. I saw them myself."

"How?"

"I snuck in," Eddie said. "She's there, and Jorge is getting better, but I couldn't find Jonathan or Nami. They're gone."

"Maybe they moved them. Or they got better and are in permanent housing."

"I don't think so. I overheard the medic talking about the cemetery, and when I looked, I found several fresh graves there."

Susan sucked in a sharp breath. "You think they're dead?"

Anguished sounds came from both girls' throats.

"Jonathan was very sick," Kari acknowledged. "You remember how bad it was at the height of the flu epidemic. Millions died. And from what Nami told us, Jonathan was never immunized against it. Even Cheever was afraid he might have it. And he still refused to take anything for the fever."

Again, Eddie shook his head. "Wainwright told me he was getting better."

"So, he lied to you? Why? You think someone is picking us off? Why would they do that? To what possible end?"

"I don't know, but the bus has been sitting in their maintenance bay for three days now and as far as I can tell nothing's been done to it. They don't seem to be in any hurry to fix it."

"What do you suggest we do?"

"I need to speak to the rest of the crew — the Rollinses and Harrison — but I think we need to demand answers, not that I expect them to tell us the truth. But if on the off chance that our people are still alive, that they've been hidden somewhere, then we need to get them back."

"Then what?"

"Then we leave." He sighed. "Tomorrow, if possible."

CHAPTER
24

"WHO'S THERE?" FINN DEMANDED, CROUCHING LOW where he had fallen and extending his hands out before him in a defensive posture. He could feel Bix lying motionless between his feet. He didn't know how badly he was hurt. He could have easily broken his neck falling down the steps. "I'm warning you, stay away!"

Rustling noises came to him from several directions at once, giving him a better sense of the size of the underground chamber. It seemed fairly large, and there had to be at least four others in it with him and Bix.

But other *what*? That was the question. Were they people? Wraiths?

Something moved off to his right, making a fluttering, scraping sound that rose the hairs on his neck. He spun around to face it. He heard a sharp inhale, and the air stirred near his face. He recoiled and tripped as his feet hit Bix's body. But whatever it was, it had moved away again.

It's like Eddie, he thought, remembering the day he'd found Doc Cavanaugh's murder scene. Eddie had moved as silently and stealthily as whatever was in the room with him now.

"Bix," he whispered. He put his mouth as close to Bix's ear as he could. His friend's eyelashes fluttered against his cheek, and he raised his hand to push Finn away. Relief flooded into Finn. *"Shh. Don't move, Bix. Be quiet."*

The two boys remained silent and still, waiting and listening. It seemed the others in the room were doing the same. All movement had stopped, and the only sounds arriving in Finn's ears were the rush of blood through his head and the air moving through his open mouth.

He stayed like that for a long time, waiting for something to move, to attack him, to touch. And for a long time, nothing happened.

* * *

"I don't think they mean to attack," Bix finally said.

Finn jerked up, startled by his friend's voice. Despite speaking softly, it had sounded like a shout in his ears.

"And you're totally crushing me," Bix added.

"What?"

"Get off. I can barely breathe."

Finn sat up. Almost immediately, the other things in the room began to move, as if spurred by his actions.

It's your mind playing tricks on you, he thought. But then he remembered Bix had heard them, too. Were they other prisoners like themselves?

"How long have we been lying here?" he asked Bix. He honestly had no idea. It felt like hours.

"Beats me. I think I may have passed out. I might even have peed my pants."

"Jesus, man!" Finn exclaimed, pushing away in disgust.

"Nope. Or maybe just a little. A few drops."

"Stop it!"

"Sorry, I can't help it," Bix said. "Are you okay? I think I might have a concussion."

"I'm all right."

Bix pushed Finn away and tried to sit up. "Had the damn wind knocked out of me."

Once more, the other things in the room shifted, sending shivers through Finn's body. "We're not alone," he said.

"Yeah, I know. I sort of saw them when I fell."

"Them?"

"At least two. I don't know, maybe three."

"More like four, I think."

"Oh, now you're just being competitive."

"Am not."

"Should we introduce ourselves?"

"What? No!"

"Who are you?" Bix asked, louder. "What's your name?"

The rustling noises resumed, followed by whispering.

"We won't hurt you," Bix added.

Yeah, as long as you don't hurt us, Finn wanted to say.

"You first," came a deep voice out of the darkness. "Who are you?"

"Bix," Bix said. "And this is Finn."

Finn hissed his disapproval.

"Byron," the man answered.

"And the others?" Finn asked. "How many of you are there?"

"Three," the man said.

"Told you," said Bix, nudging Finn.

"Four, actually," he corrected himself, and Finn nudged Bix back. "They threw someone else down here before you two showed up. Maybe a day before, don't know, can't tell.

He's hurt though, badly. Came to a few times, mumbled something unintelligible. Think it might've been his name, then passed out again. I don't think he's going to make it."

"Jesus," Finn repeated.

"Think it might be the other guy from the dock?" Bix whispered. "The one we saw last night."

"Might be."

"Yeah, they brought us in on boats, too," Byron said. "Blindfolded us and threw us down here."

"How long have you been here?" Bix asked.

"Well, judging by the position of the sun, I'd say I have no clue."

"He's got your dry sense of humor," Finn muttered.

"Hey, my sense of humor is all I got. At least it's keeping me sane."

"Can't have been more than a couple days," Byron said. "Otherwise the stink would be worse than it already is."

"And who are the other two?" Finn asked, once more wrinkling his nose. The air did smell pretty ripe.

"Jerry and Charlie."

"How'd you end up here?"

Byron didn't answer.

"Did you know Adrian and Jennifer before?"

"Never saw any women. Just men. Don't know their names."

"A bunch of men picked us up on the road," a new voice said. It sounded young and scared. "We weren't doing anything, just trying to escape from—"

"Charlie," Byron quietly said. "Zip it."

No one spoke for several minutes after that. Then Finn said, "It's okay. We wouldn't trust us, either. Not in this world, but especially not after being lied to by those people up there and shoved into this hole down here."

"They're going to kill us!" Charlie said, his voice drawn thin with panic.

"Charlie Michael!" Byron snapped. Then, in a softer voice: "We're going to get out. I promise."

The shout made their ears ring.

"Charlie's your son?" Finn asked.

"Yes. Both he and Jerry."

"How old?"

Byron hesitated. "Eight and eleven."

"Jesus."

"Father Adrian wouldn't like you taking the Lord's name in vain, Finn."

"Father Adrian can kiss my—"

"Shouldn't we be figuring out how to get out of here?" Bix asked.

He leaned on Finn's shoulder as he stood up. There was a thump and he swore under his breath. "Ceiling's low," he said. "Barely five feet. Some boards . . . rafters, maybe. Feels like dirt between them. Maybe we can dig our way out."

Something spilled down on Finn's head and he shook it out. It did feel like dirt.

"It's sound proofing material, I think," Byron said. "There's wood if you dig up through it. I already tried."

Bix was moving about the room now. "Steps are over here." His feet scraped as he ascended them. "They're steep and narrow. The door at the top feels solid."

"Steel," Byron said. "And with narrow steps and double doors, we can't easily force our way out."

Bix came back down again. Finn could hear him moving away, crawling over the floor. "There's a wall here. I make it about fifteen, eighteen feet on edge."

"Have you found anything you can use for a weapon?" Finn asked. "Anything to break out?"

"No. Nothing. Careful over there," he called out. "We use that corner as the bathroom. There's a small hole hollowed out in the ground. We've covered it with a blanket or something we found down here."

"Great."

"Do you know what they're going to do to us?" Charlie asked.

An image of the cage came to Finn, of the man they had shoved inside. His skin turned to ice.

"No," Bix quickly said. He was heading back around the room in the other direction. "This side's shorter. And— What the hell?"

"That would be the other guy," Byron said.

"You could have warned me!"

"I told you about the toilet corner."

"He's alive," Bix said. "He's breathing."

"You said he spoke his name. What was it?" Finn asked.

"Not sure," Byron replied. "He was mumbling and it sounded like Jones. Most of it was babble. It didn't make any sense."

"Not Jones," Charlie said. "Jonah."

CHAPTER
25

"YOU KNOW HIM?" BYRON ASKED, RESPONDING TO
Bix's surprised exclamation.

Guided by Bix's voice, Finn felt his way over to the man
lying against the wall. He could hear Bix shaking him, trying
to rouse him. "We know a Jonah."

"He smells like blood," Bix whispered.

"Jonah?" Finn said. He reached out and found an arm,
traced it up to the shoulder. The shirt felt wet, but when he
rubbed his fingers together, the wetness turned sticky. "He's
bleeding."

"You figure that you've been here a couple days?" Bix
asked of the others.

"No more than that. They've fed us twice. Not a lot, just
enough to keep us from starving."

"And they brought Jonah in after you arrived?"

"Yes."

"Timing's right," Bix mumbled to Finn.

"Except it's not him," Finn replied. "It's not our Jonah."

"How can you tell?"

Finn found Bix's hand and guided it to the top of the
man's head. "Curly hair. Jonah's is straight."

"Damn," Bix breathed. "What're the chances of that, coming across someone else with that name?"

Finn turned around. "What exactly did he say?"

"It was just mumbling, mostly," Byron answered. "He was pretty beat up and barely made his way over to the corner there. Kept saying something about sheep or something. Rams and breaking the bike. That mean anything to you?"

"No," Finn replied.

"Like I said, it was mostly nonsense. When I asked for his name, he just kept saying Jones. Or Jonah."

"Well, this isn't the guy we know," Finn said.

"Jone . . . *uhs*," the man mumbled. "Rams say . . . kill . . . him. Broke . . . bike."

Finn got slowly to his feet. Crouching, he slid his feet forward until he came to the wall, then followed it until he came to the steps. By touch, he could tell that it was all made of wood. He felt for the edges of the boards.

"What are you doing?"

"We need weapons, some way to defend ourselves. If I can pry some of these steps off—"

"I already tried that. They're screwed in, and there's no way to pry them off, believe me. My fingers are bloody from trying."

"Anything in your pockets? Did you have anything with you when they put you down here?"

"Emptied us out."

"Bix?"

"I've got a couple nails from the barn."

"That's a start. Let me have one." He went back over, more confident in the pitch dark, now that he had a better sense of the room's layout. "Check the other guy's pockets."

"Aw, dude. Why me?"

"Just do it."

There was some shuffling, then: "Nothing."

"Check the shoes."

"No good. Just your standard sneakers. Not much tread left."

"Thanks, that's helpful."

"Hey, you said check his shoes."

"To use, not to steal."

Finn returned to the steps, mounted them, then felt around the door at the top. It was smooth and cool to the touch. Knocking on it produced a solid sound. There was no handle, no way to pull it open. He tried digging the nail head into the space around the edge and pulling, but the thing was sturdily mounted in a metal frame and the door didn't yield even in the slightest.

He ran his fingers all the way around it, found three hinges, and pressed his fingertip against each of the mounting screws in turn. There was no give to them.

"I might be able to unscrew the hinges," he said. "But it'll take a while, and we may not have the time."

After only a few minutes working on it Finn's fingers were growing numb. He felt the area around the screw and frowned. There were barely any scratches from the nail. "It's not going to work."

"Let me have a go," Bix said.

"Hold on." He ran his fingers over the middle hinge, wondering why it was easier to picture something when he had his eyes closed, even in the dark. "I've got another idea." He pressed the tip of the nail against the bottom of the hinge and pushed.

"What're you doing?"

"Checking if I can remove the pins from the hinges. There's three."

"Is it working?"

Finn pressed harder, but the pin wouldn't budge. "I need a hammer or something to hit it with."

He felt something press against the back of his leg and heard Byron say, "Here, try this. Place it flat against your palm."

"What is it?"

"Belt buckle. The boys gave it to me for my last birthday . . . before."

Finn did as he suggested and tried to hammer at the nail, checking every few hits to see if the pin was moving.

"Is it working?"

Finn tried to hammer harder. So far, the pin hadn't budged, and he feared it might not be possible to remove it. But his heart nearly skipped when he found a tiny gap between the pin head and the hinge body. "Maybe."

A couple minutes later, the pin was halfway out. "There's a problem," he said, breathing heavily. The room seemed to have grown hot and stuffy. Sweat poured down his face. "The nail's not long enough. And now it's stuck. I can't get it out."

His fingers were sore, but he refused to give up. He pulled on the pin with all his strength, wriggling it. It still wouldn't release.

"Want me to try?" Bix asked.

"No. Give me another nail."

Bix handed it over, and Finn positioned it under the pin head and began to hammer up on it. "It's working!"

The pin popped free after a few more minutes and rolled down the steps.

"One down, two to go!" Bix cheered.

"Yeah, but unless I can get the first nail out, it's not going to do us much good."

He handed the nail and buckle over to Bix, who worked the bottom hinge for a while before taking a break. "I can feel it starting to—"

Above them, they heard the outer door open and keys being shaken out on a ring.

"Get down here!" Finn hissed.

The door flew open just as Bix stepped away from the bottom step. After hours in the pitch black, the light was blinding.

"You boys!" Luke shouted down at them. "Git on up here!"

"No!" Byron cried. He charged clumsily up the stairs shouting that they couldn't take his children. There was a *snap!* and several rapid clicks and he fell back into the room writhing on the ground. The kids tried to scramble toward their father, but Bix and Finn pulled them back, yelling at them not to touch.

"I didn't mean the little ones!" Adrian yelled from behind. He pushed Luke to the side and pointed at Bix and Finn with a rifle. "I meant you two. One at a time. And no funny business or I'll shoot ya fer real. And as far as I know, there ain't no comin back from a shotgun blast to the head."

* * *

"What are you going to do with us?" Finn demanded. He stumbled over the rough ground just outside the shack, unable to see the groundhog mounds in the dark. He

185

thought about shouting at Bix to run, but he knew it wouldn't work. They'd probably just get shot in the back.

"Time for yer first lesson in humility, boys," Adrian told them, and placed a lariat over each of their heads and tightened it. "Now march!"

He didn't have to tell them where they were going. They knew. They could see the flood lamps through the trees. Twenty minutes later, they emerged into the clearing. Several people were already gathered inside the barn. They raised a cheer when they saw Adrian approach.

Inside the cage were two naked figures. One was the man from the night before, except he wasn't a man anymore. The other was the second Wraith the boys had seen inside the animal barn the first night. Both Wraiths now threw themselves at the wire as the crowd cheered and jeered.

Billy sat on the edge of the cart on the other side of the barn. He stood up when they entered, a cattle prod in his hand. Finn noticed that he was limping noticeably from the wound on his leg, and beads of sweat stood out on his forehead. He returned Finn's glare with a murderous look.

Adrian shoved them toward the cage so violently that both boys fell onto their knees in the dirt. The Wraiths were there in the blink of an eye, hissing at them, thrusting their arms through the chain link to get at them.

Both boys recoiled, barely managing to avoid being touched. Behind them, the crowd roared.

"You sure about this?" Billy asked, hobbling over to Adrian. "Jennifer won't—"

"Shut up!" His face was red, and his eyes gleamed with a wicked spark. "Give em the prods," he said. "Now!"

"No!" Finn yelled and tried to scramble away.

But Billy was quicker, even with his injured leg. "Get up," he growled. Grimacing, he pulled the boys to their feet and removed the ropes from around their necks.

Finn spun around to lash out, but Adrian had raised the rifle into his arms and was cradling it in a threatening manner, a grin smeared across his lips. He looked like he wanted an excuse to fire it.

"Is this what you've become?" Finn screamed, addressing the crowd. Bix was shaking like a leaf on a tree, his face white with terror. "Murdering innocent people? You're no better than they are!" he said, pointing at the Wraiths inside the cage.

Several people in the crowd cursed at him, called him a sinner. "It's time for your judgment!" they cried.

"No!" Bix yelled. "Please, no!"

Billy shoved the cattle prod into Finn's hands, then stepped quickly away. "Use it!"

Finn turned to Bix in confusion. Bix's eyes widened, and he shook his head at his friend.

"Finn? Please, don't."

Finn looked down at the weight in his hands, not understanding. Was he supposed to use it on Bix?

But before he could move, Luke shoved a second prod into Bix's hands. Like Billy, he stepped swiftly away.

"Bring out the subjects!" Adrian cried.

Behind him, the crowd turned and parted. Adrian never took his gaze — or the rifle — off the boys. He gestured at Finn to go around to the right side of the cage. With a rifle now in his own hands, Luke gestured at Bix to go around to the left. The boys obeyed.

Six men marched through the door into the barn, two pairs each holding a third man, who was blindfolded. They passed Adrian, then spread out and turned to face the crowd.

"You two have been charged with crimes against yer fellow man," Adrian stated. "How do y'all plead?"

The crowd hushed in anticipation for answers that never came.

"Very well. Y'all must be punished. Fifteen seconds each in the cage. If y'all can put the ferals out of their misery before then, yer debt'll be repaid."

Bix stared at Finn through the wire mesh. The Wraiths were prowling inside the cage like animals, hissing and snapping. One threw itself at the wire and scaled it in a flash. It crawled across the newly-installed top as easily as if it were crawling along the floor. Finn shivered and tried to back away, but someone shoved him forward.

The two men, their heads still covered with the hoods, were stripped of their clothing. They cried out weakly, but the fight seemed to have been beaten out of them. One coughed, his loose skin swinging over his bones. Both were horribly emaciated and shook visibly.

Adrian turned to the boys. "If'n these men are gonna have any fightin chance at redemption, you'll shock the ferals at the same time."

He grinned and the crowd broke out in laughter.

"Good luck."

CHAPTER
26

MORNING WAS STILL AN HOUR AWAY, BUT THE CLOUDS above the base glowed with an eerie fire, reflecting the stray light from the flood lamps. Jonah had seen the encampment from five miles away, which was a relief, as the trail of oil droplets and tire tracks had become harder and harder to follow.

He crept over the packed sands, scurrying from tumbleweed to rock, running along in the shadows through the dry gullies, until he was within a hundred yards of the front gate. Only then did he take a moment to drink some water and eat the last stale protein bar he'd taken from Vinnie's pack.

He still felt guilty for what had happened back there, but what other choice had he? It hadn't taken them long to realize they'd been betrayed.

The question was, why?

So Jonah told him. He said that he'd overheard them talking back there in town. He knew what they were planning on doing with the girls. "Ramsay figured out I knew."

"It was just Ramsay talking!" Vinnie had insisted. "We don't do that! I don't!"

And instead of blaming his colleague, he'd blamed Jonah for putting the sand in the tank.

They'd fought then, exchanging blows. The man was tough in the way that surviving in a dead world taught a man how to be tough, but Jonah knew right away that he was no killer. He'd easily overpowered the older man.

He hadn't wanted to kill the guy, so he left him in the shade, his hands and feet bound so that he wouldn't follow. *Someone'll come after him*, he thought. Sooner or later someone will come looking for the two of them.

And they had, early the next morning, passing him but not seeing him. They showed up a little while later going in the opposite direction, but Vinnie hadn't been with them.

Jonah hadn't killed the man, but he sensed that the man was dead anyway.

You're no better than Seth Abramson.

The words plagued him as he continued his terrible trek after the bus.

He had kept off the road, returning to it whenever there was a junction so that he could check that he was still on the right trail. It was physically draining, having to make his way over the rough ground in the blazing heat of day. And it was mentally exhausting, always having to worry that he was going in the wrong direction, that he was following the wrong trail, or even a phantom trail, his nerves as frayed as his senses.

He didn't see a single Wraith the entire time, except maybe once, though it was a long way off. It certainly moved like one, and he couldn't imagine some other poor, lost sap wandering about the desert like he was.

He did see more bikers, however. Several each day. They were easy to hide from as he could hear them coming from miles away.

The compound was double-fenced, the runway between the barriers patrolled by dogs. Through the binoculars he'd taken from Vinnie, he saw the high-voltage warning signs posted periodically along the perimeter, and he assumed that it only pertained to the outer fence. The dogs knew not to touch the wire, but humans were either stupid or lacked some sensibility that the animals had for sensing electrical current.

In the half hour that he sat there on the sand leaning his back against a rock, he had seen no less than four foot patrols and two trucks. All of them carried automatic weapons, either in their hands or mounted on the vehicles. And he wondered which they feared an attack more from, Wraiths or other people.

The bus was nowhere in sight, but the base was sufficiently large that it could be anywhere, perhaps even inside a building somewhere. He was sure it had to be there, but until he set eyes on it or on someone in his group, he couldn't be certain that they had been brought here.

Or, if they had been, that they were even still on the premises.

Leaning his head back, he shut his eyes to rest them. The desert sun and dry air had chapped and swollen the skin around his eyes and lips. His throat was scratchy, and his nose had bled. And the whole time he was walking, he wondered what he'd do when he finally caught up. He still didn't know.

A faint scratching noise caught his attention. He cocked an eye open and, at first, saw nothing. But then he felt it, a finger of weight on his shoulder. He didn't move, just waited. The movement shifted to his ear, then ascended to the top of his scalp.

His first night in the desert alone had been a test of his resolve, more than the days had been, even though the latter were certainly more grueling. That first night, he'd fallen asleep leaning against an outcropping of loose sandstone, and he'd woken the next morning when some of it crumbled onto his face. In a panic, he pushed himself away, and by the time he heard the rattle it was already too late to escape the strike.

The snake attached itself to his leg, injecting its venom into his flesh. All he could do was stare stupidly at it.

Only when it released him and drew back did he react. He lashed out, more in anger than to defend himself. His foot came down on the rattler's head and crushed it. The rattle shook as the animal writhed in its death throes. By the time it went still, he'd regained control of himself.

He considered himself lucky. It seemed the snake had recently expended the bulk of its venom in another victim, and, indeed, there was a telltale bulge in its belly. The wound on his leg swelled and ached for most of the next day, but the poison hadn't spread. He hadn't had much trouble with it since.

He cooked the snake and ate it, including the partially-digested jack rabbit it had consumed earlier.

That whole experience had taught him a valuable lesson, that his greatest weakness was fear. So, as he sat there, the army base aglow a hundred yards away and something crawling over his skin, he didn't panic. And, just as he expected it to, the scorpion eventually lost interest and wandered away.

Off in the distance to his left, the first signs of dawn appeared in the sky, and he realized that it was time to move. He couldn't risk being stuck where he was once day broke. There was no place to hide, whether from the base patrols or the merciless sun.

He leaned forward and stretched his aching muscles. He would have to backtrack or go around and hope to find a weakness he could exploit. He might last another day without water, but it would only weaken him further.

Then what?

The whine of an engine drew his attention. Inside the fence, a large army truck appeared. It pulled up to the gate and shut off. A man got out of the cab and walked over to speak to the sentries.

Two more people caught Jonah's eye. They had exited from the central building, which appeared to have once fulfilled an administrative function in the past. An empty flagpole stood in front. The two, one tall and male, the other smaller and female, walked toward the truck. They joined the driver at the gate.

Jonah pulled out the binoculars again and trained them on the trio, but they were in shadow and he couldn't make out their faces.

One man stepped away at the same time that several riders on motorcycles appeared. He spoke to one of the bikers, then disappeared around the back of the truck. A flap lifted, and four people jumped out, two men, and two women. They all carried rifles and sidearms.

Garbled sounds and laughter reached Jonah's ears. Everyone seemed to be in high spirits. They all milled about for several minutes before the first man reappeared.

"Where's the other vehicle?" he shouted.

"Coming!"

A moment later, the bus appeared. Jonah pulled the binoculars back up to his eyes. It was theirs all right, but the man behind the wheel was a stranger. It pulled up behind the truck and idled.

"Are we ready?"

The soldiers shouted in unison that they were.

"Then wind her up!"

The guard returned to the gate and it began to open. The truck driver stepped into the cab and started it up. The four from the back of the truck returned.

The last figure, the woman who had accompanied the man, walked over to the bus. The doors whispered open and she stepped onto the first stair. Then, just before going inside, she turned to say one last thing to the man who'd accompanied her. The image in the binoculars was unmistakable.

It was Bren.

CHAPTER 27

FINN FEARED THAT THE CROWD WOULD RIOT IF HE AND Bix didn't neutralize the Wraiths soon. He had tried half-heartedly several times, but the creatures were simply too fast and too wary of the prods. Twice he'd come close, and the third time would have succeeded had he not been foiled by the chain link. The crowd's boos grew louder with every failed attempt.

And poor Bix. He'd thrown the cattle prod to the ground in refusal, only to have Luke step over and sucker punch him in the gut. "Next one'll smash that pretty face of yours even more," he snarled, then thrust the device back into Bix's hands and ordered him to stand up.

For a moment, Finn was sure he'd turn it on Luke, and he shouted for him not to do it. But the yell was lost in the roar of the crowd. Luke stood there, a grin curling his upper lip, as if daring Bix to do it.

Visibly shaken, Bix turned back to the cage and jabbed reluctantly at the wire when a Wraith flashed past.

The crowd reached the end of its patience. Someone threw a stone, hitting Finn on the ear. It wasn't a large one, but it had been thrown hard. He felt a trickle of blood run down the side of his face. Or maybe it was sweat. He couldn't tell. In any case, it stung terribly.

The two naked men, still hooded and with their backs to the cage, seemed frozen in fear. Finn felt for them. He knew that Adrian had been right, that those men's only hope rested in his and Bix's ability to shock both Wraiths simultaneously, but it seemed an impossible expectation. They couldn't even shock one. How were they going to get two at once?

At last, Adrian grew tired of their futile attempts. Or perhaps he was finished with his masochistic demonstration. He walked over to the main circuit box that he and Finn had installed just a day earlier, opened it, and flipped one of the switches.

The lights dimmed and the generator whined from the extra load placed on it. Both of the Wraiths, one climbing the wire at the opposite end of the cage and the other hanging from the top halfway between Finn and Bix, suddenly began to jerk violently. There came a series of crackles and the barn filled with the smell of burning flesh. Both Wraiths fell to the ground.

When Adrian flipped the breaker off again, the lights immediately brightened.

The cattle prods were stripped from the boys' hands, even as the crowd began to chant: "Forty-five! Forty-four! Forty-three . . . !"

Adrian snapped the box shut, then circled the cage to stand before the prisoners.

"Y'all will be unmasked before yer peers and placed into the cage fer judgment. There will be two ferals, both shocked and harmless. They cannot kill. They cannot infect. It's yer choice: executioner or not. Salvation or damnation."

"Thirty!" the crowd shouted. "Twenty-nine!"

"Y'all will have twenty seconds and nothin but yer wit and bare hands. Understand?"

The men shook their heads and began to babble. One of them collapsed to his knees. The other wore a splint and seemed unable to move, even if he wanted to.

The men flanking the prostrate figure pulled him up again.

"Twenty-five! Twenty-four!"

"Open the gate!" Adrian shouted.

The gate was opened.

"Remove their hoods!"

The black bags were pulled away. Both men lowered their heads to shake the sweat out of their eyes. Then, just as the count reached twenty, they were spun around and shoved toward the opening.

Finn's eyes widened in shock. He looked over at Bix and tried to cry out, but the crowd noise was too great, and his voice was lost in the roar.

But Bix wasn't looking at him anyway. He was staring at the men with the same utter disbelief that Finn felt.

The two men stumbled in. Locked in their own version of Hell, neither acted. They simply pressed themselves against each other for protection and eyed the bodies of the Wraiths.

As if on cue, both boys screamed for them to hurry up. The crowd screamed, too. Time was running out. The count was already down to fifteen. But neither Nami nor Jonathan could hear them. They stood and stared and at first did nothing.

Nami was the first to snap out of it. He slowly turned, his gaze sweeping the crowd. It touched Finn and continued on without recognition, and Finn thought that the man's mind had simply shut down from shock. But then it snapped back in surprise.

The count was down to twelve.

Finn jabbed his finger at the Wraith a few feet away from Nami and screamed for him to break its neck.

Nami looked at it, then back at Finn. Finn nodded and made a snapping motion with his hands.

"Eleven!"

Nami leaned stiffly over and screamed something into Jonathan's ear, then limped over to the Wraith Finn had indicated. The crowd went wild with excitement. Someone jostled Finn roughly, and he fell forward onto his knees.

Nami grabbed the Wraith just as it began to move. Jonathan looked on with horror.

"Nine!" the crowd screamed.

In a flash, Jonathan turned, and for a moment, Finn feared he was going to try to run away, except there was nowhere for him to go. He saw the other Wraith and started to go for it, hesitating only momentarily when it, too, began to rouse.

"Seven!"

Finn looked over at Bix and saw the horror he felt reflected in his friend's face. There wasn't enough time for their fellow survivors.

A flash of movement caught Finn's eye and he turned in time to see Nami snap the Wraith's neck. The count reached five. At the same moment, Jonathan slammed his foot down onto the neck of the other. Both were free of the creatures as the forty-first second died on the crowd's lips.

Only Jonathan's wet cough broke the silence.

Both men backed away from the lifeless forms. Their chests heaved. The crowd was frozen, waiting. Forty eyes studied the four inside for signs of infection.

Jonathan stumbled over to the gate. "Let us out," he begged. "We did your dirty work!"

Adrian slowly walked over to him. He seemed genuinely surprised at what he saw. He checked Jonathan's face for several seconds, then turned to the crowd. "Salvation!"

The crowd erupted.

"Let him out," Bix screamed. His voice sounded hoarse and far away. Nobody heard him. "He's not infected! Let him out!"

But while everyone was looking at Jonathan, Finn was looking at Nami. The man had fallen to his one unsplinted knee in exhaustion, his head lowered. Slowly, he raised his face, and a chill descended over Finn. Death was in the man's eyes, the blackness of the Flense.

"Oh no," Finn moaned. "No!"

The crowd was quick to notice the change. The cheers rose once more.

"Get him out of there!" Finn tried to scream. He turned to Jonathan and shouted his name and pointed behind him. "Look out!"

Bix was shouting and pointing, too. Jonathan whipped around and finally saw. He grabbed the wire of the gate and shook it. There was a new fire in his eyes, not the blackness of death but the vibrant red and white of terror. "Let me out!"

His arms quavered and his knees collapsed beneath him. Still weak from the lung infection, he fell to the dirt, coughing and spitting.

A gray husk swept over Nami's skin. His nails turned black. He raised his head in agony, but no sound came out of his mouth.

Finn tried to get to the gate, but he was tackled and thrown to the ground. Something slammed into the back of his head, and for a moment he saw stars. But he got back up and tried again. Once more, he was hit hard and knocked onto his side. This time, he could only crawl.

The crowd was drunk with bloodlust.

Bix had been bound, his wrists tied behind him. He was screaming, but no one could hear him. Finn read the words that formed on his mouth. He was begging Jonathan to turn around, to kill Nami.

Billy pressed Finn down, a handful of his hair in his fist, twisting. The pain was terrible, but not as bad as his anguish. He forced his head to turn despite Billy's resistance. He needed to see.

Nami's transformation was progressing, faster than it should, it seemed. The changes swept over him in the space of a few minutes.

On the other side of the cage, Jonathan had finally pulled himself up again to his feet. Slowly he turned, as if finally resolved to his fate. He took a step toward Nami, then stopped as indecision crossed his face.

But it was too late for any salvation now. Everyone knew it. Finn watched as Jonathan stumbled over to Nami and grabbed his friend's head in his arms. But he was too weak, and Nami was too far along, less himself than the monster he was becoming. The struggle went on for a very long time, with Jonathan growing weaker and Nami growing stronger.

Then, at long last, Nami extracted himself. Jonathan collapsed to the ground, no longer able to fight. He began to pull himself over to a corner of the cage. Outside the wire the crowd seethed like a living thing, a single mindless organism, a shapeless parasite engulfing its prey.

Nami began to move toward Jonathan, stepping jerkily, as if the monster inside of him still wasn't fully in control. It seemed to consider its old friend for a moment. And when it reached down, its hand hesitated for a moment. Then it turned its face toward the crowd and hissed.

Everyone went silent. Everyone waited.

"Do it!" someone whispered. *"Touch him."*

The thing that had once been Nami twitched at the sound. It slid over the ground toward the crowd, then seemed perplexed when it couldn't go beyond the wire.

"Touch the fucker! Do it!" a man screamed. He threw a handful of dirt. It hit Nami in the face and bounced off. More people picked up the chant: "Touch him! Touch him!"

Finn knew the instant the change happened. He saw it take hold of Nami. The slack muscles quivered and tensed, turning to fury. His whole body seemed to expand, filling with rage. It growled.

"Yes! Yes!" the crowd screamed. "Touch him!"

The Nami-thing began to scramble about the cage, trying to get out, wanting to get out. Like a spider, it scrambled across the wire fencing, onto the mesh on top.

The crowd came alive. "Touch him!" they chanted, pointing at Jonathan. But Nami seemed not to notice the man inside the cage at all.

Not until Jonathan moved.

In a flash, the Nami-thing was by his side. This time, it did not hesitate. It didn't reach out to touch him. It wasn't interested in spreading its disease to him anymore. Instead, it slammed its fist down through Jonathan's back, through spine and ribs alike. Blood spurted into the air, and the crowd backed away with an utterance of awe.

"No!" Finn cried. He tried to reach the fence, but he was dragged away instead. The crowd swallowed him up, trampling him. It cheered and slapped him where he lay. All he could do was try not to be crushed beneath their feet.

He covered his head, his face, his ears. But the noise couldn't mask the sounds that came to him from inside the cage, the snapping bones and the muscle torn away from them. He could not unhear Jonathan's shrieks of pain or the echoes of the manic cheers filling the barn.

CHAPTER
28

NEITHER BIX NOR FINN STRUGGLED AGAINST THEIR captors as they were returned to the underground chamber. Their shock and despair were too great, crushing even their will to survive.

Finn barely remembered the long march through the woods back to the house. He knew night was drawing to an end, as he could see where to place his feet. And he remembered emerging into the clearing near the house to find the scene etched in the sterile metallic gray of pre-morning. The monochromic tone mirrored his emotions, cold and hard, colorless. He knew he should feel anger and fear, but his utter disbelief at the horrors he had witnessed smothered his ability to summon anything from within, much less a sense of urgency.

He lay on the cool dirt floor in the absolute darkness, vaguely aware that someone was shaking him. He didn't care. He was dead, beyond dead. He was in some sort of living purgatory tormented by questions. He could feel them, worming their way into his mind, prying at the flimsy glue that held his sanity together. How could people do such horrific things to each other? How could people stand around and cheer?

How could it be possible that Nami and Jonathan were there?

And on the heels of that: Where was the rest of the group? Were they here, too, at the ranch? If so, where?

He remembered a locked door at the far end of the animal barn. He'd thought it led outside, but now he wasn't so sure anymore.

The shaking became more insistent. *Hey,* someone asked, *what happened out there?*

The absolute darkness of their prison made a perfect canvas for Finn's worst imaginings. They were all dead—Bren and Hannah and Bix's father and . . . . All of them. They had been turned into Wraiths.

He could picture Bren in some dark room, just like this one, terrified. Where was she? Had they killed her? Had she been made into one of them?

Finn cowered deeper inside of himself, ashamed of what he'd done, bringing them all out into this terrible world. The bunker had been safer, even with that murderer inside.

Snap out of it!

His head rocked to the side from the force of the slap, and like a sudden flash of light piercing his eyes, he rose up out of his stupor. It wasn't like coming to the surface of a deep lake as it was an abrupt thawing, or an explosion of air entering what had been a vacuum.

He gasped and pushed himself upright again, coughing and heaving.

"What did they do to you up there?" Byron asked.

Finn couldn't see the man, but he could feel and smell his rancid breath on his face, could feel the grip of his hands on his arms as he shook him. He turned to the side, pushing Byron away.

"B-bix?"

"Answer me! What the hell did they do to you?"

Somewhere in the darkness, on the other side of the room, someone wept.

Finn pushed Byron aside again. "Bix? Bix, is that you? I can't find you."

"That's my son," Byron said, still gripping Finn's arm. "He's scared."

"Where's Bix? Did they take him?"

"F-finnnn . . . ?"

He spun his head to the left. "Bix?"

"I can't . . . " There was a groan, and Finn tried once more to move toward the sound of the voice.

"That's not him, either," Byron said, and pulled him back. "Bix is over there, on the other side."

"Finnnn . . . ."

Confusion wrapped its iron fingers around his mind. If Bix was to the right, then who was to the left?

Jones. Or Jonah.

There was a slow, dry hiss, the sound of air passing through swollen lips and the rustle of a body trying to move.

"Who are you?"

"Finn, it's me," the man said. "D-danny."

* * *

News trickled out of Danny like tree sap, coming slowly a drop at a time. Finn had to be patient, and between careful sips of the precious few ounces of water Byron and the boys had saved from the last time they'd been fed, Danny told them what had become of the other survivors.

Allison had died. He and Jonah had been marooned in an empty town overnight during the same attack. The bus had tried to draw the Wraiths away, only to be attacked again. They'd been rescued. The survivors were taken to some old army base.

"They were lucky," Danny said, his weakness leaking out of him as slowly and steadily as the information.

He told Finn how a couple men had returned on motorcycles to find them. "Jonah warned me not to talk to them, not to share any details. He didn't trust them, though he didn't explain why. He was right."

"Where's Jonah now?"

"Dead. Ramsay broke the bike." His body shook. "He left them out in the desert to die."

Finn realized the man was crying. "Tell me what happened."

"He bragged about it, Ramsay did. He said Jonah would ruin everything."

"Ruin what?"

"I don't know. He tortured me, Finn. He wanted to know where we'd come from and if there were more of us there. I tried not to say anything, but he . . . he burned me."

"What did you tell him?"

"Everything," Danny sobbed. "The dam. The bunker. The people inside. He promised to let me go. I couldn't help it, Finn! It hurt so bad!"

"*Shh*, okay. Listen, Danny, it's okay. We'll figure it out. But first we need to get out of here."

"H-how?"

"Byron's working on it."

"These other hinges won't budge," Byron said from the direction of the door. "I worked on them the whole time you were gone."

Finn went over to Bix. It took a long time to elicit any kind of coherent response from him. He seemed to be aware, he just didn't seem able to move until Finn grabbed him by the shoulders and shook him.

"We need to get out of here, Bix! Before we end up like—"

He stopped himself, not wanting to say the names of their dead colleagues.

"We need to get that door off. Do you think you can help Byron with it? Bix?"

"Y-yes."

"Good." He returned to Danny and asked how he'd gotten here.

"Private Ramsay. When he was finished with me, he turned me over to some men. They brought me in the back of a pickup truck. I tried to escape. That's when they beat me. They—" He choked back a sob.

"What, Danny? What about them?"

"They said they were going to sell me, like a slave. Said they'd already sold others. Except for the women and girls. They were going to—"

"No." Finn didn't want to hear.

"Why? Why are they doing this?"

"Tell him," Bix said. His voice sounded hollow. "Tell him about Nami and Jonathan. What they did to them."

"Nami?" Danny asked. "Jonathan? You saw them? They're here?"

"They were," Finn whispered, and he silently cursed Bix for speaking out. Danny didn't need to hear this right now.

He was too close to slipping away, and if they were going to get out, they all needed to focus. "They were brought here. They died last night."

"Died? How? Did they beat them, too?"

"I don't think so."

"But Nami wasn't hurt that bad during the Wraith attack. And Jonathan was getting better."

"Better?"

"The flu. He was never vaccinated. But they gave him antibiotics."

Finn was silent for several minutes. He hadn't wanted to tell Danny what had happened overnight, but now he felt compelled to. "I couldn't understand why Nami wasn't interested in Jonathan after he was infected, but I have an idea. Remember what Seth Abramson said about the things in our bodies?"

"The nano things?"

"Nanites," Finn corrected. "Tiny machines in our blood. He implied that they were somehow connected to the Flense."

"Yeah, but he didn't say how. And he also didn't explain how they got into all of us."

"I thought I knew. I thought it might've been the shots at the evacuation center, and that they made us susceptible to the infection."

"Except the Flense was worldwide and happened before we got those shots."

"Yes. But remember, Seth said the government authorized broad distribution of the nanites, he just didn't explain how. I now think it was the flu immunizations. The nanites must have been in them. If Jonathan was never immunized, he was nanite-free. I think it's why Nami wasn't interested in touching him. He was immune."

"Nanites in the vaccine? The government wouldn't—"

"What? They forced everyone to receive it, Danny. Remember? Not just us, but everyone everywhere all over the world. If you didn't get the shot, you couldn't work or go to school. You couldn't travel."

"Millions were dying from the flu. Hundreds of millions. They were trying to control the spread. It's not because of the shots! It can't be."

"Finn, we don't know if Jonathan was immune at all," Bix said from the other side of the room. "Maybe it was the electrical shock—"

"It wasn't."

"Then how do you explain Billy?" Bix quietly asked. "He touched one, and he wasn't infected."

"The wound on his leg."

"Excuse me?"

"The wound on his leg means he doesn't have those nanites in his body, either. He was injured before Adrian got the cut on his forehead. And yet Adrian is almost healed. And remember what Jennifer told us about Luke and Billy, how they take forever to heal? Thing is, they don't heal slower, they just heal normal. It's everyone else who heals faster."

"Let me get this straight," Byron interrupted. "You're saying anyone immune to the flu is sensitive to the Flense. And anyone sensitive to the flu is immune to the Flense?"

"Yes."

"I was never vaccinated," Bix said.

Finn had suspected as much. Doc Cavanaugh had told him that the nanites weren't in Bix's blood. "It's just a theory," he warned. "It doesn't mean anything until we can prove it."

CHAPTER

THE THREE OF THEM WORKED AT THE HINGES FOR several more hours, switching places when their hands cramped or grew too tired. But the top and bottom pins simply wouldn't budge.

Danny attempted to help, but though his recovery seemed extraordinarily rapid — which Bix saw as more proof of Finn's theory — he remained weak and sore.

They had just about given up in frustration when Bix heard the outer door being thrown open. He hurried down the stairs before the inner door could be unlocked.

Once again, the light that spilled down blinded them. Something heavy tumbled down the steps wrapped in a burlap sack. This was accompanied by Luke's laughter.

From further out, Billy shouted at them with considerably less humor. "Y'all better enjoy yer last bit of daylight," he growled, "cause soon y'all are gonna be the main attraction."

Then the door slammed shut, and darkness and silence swept over them.

"What do you think he meant by that?" Bix asked.

No one answered. It seemed obvious enough.

"Well, I don't mind being the main attraction," he went bravely on, though his voice shook. "Now, how about we see what they got us."

"Don't touch it," Finn warned. "Bix, don't!"

"Too late. I'm already on it."

They could hear him moving about and mumbling to himself as he tried to figure out what was in the sack.

"Those idiots tie knots like kindergartners. And . . . it's food. Smells okay."

"Food?" Charlie asked, and scurried over from where he and his little brother were sitting.

Jerry hadn't spoken a single word the entire time Finn and Bix had been down there, and he still didn't. Finn couldn't help wondering what the boy's issue might be, but he didn't want to pry.

"What kind of food?"

The last meal kind, Finn thought. He didn't say it out loud.

"Roast beef. Baked potatoes. All cold, of course." Bix took a deeper sniff and groaned. "Ugh. It might be spoiled."

Finn's stomach rebelled. This seemed especially cruel.

"Well, beggars can't be whiners."

"Don't eat it, Bix. You'll get sick."

"I don't care. I'm starving. And there's plastic bottles of something." He shook one. "Sounds like something to drink."

"We had all better eat," Byron said. "We need to keep up our strength."

"Mm, yeah, go ahead," Bix said around a mouthful. "There's enough for everyone."

The roast did smell a little off, but it didn't taste bad. Finn ate what he could, and within a few minutes, he felt his strength returning.

The liquid in the bottles turned out to be water. It also tasted all right, though he was glad he couldn't see it. He'd bet it was probably from the lake.

The food sat like a lead weight in Finn's stomach. He felt like puking. The thought of what was waiting for them above sickened him. He went to Bix and asked how he was doing. He could hear his friend breathing funny— short, rapid breaths. "You going to be sick?"

"No." But he sounded like he might. "I . . . . Listen, Finn, no matter what happens, I want you to know it's okay. This was my choice."

"You'd still have been in danger, even if you'd stayed on the bus. I'm glad you're here with me."

"That's . . . not what I meant, but okay. I was talking about tonight."

"What about tonight?"

"What you said earlier."

"About what?"

The inner door slammed open, surprising them all. Finn instinctively shielded his eyes.

"Everyone against the back wall!" Luke shouted down at them. "Y'all try anything, I'll pump yer ass full of lead. Now move!"

The prisoners joined Danny along the far wall. It was the first chance Finn had to look at everyone's face. The bruising around Danny's eyes and the amount of dried blood that had soaked into his clothes shocked him.

"Time fer asking forgiveness of yer trespasses!" Luke said, descending the steps. "Time fer damnation or sal-vation."

"Now, let's not get ahead of ourselves," Adrian interjected, following on his heels.

Billy came last, still clearly limping. All three held semi-automatic weapons in their hands instead of the stun guns. Finn eyed them warily.

"You!" Luke said, pointing at Danny. "On yer feet."

"He's hurt!" Finn objected. He pushed himself off the floor, but Billy stepped forward, moving fast despite the wound, and slammed the stock of his rifle into Finn's face. He crumpled to the dirt.

"Damn it, Billy!" Adrian cried. "I told y'all to keep yer wits!" He sighed and shook his head. "Pull him up!"

Luke went over to Danny and yanked him to his feet, the muzzle of the rifle digging into his side.

"He cain't barely walk," Adrian growled in frustration. "I told them people not to bring me them half dead."

"You don't have to do this," Finn said from the ground. The hit hadn't broken skin, but he could feel the side of his face swelling up already. His jaw ached.

"What should we do, boss?" Luke asked.

Adrian studied the huddled group for a moment, scratching his chin on his arm.

Billy pointed at Byron. "What about him? They been in here the longest."

"The blind man?" Adrian said, laughing derisively. "Another waste. Wouldn't have much of a sporting chance. No, we'll save him and the boys fer somethin else. I got to think what, though." He swung around again and pointed at Finn. "Take him."

"No!" Bix jumped up and slammed his body into Adrian, driving him across the room. The two lost their footing and went crashing against the wall.

Charlie tried to jump up to help, but Byron held him back, hissing for him to sit tight. Finn struggled to stand, but the room was still spinning.

"Get yer ass offa him!" Luke growled. He kicked Bix in the side. Bix cried out and crumpled to the floor, coughing and groaning and clutching his stomach.

"You rotten stinking bastard," Bix spat. "You're an abomination!"

"He's got some fire!" Luke said with glee.

"I don't care, I want him!" Adrian shouted, still pointing at Finn.

Once more, Bix charged at the man. Once more, Luke kicked him in the back.

"Enough!" Adrian screamed, and grabbed Bix by the hair. "Y'all just took yer friend's place."

"No! Leave him alone!" Finn shouted. He fell again when the world tilted beneath his feet.

Luke laughed. "You cain't even stand, neither."

"Y'all heard the man. Get up," Billy ordered Bix. "Yer gone be tonight's spotlight attraction."

"No, please!" Finn said. "Take me instead."

"Oh, we will," Adrian replied, dusting himself off. "Don't y'all worry 'bout that. Yer time'll come soon enough."

He stomped up the steps, followed by Bix at the end of Luke's rifle. A moment later, the door slammed shut.

* * *

An hour passed. Maybe two. Or maybe it was only ten minutes. Finn couldn't tell. Nobody came for him.

He redoubled his efforts on the door, but it all seemed for naught. He'd managed to get the top hinge pin to move about a quarter inch, but no more. He screamed out in frustration, then silenced himself worrying he was frightening the children even more than they already were. He couldn't stand not knowing what was happening to his friend.

You know what's happening to him. He's going to die.

Tears and sweat dripped from his face, made his hands slippery. He cursed his inability to escape, cursed his decisions, cursed the world for what it had become and what it had forced him to do. He cursed his father and the decision he and his mother had made all those years ago. He cursed that it had all gone wrong, despite their careful planning. He cursed his father for discovering the nanites in their blood.

He cursed that it hadn't been his little sister instead of his father in that bunker with him, like it was supposed to be. If it had been Leah, none of this ever would have happened. She knew him, knew his weaknesses. She accepted him as he was and would never have pushed him like his father had, urging to be more than he was.

More like Harper.

None of them would have died if he'd just remained like the old Finn— cowardly, indecisive, alone.

Finally, he cursed his brother, not for being better, someone to aspire to, but for simply still being alive and inside that other bunker, making Finn believe that he could, for once, be the hero.

Harper would have come up with a plan to escape and save his friend. In fact, Harper would never have gotten himself into this situation to begin with. Had their roles been switched, Harper wouldn't have allowed himself to be distracted. He would have seen right through Father Adrian. He would have already made his way to Bunker Two, found Finn, and saved him.

Harper would have done everything right.

But it wasn't Harper, it was Finn. And he had done everything wrong.

Please, please, he silently begged. *Please let me be right about the immunity.*

At last they returned for him. Finn hadn't heard them coming. So deep in his despair was he that he hadn't been listening. And so, when, in a rush of air that smelled of rain, the door flew open and knocked him down the steps.

The buckle and nail flew from his hands as he tumbled. Luke was there in an instant, descending in a rush. He saw the objects and guessed immediately what Finn had been doing. "Check the back of the damn door, Billy," he shouted. "They was trying to break out!"

"Don't see nothin," Billy said. His voice was filled with scorn. "Stupid boy thinks he can scratch his way through a steel door?" He laughed.

Luke kicked Finn in the thigh. "Don't you move a muscle!"

Finn didn't. What was the use? If Harper had been there instead of him, he would never have been caught unawares. He would have expected them, been waiting for them. He would have been ready. He would have figured out a way to overpower them and escape.

But he wasn't Harper. He was Finn.

"Cover him!" Luke yelled at Billy. "I'm goin to check and see if they's hidin anymore secret tools."

Finn could hear him slapping the boys around, calling them freaks. Byron yelled. There was another sickening crunch as something hard and heavy hit bone. Charlie shrieked to leave them alone.

A moment later, Luke was back, pulling Finn to his feet. "It's yer turn, boy!"

Finn had one final glimpse of the remaining prisoners before being dragged up the steps. Byron lay on the floor along the wall opposite where Danny lay. Fresh blood trickled from a new wound on his forehead. Charlie lay draped over his father's chest, shaking him and screaming for him not to be dead.

In the far corner cowered a tiny boy, his face white with terror. With a shock, Finn realized that Jerry, like his father, was blind.

Luke and Billy wrestled him to the ground outside the shack and bound his wrists and ankles. Thunder rolled across the sky, and the air smelled of electricity. The wind blew, stirring up the horses.

When they finished trussing him, they threw him into the cart.

"What have you done to my friend?" he cried.

"Oh, he's just fine," Luke cackled. "That boy's a natural-born killer, all right. Didn't take him but two seconds to finish off his feral."

"He's okay?"

"He ain't dead, if'n that's what you mean. But he ain't been saved, neither."

Finn moaned.

"Yep," Luke replied, mockingly. "Took him too damn long to get started. Then another damn long time to turn. Drove everyone nuts. But that's what the reverend likes."

"After he did turn, it just sat there in the middle of the cage, sitting on top of the other body, like it were some kind of trophy or something."

The cart jounced over the uneven terrain, making it difficult to understand his words. He turned and gave Finn a wicked grin.

"Maybe y'all will be saved tonight. I doubt it, though.

"Noooo," Finn wailed. "Bix, no!"

"He's waitin fer y'all to join him in the cage," Billy said, turning around. Lightning flashed, illuminating the mad grin on his face. He blinked as the first drops of rain hit his face. "What do y'all think, Luke?"

"Yup, I think he's waitin all right."

"You made the reverend so mad he changed his mind about doin only one sacrifice tonight." He snickered, and Luke joined in. "No sense keeping the boyfriends apart."

They arrived at the barn just as the rain began to grow heavy. They yanked him off the cart by his bound feet, letting him drop heavily to the ground. The fall knocked the wind from his lungs, and before he could recover, his ankles were unbound and he was yanked upright and turned toward the barn.

Run! his mind screamed. He could. He knew the path. But he also knew it would be impossible the moment the thought entered his head. He remembered how quickly Luke and Billy had followed them through the woods that first day. Even if Billy was injured and couldn't run, Luke was healthy.

They shoved him toward the door, and the crowd parted. Adrian stood at the far side, watching them over the top of the cage. "Idiots!" he shouted. "Y'all forgot to put the damn hood on him!"

Billy and Luke hesitated a moment.

"Never mind! Just bring him forward."

The last of the crowd parted, revealing the scene inside the cage. Bix, his head down like he was resting, crouched on Nami's back. Nami's head was twisted around at an unnatural angle. Dried blood from the night before caked the corners of his mouth. His dark eyes held no expression at all. Both were naked except for their underwear.

"No!" Finn screamed. "You murderers!" He collapsed to his knees in anguish, but was immediately wrestled back to his feet.

"Strip him down!" Adrian shouted, and the crowd roared.

They pulled off his shoes, socks, and pants. Then held him down as they unbound his wrists and removed his shirt.

Adrian bent down to speak to him. "I ain't never seen a smart feral before. Then again, I ain't no one ever been saved like we saw last night. Too bad it was fer only a couple minutes, though. He shoulda killed the other when he had a chance."

He stepped to the side so Finn could see inside the cage again. The thing that was once Bix still hadn't moved.

"Cain't get to it with the prods when it's just sitting there like that, not near the sides, not touchin the wire. Smart. Cain't get it to come no closer. Y'all know what that means? Means we cain't zap it. So, what're we gonna do? How y'all gonna be able to redeem yerself?"

"It's all a lie anyway," Finn growled. "You know it doesn't work that way."

Something flickered across Adrian's face, a sense of doubt, perhaps, or irritation. It was gone before Finn could really get any sense of what it was.

"These people," he quietly said, gesturing at the crowd, "they're payin customers, and I don't intend to disappoint them."

"But you will," Finn spat. "Because it's all fake! They bought into your religious lies. They came looking for salvation. Why? Because if they see it, it means there's hope for an end to this nightmare. But you know the truth, don't you? There's no cure, no salvation!"

Adrian sneered at the boy. "I do believe you're right," he said. "They want somethin to hold onto, somethin to hope fer. I give em a good show, a reason fer them to come back. So here's what we're gonna do. We're sending y'all in with a stun gun to zap it yerself. You should be happy, havin a full forty-five seconds instead of the usual fifteen to kill it. Them's pretty good odds, don't you think?" He smiled tenderly, then stood up and gestured. "The crowd'll pay more to see a salvation."

Billy hobbled over, a cattle prod in his hands and stood by as Adrian unlocked the gate. They kept their eyes glued to Bix's body, ready to slam the gate shut in case he moved. The crowd stood in hushed anticipation.

The Bix-thing in the cage remained still, not even a sudden peal of thunder seemed to affect it.

Finn was lifted up by a wrist and ankle and heaved inside. The gate clanged shut behind him just as he hit the dirt.

Only then did the thing that had once been his friend begin to stir.

CHAPTER

JONAH KNEELED IN THE DARKNESS IN A SMALL DRY creek bed and trained the binoculars on the gate.

A pair of trucks had just arrived. He'd seen them coming from a couple miles away, the sand and dust blown up by their tires from the road turning the beams of their headlights into ghostly shapes.

Above him, storm clouds raced across the moon, masking it more often than not. He hoped for rain. He wouldn't make it another day without water.

The trucks were inspected by several armed guards and sniffed by dogs before being allowed to enter the compound, where they stopped and disgorged about a dozen people. Most of these appeared bewildered, stepping out and turning in circles to inspect their surroundings, as if it was all new to them. Some appeared frightened.

One couple, a man and woman with a girl huddled tight against their legs, were talking with a pair of heavily-armed men. Jonah couldn't be exactly sure if they were arguing, as he couldn't hear them over the rumbling of the trucks' engines.

The door to the administrative building opened and a figure hurried out and down the steps. He shouted something, and the trucks shut off.

"Everyone, may I please have your attention?" His voice boomed over the desert sands, clipped and full of assurance. "Thank you. My name is Captain Cheever. On behalf of Colonel Wainwright, please allow me to formally welcome you to Westerton Army Base. I'm sure you're all exhausted after your long journey, so I'll keep this brief.

"My people will shortly escort you to your temporary quarters. For your safety and for the safety of the residents of this community, you will be quarantined in separate barracks until you can be examined by our medic tomorrow. I appreciate your understanding in this regard. We'll have you all back with your families and friends soon enough. There will be a briefing first thing in the morning. Good night."

Jonah didn't recognize any of the new people. He had hoped to see Bren, but she wasn't among them. Wherever she'd gone the night before, he hadn't seen her return, though he knew it was possible she'd come in while he had been scouting the perimeter for a way inside or else napping in the shade.

He'd determined that the compound covered just over a hundred acres of the desert's ancient seabed, stretching roughly a half mile by a third. Save for a few scrubby bushes and rocks, the installation was surrounded on three sides by flat, barren ground scored by a warren of dry cuts.

The fourth side was bounded by a narrow arête of exposed rock, the tail end of the mountains rising fifty miles in the distance, and it was in this maze of outcroppings and fissures that he had spent the bulk of the day, mainly searching for pools of water and staying out of the blazing sun.

He had also concluded that the perimeter could not be easily breached. The outer fence rose at least twelve feet high and was topped with razor wire. It had been buttressed along its length with wooden boards propped up against it. A set of black cables connected it to a large shed from which the constant hum of a generator could be heard.

The inner fence was only slightly shorter. It too was similarly topped, though it wasn't electrified.

Between the two fences ran several dozen very hungry-looking German shepherd guard dogs. There were only two places where the animals didn't have access. One was the main gate; the other was an unused gate in back, which did not appear to be guarded. Instead, barriers had been erected around it on the inside, and signs were posted warning people to stay clear, suggesting the presence of booby traps.

He had slept little, napping whenever he could, waking when he heard the sound of vehicles. But though he hadn't seen Bren, he had caught sight of a few of the others from Bunker Eight. In particular, he'd spotted Hannah and the two Rollins boys and their mother entering what appeared to be a series of greenhouses along the southern fence. And he thought he'd seen Eddie slinking around near the back gate, though by the time he managed to untangle the binoculars and raise them to his eyes, the figure was gone from view.

There appeared to be only one option for him to gain access to the base, and it wasn't one he favored. He would have to walk up to the front gate and ask to speak with this Captain Cheever or Colonel Wainwright. Based on what he'd heard Ramsay say back in the town, he wasn't sure either of them could be trusted.

He gathered his pack and tossed it onto the raised ground before him in preparation for climbing out of his hiding spot. From somewhere to his right, there came a small clatter of stones tumbling to the floor of the arroyo. He froze and stared into the night. Nothing moved.

Vinnie's pistol pressed against his spine inside the waist of his pants. He thought about retrieving it.

A hundred yards away, the new arrivals were being led toward a pair of one-story buildings. Their shadows, fanned by the flood lamps topping the fence posts, danced over the desert sands.

But Jonah didn't see any of this. His eyes remained glued to a spot of darkness some twenty feet away, where another patch of sand and gravel suddenly collapsed down the embankment.

Then came another, a few feet closer.

Something was making its way toward him.

Jonah planted his hands on the sand and kicked a toe into the side for a foothold. He could feel the earth crumbling beneath him, threatening to spill him back into the dry bed. With a grunt, he jumped, landing flat onto the desert floor, and rolled.

But something grabbed his leg. He kicked out, felt his heel connect. The ground collapsed beneath him, pulling him down. He slid into the arroyo and was immediately smothered beneath an avalanche of sand. Darkness in the shape of a human swept over him.

Jonah struggled to reach for the gun, but a hand with the strength of steel clamped over it. Another grabbed his face, choking him.

"Dammit, Jonah! Keep quiet."

The hand slowly peeled away from his mouth.

225

"Eddie?"

Jonah tried to wipe the sand away, but it clung to his sweaty skin, got in his eyes and blinded him.

"Let me help," Eddie told him. "I've got some water." He formed Jonah's hands into a cup and poured a little in.

"You scared the crap out of me," Jonah sputtered. "I thought you were a Wraith."

"There aren't any around."

"How do you know?"

"Trust me."

"You could have let me know it was you before grabbing me."

"How? I couldn't very well yell now, could I? Not without them shooting at us. Sound carries out here."

Jonah snatched the bottle from Eddie's hand and put it to his lips. "God, that tastes good," he said after swallowing several mouthfuls of the liquid. "What are you doing out here anyway? And how'd you know it was me?"

"I saw you up in the rocks on the east side of the base this afternoon. Been watching you ever since."

"You saw me?"

"Well, smelled you first, actually."

Jonah sniffed his arm pit, then wrinkled his nose. "Is it that bad?"

"To me, yes." He took the bottle back and shook it. There was only another mouthful left. "We thought you were dead."

"Alive and kicking, although they did try."

"That's what I figured. The search team that went out looking for you reported that you'd been attacked and killed. You and the other biker scout. I had my doubts."

"They found him?"

"Nothing but the bike and a bloody mess. The team claimed it was Wraiths."

Jonah shook his head. "I didn't want to leave him, but I had no choice. I couldn't trust him. He was alive when I took off."

Eddie's eyes glistened in the darkness, reflecting the stray light from the base. He seemed to be searching for something in Jonah's face. "Why'd you come here?"

"What other choice did I have? It's not like I could go back. Where else could I go?"

"It's just that . . . ."

"That nobody here likes me? Hate to break it to you, but they can't stand me back at the bunker."

"You know that's not strictly true. Hannah has always had a soft spot in her heart for you."

"But not you."

"You haven't always made it easy for people to like you."

Jonah looked away. "Can we talk about this later?" He stood up and turned toward the army base. The streaks on his face made it look like he'd been crying.

"If you're thinking about going in there," Eddie said, "that's not a good idea."

"Up until a minute ago, it seemed like the only idea." He turned to Eddie. "Why not?"

Eddie stood beside him. He was shorter than Jonah, yet he seemed larger. "It's dangerous." His face was pale in the wan light, though not as translucent as it had been just a few days before.

"You're changing," Jonah observed.

"Still no hair." He turned to Jonah. "Something bad is going on here. Our people are disappearing. First, it was Danny."

"Danny made it back? Did he say anything to you about why they tried to get rid of me?"

Eddie shook his head. "I never got a chance to talk to him. He was here, then gone."

"Where?"

"I don't know. They claimed he left on his own."

"He wouldn't."

"Yeah, I know. He's not the only one."

"Who else is gone?"

"Jonathan and Nami. When I confronted Cheever, he tried to say they'd died, but I went to the graveyard. There were new graves, but our people weren't in them."

"How do you know?"

"The smell."

Jonah frowned. "You could smell them through the dirt?"

"I know it sounds ridiculous."

Jonah shook his head. "I guess if you could smell me at that distance, then why shouldn't you be able to smell through the ground."

Eddie didn't respond.

"Those nanite things really did a number on you, didn't they? The ones Bren's dad was talking about in your blood. They really did make you . . . better."

"Some people wouldn't say so." Eddie sighed and shook his head. "They made me . . . more, yes. But maybe not better."

"Anymore disappearances?"

Eddie nodded. "Last night. The group's really spooked by it. We've been demanding that they tell us what's going on, but neither Cheever nor his boss will say. I was planning on breaking into their office tonight and taking a look around, but one or the other has been inside it all day. And now this." He gestured at the activity in the camp. "I'm going to try once things settle down."

"Who was it this time? Harrison?"

Eddie studied Jonah's face for a moment. "It was Bren."

Jonah frowned. "Well, at least we know she's not in the cemetery. I saw her leave with a bunch of people last night. They took the bus and a truck and several motorbikes."

Eddie's face tightened. "Dammit."

"Why, what's the matter?"

"I think she took them to Bunker Eight."

CHAPTER

RISING SLOWLY TO HIS FEET, **F**INN'S EYES NEVER BROKE away from the creatures at the center of the cage.

I'm so sorry, Bix. I was wrong about the nanites. Goddamn it, I was wrong about everything.

The din from the crowd behind him began to grow. He could feel their nervous energy, their need for violence, and he wanted to shout at them to shut up, but he knew it would only make them even louder. They were looking for a show, not a quick and easy kill. They wanted blood and murder.

They'll get it either way, Finn thought, *whether I deliver it or not*.

He edged backward, moving toward the gate until his heel contacted the metal. "Give me a cattle prod," he muttered, and reached a hand back.

"Screw you," Luke replied.

"Adrian said he'd give me one."

"Use yer hands."

"Aw hell," someone in the crowd said. "At least give the kid a fighting chance. That thing isn't going anywhere near the wire."

"Give me a cattle prod," Finn repeated.

Something hit the ground beside his foot. Moving slowly, he reached around and found a stun gun instead. He brought the pistol-like device forward, bracing it against his belly. It was good for a single zap. But to do it, he'd have to get close enough to almost touch.

Better not miss then.

Luke poked him in the back with the end of his cattle prod. "Get moving, boy," he growled. "Or else I'll shock you."

Finn shuffled forward, raising the weapon. His hands trembled. He placed his finger on the trigger and took another step.

What good will it do? All it'll do is buy you a few seconds. Then what? There's no place to run.

He knew with absolute certainty that it was all a charade. He'd seen the truth in Adrian's eyes when he told him as much.

You don't know. It might work. Shock Bix and then—

He nearly tripped on one of the buried electrical cables. It had come loose during an earlier scuffle. He caught himself and cursed.

It's not Bix, not anymore. Bix is gone so don't call it that.

He wanted to lie down and die.

Just zap it. You can figure out what to do then.

Zapping it would give him — what? — a half minute to come up with an escape plan? That wasn't enough time. Maybe he could use the butt of the gun to smash in Bix's head without touching him.

It's not Bix!

He wanted to throw up. There was no way he could do it.

231

The Bix-thing slunk toward him, edging closer on all four limbs. It slid a little to Finn's left, forcing him into a corner. Finn stepped forward deliberately. He needed it to get within ten feet to be sure the darts embedded in its skin. Even at that distance, however, he didn't feel confident enough in his aim, not with his body shaking as much as it was.

The Wraith matched his movements, and Finn instinctively edged even further to the right, keeping the distance between them constant. He didn't dare blink, afraid that it would charge at him the moment he did. He knew how quickly and suddenly they could move. He had witnessed it too many times.

"Get to it!" the crowd screamed. Something hit the cage and bounced away, sending a ripple across the fencing. The Wraith didn't seem to notice it at all. Its focus was entirely on Finn's feet and nothing else. For every step Finn took away, it edged the same distance closer. "Zap it! Zap the feral! Zap it dead! Kill it!"

The two boys circled each other, pivoting around Nami's body. Out of the corner of his eye, Finn saw Luke standing just outside the cage, the cattle prod held at the ready. He slid his body toward the Bix-thing, taking advantage of its blind spot to edge close enough to reach through the wire. He really wanted to be the one to shock it.

Outside, the storm was building. Wind battered the sides of the barn, making it creak and rattle. Someone went over and slid the door shut.

Finn made eye contact with Luke, then twitched his head slightly to the left, directing the man to that side. In the background, Adrian shouted at him to step away, to leave them be, but his voice was lost among the many shouts coming from the crowd.

Finn saw an opportunity in Luke's impatience. If he could draw the Wraith close enough to the fence, Luke wouldn't be able to resist. He'd strike first so he could claim credit for knocking the Wraith out. Finn actually hoped he would. With his stun gun unused, he'd still have it for his escape, or at the very least to zap the Wraith a second time. He wondered if a second shock in rapid succession would be additive.

But what then?

His toes nudged the cable. They had buried it beneath six inches of dirt, the end attached to the wire. He filed it away as something he might use. Maybe he could tie Bix up with it, choke him.

It, not him.

He stepped to the side, bringing himself closer to the fence. Luke gave him a barely perceptible nod. The Wraith matched Finn's movement, sidling closer, and Luke stepped up to meet it. Silently, he slid the prod into an opening, edging it toward the Bix-thing's back. But just as he was about to jab, it stepped away, as if sensing the danger.

Finn tried again, circling around. He grew alarmed at how far he was getting from the gate despite his best attempts to stay close. Now he could see the crowd, could see them pressing forward. There was no barrier holding them back, none but their own fear of being touched.

On previous nights that fear had been enough. But tonight was different. Now they pushed against one another, jostling for a better view, eager for the bloodbath or the salvation. They didn't care which.

Luke tilted his head toward a spot in the corner, urging Finn to move the Wraith closer. Adrian had climbed onto the stage behind Finn and was screaming at Luke. But the man standing just outside the wire was beyond hearing anything else now. His attention was focused entirely inside the cage.

A smile twitched Luke's lips. Finn tried to maneuver the Wraith toward him, but nothing he did seemed to work. The creature acted as if it sensed his ploys and remained stubbornly just out of reach of the sides.

Finn jerked a finger to the right, and Luke nodded. Finn had angled the Bix-thing so that it was completely blind to anything but him. It couldn't see the crowd behind it, though it certainly had to sense it.

Rain lashed the side of the barn, driven hard by the wind. The men yelled even louder.

The Wraith edged closer to Finn, stepping slowly forward on all fours, sniffing at the ground. Ten feet away, nine. Finn raised the stun gun and took aim. *Just a little closer . . . .*

"Bring it over to the wire!" Luke growled in frustration, as if he could sense his chances slipping away. "Over where I can reach it!"

The Bix-thing ignored Luke. It ignored the crowd behind it. Finn's finger tensed on the trigger. He waited for it to step forward.

And it finally did, sliding to the side just as Luke extended his arm through the wire, once more avoiding the shock meant for it.

It rose up onto its feet, straightening its spine. It lifted its head and looked Finn straight in the eye.

And winked.

CHAPTER

32

FINN FROZE. *HAD IT JUST— HAD THAT THING actually—*

Their eyes met and locked, and for just the briefest of moments, he thought he saw a trace of the old Bix in them. But then it hissed, and something passed through its body, a spasm of some sort, and it took a step toward him.

In a flash, their bodies crashed into each other. Skin slapped skin. The Bix-thing howled at the same time Finn screamed. Their arms went about each other and they tumbled to the dirt.

"Kill it!" the men shouted.

The two wrestled for a moment. The Bix-thing lowered its face to Finn's and opened its mouth beside Finn's ear. The crowd saw them jolt, their bodies arching against their spines, and they both went still.

Finn lay underneath, his head flopped to the side, his eyes unseeing. His arm fell limp to the ground, still gripping the unused stun gun.

"What did you do?" Adrian screamed at Luke.

The crowd fell silent. Every man held his breath in anticipation. Wind and rain pummeled the barn and scratched at the roof. Several seconds passed before the men realized that the spectacle was already over.

"What the hell?" someone asked. "Is that it? What just happened?"

"We've been ripped off!" another cried. "He killed them both with that cattle prod!"

"No, I didn't!"

The men began to yell in anger and confusion. They pushed forward again, this time not bothering to keep away. The risk was gone. No one was going to get infected.

Adrian screamed at them to get back. He jumped from the stage and shouted, "Move away! Make a path!" But he couldn't stop them. They swept past, crushing against the chain link, rattling it. The wire bulged inward, as if the men meant to squeeze through the openings. They were enraged. They were cheated.

There was a clank as the gate latch was unlocked. Adrian screamed at Luke not to open it. He tried to stop him.

Then the man was running across the cage, his feet pounding the packed dirt. Rapidly at first, then slowing as if he realized how foolhardy it was.

"Get out of there!" Adrian shouted.

Luke stood uncertainly over the boys, the cattle prod raised. he jabbed it into the Bix-thing's back. "They's dead all right," he said, half in disbelief, half in relief. He poked again.

"Zap them to be sure!"

"Botha them's dead!"

"How could they be?" Adrian screamed. "It's not possible!"

"Zap them, Luke!" Billy cried. He rattled the fence. "Make sure!"

"Okay, but—"

"Now!" Finn yelled, and aimed the stun gun just as Bix rolled off of him, snatching the prod away. The man jittered from the electricity, his mouth agape. He stumbled backward and tore the darts from his shirt.

Bix stuck the cattle prod into Luke's belly and pressed the button. This time, the man let out a shriek of pain as he was thrown backward. Smoke rose from a hole in his shirt. He lay on the ground unconscious. A wet spot appeared on the ground beneath his crotch.

Finn reached down and grabbed the second stun gun from Luke's belt, then ran toward the gate, howling at the men who had entered the cage. There was a unified cry of panic and they turned to flee. But they were too slow, and the gate too small. They crowded the opening, punching and kicking to get through.

Finn aimed for the closest figure and pulled the trigger. The man shrieked as the darts bit into the shirt on his back, setting off a chain reaction of screams from the other men desperate to get away.

Come on! Finn prayed, as he started pummeling the men with the gun. *Come on, Bix! Hurry!*

There was a *BOOM!* and the lights above him dimmed. The stink of burning plastic and wood reached his nose. A light bulb above his head exploded, sending more sparks to the ground. Then several more blew in rapid succession. The place went dark.

Flames rose, setting the straw on fire.

Finn spun around. Bix was still jabbing the cattle prod at the fencing, trying to short the circuit. "It's blown!" he screamed.

He turned back and saw Billy pushing his way through the fray, his eyes pinned on Finn. There was no panic on his face, only the sort of clarity that hatred bestows upon the manically obsessed.

Finn stood his ground while chaos swirled about him. He didn't worry about any of the men attacking him. They still hadn't realized he wasn't infected. They didn't want to get anywhere near him.

Billy pushed his way through until they were close enough to grapple. Finn raised one of the stun guns and pulled the trigger before realizing he'd already expended the darts. Billy grinned and charged.

"No!" Finn screamed. He jammed the business ends of both stun guns into either side of the man's face and pulled the triggers. Billy screamed and went down. His body jigged on the ground.

A dozen men tried to draw the barn door open, but they had to fight against the crushing weight of those behind them. As the opening grew, they poured out through it. Lightning flashed outside. Rain washed in.

Finn spotted Adrian in the middle of the fray. He was fighting the runners, but he ended up being swept out into the night. For a moment, Finn locked eyes with his, and he saw the same hatred he had seen in Seth Abramson's a week before.

"We need to get the horses," Bix shouted into Finn's ear. He grabbed him by the arm and pulled. "We have to get to Danny at the house before the others do!"

"The key for the woodshed!"

"Got it from Luke's pocket. He didn't argue."

They waited for the men to exit, then slipped out and made their way around the side of the barn. Luke stumbled out after them, a dazed look on his face. Adrian appeared out of the darkness and tried to steady him. Through the

238

wind and rain, Finn heard him screaming for help putting the fire out, to save the equipment, to capture the boys. Flames erupted through the roof. They raced up the side of the barn. The generator shed was fully engulfed.

"Lightning strike!" Bix shouted, and clapped Finn on the back. "Nice job grounding the wires."

Then they ran.

Most of the men had scattered to the dock and were trying desperately to get into their boats. The surface of the lake was white from the downpour. A few more men ran up the main trail. They slipped in the mud and fell. The boys mounted the horses and rode after them. The pounding hooves sent them diving into the brush.

Bix screamed at them as they passed. With each lightning flash, he seemed to become more and more like a crazed phantom, his undies hanging half-way to his ankles.

"I thought you were going to zap me for sure," he shouted at Finn as they rode.

Finn thought he'd fly off of the horse's back at any moment. He gritted his teeth and replied, "I almost did. I actually thought you were infected."

"I was convincing, wasn't I?"

"That's not the half of it."

"It's because of my mad acting skills."

"Damn it, Bix. The immunity was just a theory!"

"Well, now it's a fact."

CHAPTER

33

FINN SLID OFF THE HORSE THE MOMENT THEY reached the clearing for the house. He handed Bix the reins. "Get Danny and the others out. I'll meet you at the barn in ten."

"Why the barn?"

"We need more horses!"

"Where are you going?"

"To knock out the main generator!"

He ran down the road toward the front entrance, the wind pelting his skin with rain and leaves. Careening down the path, guided only by the few lights Adrian had strung along it, he swiped at his eyes.

Finally, he came to the path he'd seen Billy using the day after they arrived. The red five-gallon fuel cans in his hands had told Finn that there was a storage tank somewhere back in the trees. And the thick insulated cables laid along the ground betrayed their purpose. The path led to the main generator powering the house and fence.

"Hurry your ass up, Bix," he muttered, then plunged into the wood. He prayed that Adrian and the others would remain behind to put out the fire at the barn. He and Bix needed all the time they could get to make their escape.

The muffled clatter of a large motor grew louder as he approached the building, guided once again by the faint glow of a bulb shining through the trees. Finally he emerged from the trail.

The lamp illuminated the front of the brick structure. He stepped up to the heavy panel door and frowned at the thick padlock. The door was too solid to force open with his shoulder. It barely shook when he tried kicking it. And there were no windows to break.

He searched the ground within the sphere of light for a sizable rock, but there was none, forcing him to look deeper into the darkness. He could almost feel the night on his bare skin as he searched on hands and knees, sweeping his half-frozen hands over the soggy ground, sensing the invisible things that might be watching him from the shadows.

"There's nothing out there," he told himself. "No Wraiths, so stop psyching yourself out."

There was no time to worry about it anyway. He needed to get that door open.

At last he found a rock and hurried back to the building with it cradled in his arms. The latch was recessed into the corner of the doorframe, underneath the knob and well out of reach of the rock.

Finn growled in frustration and hammered at the knob anyway. It bent after the first blow, then broke off from the second and landed onto the cement pad by his bare foot. The knob was gone, but the latch and lock remained intact.

He continued hammering, hoping to break the deadbolt instead. The door shuddered with each blow, denting but not breaking. The booms sounded dull in the storm. The latch bent. The screws holding it in place started to strip out of the metal.

"Put it down!"

Finn froze at the sound of Jennifer's voice.

"I said, put it down!"

He turned to find her standing at the end of the trail, a dozen feet away, a plastic raincoat shedding water in streams. She held a rifle in her hands, and it was aimed at his chest.

"What you're doing here is wrong," he shouted.

"Put the damn rock down, Finn. I don't want to shoot you."

Still facing her, he backed up to the door again and swung the stone. The door shook. The padlock jumped and fell back.

"Finn—"

"You won't shoot me!" He swung again: *BAM!*

"Yes, I will." She stepped forward, her boots squishing in the soggy ground.

"I see the way you treat Luke and Billy," Finn yelled. "Even Adrian. I've seen the sympathy on your face when you look at the Wraiths."

He swung — *BAM!* — and the top two screws of the latch pulled a quarter of an inch out. The rock nearly slipped out of his grip. If it landed on his foot—

"You know what they're doing in the barn is wrong!" he shouted. "The way you cared for Bix the other night. You're not like them, Jennifer! You're not a killer."

He regripped the stone and swung: *BAM!*

"It's not killin. We're rehabilitatin them. We're savin them!"

"No, you're not! You're *using* them. And Adrian's using you. That's why you won't stay there and watch. I saw the disgust on your face."

BAM!

242

The screws were nearly out.

"I can't let y'all leave. Adrian won't let you."

BAM!

Finn kicked at the door, and the lock rattled, but the latch stubbornly held.

"Finn, drop the rock." She stepped forward again and raised the rifle to her side. It was now pointed at his gut. "You don't know what you're doing."

"You're going to shoot an unarmed boy in nothing but his underwear?"

She hesitated. Then shook her head. "Don't Finn."

He considered swinging the stone again, then dropped it onto the concrete pad. "Shoot me then," he said, and raised his hands. "Shoot me, or let us go."

She didn't move. Emotions contorted her face, and for a moment, he believed — truly believed — that she'd let him go.

"Y'all don't know what yer doing," she said. "Or what yer startin. Lord help us all."

With a thunderous clap, the gun jumped in her hands. The lightning flash blinded them both.

Behind Finn, the latch exploded and the door flew open. Shards of metal shrapnel peppered his bare back. He ducked away, staggering, as his blood sprinkled the ground. When he raised his head again, she was gone.

CHAPTER

34

SHUTTING DOWN THE GENERATORS EXTINGUISHED THE pathway lights and threw the entire compound into darkness. Only the sporadic flashes of lightning helped guide Finn's way back to the house. The whole time he feared blowing himself up into little pieces because he'd strayed too far off the path.

When he emerged from the trees into the clearing surrounding the house, he first thought that the light coloring the sky was the clouds parting and the first traces of morning. But the glow came from deeper in the woods. Despite the rain, perhaps aided by the winds, the fire was spreading.

Two large shapes lay in the middle of the clearing, and in a flash of lightning he saw that they were the horses they had ridden. The side of one heaved, spurting blood from a terrible gash in its side. Steam rose in the cool night.

The other horse was dead from a massive wound in its neck. The flesh was shredded.

Claymore mine? Shotgun?

Who would shoot it? And why?

"Bix!" he screamed, scanning the grounds.

The house was pitch black — no sweeping flashlight beams or the dull glow of a gas lantern in the windows — and no one came out as he ran to check around back. He pulled the axe from the woodpile before hurrying to the storm shelter. Nothing but darkness and silence greeted him inside, nothing but the hot, thick stench of their waste.

"Bix? You down there? Anyone?"

He picked up a handful of dirt and cast it into the darkness. The bits rained down the steps. Nothing moved. Everyone was gone.

Or dead.

He whirled around and ran for the path.

Flames leapt higher into the night. A solitary figure, half naked, stood at the edge of the yard, silhouetted in the glow.

"Bix!"

Rain pelted his face as he ran, blinding him. His feet ached from cold and the battering they received from running bare. Adrenaline had kept the pain at bay, but it was now fading.

The figure still hadn't moved. Finn stopped and called out again.

He heard the howl in the woods then, and he knew what had made the sound. He knew that the figure before him wasn't Bix. It wasn't even human, not anymore.

And he also knew what had happened to the horses.

The creature dropped to all fours and began to stalk him. Finn didn't move. He knew if he ran, it would attack. Slowly, he raised the axe over his shoulder and waited. Then, not three feet away, it stopped. It stood up. It reached a finger out to touch his elbow.

Finn swung the axe down. It embedded itself deep into the creature's skull and the thing fell into the mud.

He didn't bother removing the axe. He just ran.

Calling Bix's name, he stumbled into the clearing by the animal barn. The Dutch door that they had used that first night was open, each of the halves swinging freely in the wind. The animals inside brayed in agitation.

"Bix?" he shouted into the darkness. "Hey? Are you in here?"

From the other end of the runway, he thought he heard pounding. It was too insistent, too regular to be anything but human.

"Bix?"

Plucking a pitchfork from the wall, he entered. Chains rattled in the shadows off to his left, sounding as if they were being pulled tight. A face emerged from out of the shadows — pale and ghostly, white teeth against blackened lips, eyes that seemed to swallow light — followed by an equally pale body.

The skeletal figure lunged, but jerked back, unable to free itself. Finn stumbled away against the stall on the other side of the walkway.

"Jesus," he whispered, and hurried on.

The sound of the pounding drew him further into the barn. He edged his way past each of the animal stalls, leaving behind the wan rectangle of light behind. He wished for more lightning, but the storm was growing weaker and the flashes grew more and more intermittent.

The further in he went, the more frantic the animals became. Goats rammed their heads against the wooden boards, bleating in panic. Cows lowed unhappily. But it was the horses that concerned him. They were at the far end. He could hear them whinnying in distress, beating against the rails and walls.

"Bix?"

The banging grew louder.

He reached the far end of the barn, arriving at the second door, the twin of the one he had just come in. But no sound of wind or rain came through it, only the steady, purposeful drumming of something alive inside.

He ran his hand along the rough wood, feeling for a handle, but only found a small opening about as wide as the width of his finger. It was a keyhole.

"Bix?"

The pounding abruptly ceased.

"Anyone in there? Can you hear me?"

Now there was a new sound, low at first and indistinct. He pressed his ear against the wood and listened. The animals behind him seemed to still as well, as if they were waiting, too.

The sound was a whisper, wavering just beyond his ability to make sense of it. Then came a soft scrape of something rubbing against the door. Finn pushed himself away, frowning. A finger of ice worked his way up his spine.

"Bix?"

The door rattled.

Get out of here, Finn. It's nothing good in there.

But he needed to know for sure. What if it was the rest of Bunker Eight?

It's not!

The door rattled again.

It's not them. It's—

A howl rose on the other side, raising the hair on his neck. Finn stumbled away. *Wraiths!* And a lot by the sound of it. The scratching sounds grew more frantic, accompanied by more growls and hisses until the barn was filled with an entire chorus of them. The door rattled.

CRACK!

Dust rained down on his skin from the rafters above. The wooden frame was failing.

Time to go, Finn!

He spun around and began to run. The animals were frantic. Wood from one of the stalls ahead exploded into the runway. A pig the size of a small cow tumbled into the path, followed by a half dozen piglets. Squealing in fright, the mother trampled its young. Behind Finn, the door splintered, then crashed to the ground. Finn's legs tangled, and he fell.

He could hear them coming out now, slipping through the fractured pieces of the wooden door like steam through vents. The horses were mad with terror. They crashed and screamed. There was a noise, like the crunch of teeth on bone, and a sudden high-pitched whinny of pain. The cry rose for a moment, then abruptly stopped.

Finn scrambled to his feet. They were coming down the runway, driving the animals mad with fear as they came. They fed on them, physically, psychically. But it was him they wanted, him they wished to infect.

He pistoned his legs, trying to gain purchase on the slick floor with his bare feet. Another stall behind him collapsed, letting loose a cacophony of bleating cries and trampling hooves.

He was almost to the door, not caring about the crushed piglet bodies beneath his feet, when a shadow stepped into the opening. Without hesitation, it entered. Finn didn't stop. He charged straight at her, the pitchfork held out like a lance.

"No!" Jennifer cried, as the tines entered her belly.

Finn let go of the pitchfork in horror and backed away.

"Go," Jennifer gurgled. She yanked the pitchfork out of her stomach and shoved the object in her other hand into his arms. "Take it. It's the only thing that stops them."

Then she pushed him toward the door.

He was outside when he heard her scream. Slipping and sliding through the mud, his feet torn to shreds by the rough ground, he tried not to hear. An unholy sound erupted from the barn, filled with a mix of anguish and fury.

She screamed for a long time.

He ran to the road, not knowing where he was going. He ran to get away from the things that would soon follow after him. He ran until he knew he was being followed.

He felt its presence coming up behind him, heard the terrible growl, so loud that it shook the ground. He ran until he couldn't run anymore. And then he turned, holding out the object Jennifer had given to him as a sacrifice.

The vehicle slid to a stop a few feet away, spraying him with mud. The passenger door slammed open.

"Get your ass in here!" Bix shouted out at him. *"NOW!"*

CHAPTER
35

"HOLD ON TO SOMETHING!" BIX YELLED AND STOMPED on the accelerator. The van leapt forward, fishtailing on the slick surface.

Something slammed against the back doors, prompting Little Charlie to scream at them to hurry.

More figures rose up out of the night, crystallizing from the pouring rain. They surrounded the vehicle, attacking it with their clawed fingers and bared teeth, grabbing anywhere they could gain purchase.

The door beside Finn popped open and something reached in. A pale hand brushed the air in front of his face, coming within an inch of touching him.

"Go!" he shrieked, and pulled back just as a blast came from the seat behind him. The figure leaning in jerked out of the car in an explosion of red, splattering Finn with gore.

The van sped away, thumping over more Wraiths, flinging them aside or under its tires. Finn sat in shock, not seeing any of this, not sensing anything but the droplets burning on his skin. *I'm infected*, he thought. *Oh my god! I've been infected.*

"Shut the damn door!" Danny yelled. He reached forward and shook Finn. "Shut the door! Lock it!"

"I'm infected!" he yelled back. "Stop the car! I have to—"

"No!" Bix roared, and skidded around a turn in the road that almost cast Finn out anyway. "It doesn't work that way! They have to be alive to infect you!"

"What? How do you know?"

"I saw one of the men trip over Nami's body. Skin to skin. Nothing happened."

"Why not?"

"I don't know, Finn! Just shut the goddamn door and get your seatbelt on!"

He did as Bix said without thinking, even though he knew his friend was wrong. It didn't work that way. How could it?

As the blood and tissue dripped down his rain-soaked skin, he tried to feel the infection passing into his body, tried to predict when the moment would come when he'd no longer have control over himself. But he was too wired, too cold from the rain, and everything hurt too much to know whether anything he felt was Flense or not."

"Everyone okay?" Bix called out. He didn't look away from the road.

Finn spun around and saw Byron two seats back, his boys on either side of him. Danny occupied the middle seat. Both men held rifles in their hands, though clearly Byron wouldn't be shooting anything. A thin wisp of smoke rose from the muzzle of Danny's.

"Here we go!" Bix said. "Brace yourselves!"

Finn turned back in time to see the gate rising up before them. "You're going to crash!"

"That's the point!"

They hit, and Finn flew into the dash, slamming his head on the windshield before being jerked back by the belt. The pain blinded him, a flash of white so brilliant it felt as if his head had exploded.

Bix spun the wheel. "Told you to put your belt on!"

"I did," Finn groggily replied. He pulled it tight and tried to blink the pain away.

"You're bleeding."

He raised a hand, intending to press it against the gash on his forehead, then dropped it to his lap before making contact. More blood spotted his palm, blood from the Wraith. He suddenly felt like a walking time bomb, like he was covered in something that had the potential to turn him and everyone else into killers.

"First chance you get, Bix," he mumbled, "pull over. I need to wash this crap off of me."

He also needed to throw up.

* * *

We found the van parked outside the house," Bix explained. "The keys and rifles were inside, just begging to be taken."

"Probably belonged to someone in tonight's crowd," Danny said.

Bix agreed. "Wasn't Adrian's. He doesn't trust cars. Too unreliable. And he doesn't know how to fix them." He seemed unable to shut up as they tore down the leave-strewn road. "Horses don't break down, don't need gas stations and oil changes. And they make more of themselves."

"Jennifer's dead," Finn interrupted. He stared at the box-shaped object on the floor at his feet and repeated himself. He didn't know what the device was, or why Jennifer had given it to him, but her last words rang in his ears: *It's the only thing that can stop them.*

Why had she sacrificed herself? Why had she let him go?

"And I say good riddance," Bix replied. He looked over.

"She wasn't . . . . She didn't . . . ." But Finn let the thought go without finishing it.

They drove for about twenty minutes, soon emerging from the trees, then arriving at a lookout point somewhere near the cable bridge they had crossed a few days before. Neither boy said anything to the others about what they'd seen down below.

Bix stopped in the middle of the road and suggested that Finn wash himself off. The rains had stopped by then, and the clouds were beginning to break apart. But it seemed like the night would never end and the sun would never rise.

Using the sandy water from several puddles, Finn scrubbed his skin clean of the gore. He was almost certain he hadn't contracted the Flense by then, but given that he was still technically within the window of time it took for the infection to complete, he didn't feel comfortable being around the others.

As they gathered around to discuss their plans, he wandered away from them and stared out over the rail into the gorge. He shivered at the secrets he knew it held.

"I think we've decided that our first priority will be to find clothes," Bix said, coming up beside him. "Those boxers just aren't cutting it, bro. Can't be seen around you looking like that."

"Says the man wearing the tightie whities with holes in all the wrong places."

Bix grinned. "Gotta let the boys breathe." But the smile slipped away. He leaned his elbows on the cold metal and sighed. "That was some wild ass shit back there."

Finn was quiet for a moment. "I'm still really pissed at you. It was crazy."

"It was the only way we had a chance—"

"I could have been wrong about the immunity!" Finn snapped.

Danny and Byron stopped talking and looked over.

"You need to keep it down," Bix murmured. "We don't know what's out here. And, for the record, I never had any doubt you were right."

They piled back into the van once more. Byron and his sons took the third row, as before, but this time Danny and Bix swapped places. Danny was still sore from the beating he'd taken and felt terribly weak. But he assured the rest of the group that he was mending quickly and could drive.

"Besides," he told them, as he eased into the driver's seat with his face twisted in pain, "I'm the only one who knows where we're going."

"Where *are* we going?" Finn asked, taking a place beside Bix.

"South. To the army base."

"But what about Harper?"

"Your brother can wait," Danny answered firmly. He sighed and shook his head. "Look, I know you want to find him, but it was a mistake to split up back there like we did. And unless we hurry, we may not find anyone to rescue."

Finn sighed and shook his head in frustration. "How far?"

"Six hours by car, I think. I can't be exactly sure."

254

They rode in silence, crossing over the gorge around daybreak, then continuing on for another hour or so. Sunlight streamed into the van through the dusty windows, steaming the glass as their clothes dried and lulling them all into a sort of exhausted torpor.

Danny pulled over after a bit so they could stretch their legs. It was the first opportunity they'd had to see each other in the full light of day.

Danny insisted on driving when they resumed their trip, telling the boys that they should rest. No one argued.

Finn was nearly asleep again when he felt a hand on his shoulder. He jumped reflexively and turned to find Charlie leaning toward him in his seat.

The boy studied Finn's face intently for a moment. "You have a brother?"

Finn nodded. "My twin. Bix and I were heading north to find him when those people brought us to the ranch."

"Harper? You said his name was Harper."

"Yeah. He was staying inside a . . . a sort of special place where he could be protected from the sickness. I haven't seen him in a long time."

"Since before?"

"Yes."

Charlie sat back and nudged his father with his elbow. Byron leaned in and listened to the boy whisper something in his ear. When he was finished, he frowned and whispered something back.

"What is it?" Finn asked.

They exchanged a few more words, then Byron straightened in his seat. "Are you sure, son?"

The boy glanced over the seat again. He raised a hand toward Finn, who flinched. But Charlie didn't want to touch

255

him. He made a frame to block out a part of Finn's face. Then he nodded and said, "I'm sure, Daddy."

"Sure about what?" Finn asked.

"Is your bother Harper Bolles?" Byron asked.

"How did you— You know him? Have you seen him?"

Byron didn't answer right away. He chewed on his lip for several seconds, as if trying to decide what to share. Finally, he asked, "Where did you say you were going? And where were you coming from?"

"North," Finn replied. "To a . . . to a mine."

"Bunker Two?"

Finn's mouth dropped open. "Yes."

"Me and the boys," Byron said, hugging them to his sides, "we were there, too."

"With Harper? Were my mother and sister there?"

Byron shook his head. "He was alone. Other than to say he'd lost his entire family, he never mentioned anyone. Few of us did. We all lost people, friends and family. It sort of became an unspoken rule not to dwell on the people who'd died during the Flense."

Finn was shaking.

"How did you know he was there?" Byron asked.

"You had a man named Micheal Williams with you. He showed up at our front door, Bunker Eight, about two weeks ago. He said he was from Bunker Two. Right before he died, he recognized me. Or, rather, he thought I was Harper."

"Williams?" Byron echoed, his face tightening.

"Yes."

"What did he tell you?"

"That there was a breach and Wraiths got inside. He said he barely made it out alive."

"There was a breach." He let out a deep breath. "But they didn't."

"I don't understand. He said a lot of people were infected."

"They were, but not by Wraiths coming in. The infection was already inside."

"What?" both Bix and Finn exclaimed at once. "How is that possible?"

"I don't know. It swept through the community like wildfire, starting deep in the mine. It was Charlie who saved us." A tear slipped down his cheek. Little Jerry buried his face in his father's shirt.

"What happened to Harper? What happened to my brother?"

Byron shook his head. "The infection came from his end of the complex. No one from there got out."

CHAPTER
36

EDDIE HAD GROWN TO APPRECIATE HIS NEWFOUND abilities. They enabled him to scale walls, jump higher, and run faster than normal. They significantly improved his senses. But if there was one thing they didn't help with, it was picking locks.

He threw the paperclips down in disgust and straightened up in the darkened hallway and glanced toward the front door. He kept expecting one of the two men who occupied the office, Cheever or Wainwright, to return.

Cheever had come and gone for most of the day, but Wainwright had ventured out for only a few minutes here and there.

"Guy needs to get himself a frikkin life," Eddie had decided.

Finally, about an hour after sundown, the colonel left the building, locking the front door up tight.

Eddie had been waiting all day. He'd slipped into the building soon after it was unlocked early that morning, but rather than knocking on the commander's office door, he'd headed up to the dusty unused attic, and there he'd stayed, hiding directly above the office, listening to the two men talk. The attic was hot, and he was drowsy, as he'd gotten no sleep after leaving Jonah to prepare.

He heard the man in charge of his duty assignment come in midmorning to report that he hadn't checked in. Eddie hoped both men would leave to investigate his absence, perhaps to go searching for him in the barracks. But all Cheever did was tell him to check with the guards at the gate. "See if he left on his own."

"That group from the bus has been more trouble than they're worth," he complained to Colonel Wainwright afterward. "They have no interest in fitting in with the rest of this community. If they want to leave, I say let them."

"That would not be advisable."

"We lost a man because of them. And what do we get for thanks? The guy they saved just ups and leaves. A bunch had to be put in the infirmary, straining our limited supplies."

"And two of them have died."

"Yes."

"You know how it is anymore, Grant. The sooner the weak ones drop away, the stronger the rest of us become. They'll either realize how much they need us and settle in, or they won't."

Eddie did not like the sound of that.

"Patience. Maybe something positive will come out of this."

Eddie had warned Hannah at breakfast about his plans. He didn't tell her about finding Jonah out in the desert or that he'd seen Bren leave with the bus. He simply told her that he wouldn't be around for most of today and not worry. "You may hear rumors that I've left, but know that it's not true. I'd never leave without you."

"Where are you going? What are you doing?"

"These people aren't telling us the whole truth. I need to find out why. If anyone asks, you haven't seen me. You don't know where I am. I'm telling you so you won't worry."

She nodded and hugged him. "I wouldn't, Daddy. I know that you'll be okay. You can do anything now."

His daughter's words echoed in his mind as he stood before the locked door. "Anything except pick locks," he grumbled.

He checked the front door once more, then reached into his rucksack and extracted the roll of duct tape he'd relieved from the supply closet a few days before and began to cover the glass in the door with it.

When he was done, he pressed his palm against the surface until the window began to bow. It soon broke with a muffled series of cracks. Some of the pieces still fell away and tinkled to the floor, but it was a lot quieter than the sound of an entire pane shattering.

With the broken window held in place, he cut a hole in the tape and stuck his hand through it until he found the knob on the other side. Ten seconds later, he was inside the office.

The room was dark, but it proved to be little problem for him.

A week ago, it wouldn't have been any *problem at all*, he thought, remembering the ease with which he'd been able to move about inside the bunker despite the near complete darkness at times. He could still see clearly enough to get around now, though not with quite the same ease.

He went over to the desk and saw that it was strewn with several large sheets of thickly laminated paper. He recognized them immediately as military-issue detail maps, busy with contour lines and other labels of strategic importance. A stamp in the bottom corner said PROPERTY OF QUANTUM TELLIGENCE.

On the map topping the stack, someone had circled an area with blue wax pencil and labeled it with the number 7. A green X filled it. Below the circle was a series of letters and numbers:

$$AM - 5$$
$$AF - 7$$
$$JM - 2$$
$$JF - 3$$

He flipped the map to the side and checked the next one. Like the first, it had a point circled with blue wax. It, too, was crossed out in green. This spot was labeled with the number 2. As with the first, a similar set of codes accompanied it:

$$AM - 2$$
$$AF - 1$$
$$JM - 0$$
$$JF - 0$$

The next was labeled #1; however, the X was in red this time, and there was no associated alphanumeric column. Instead, there was an ominous notation: DESTROYED. The circle encompassed a town named HENGILL, which he didn't recognize.

He thumbed quickly through the next six maps, noting that some of them contained a single circled area, though not all. Each one, however, had its own unique number. None was X-ed out, whether in green or in red. Nor did they include a coded column.

On one of the maps, his eye caught several Chinese characters. On another, what appeared to be Russian words.

Eddie slumped in the chair in frustration. None of this meant anything to him at all. What were these people doing with maps? Some of the areas they depicted didn't even seem to be within North America. And as far as he knew, overseas trips had become an impossibility since the Flense, a relic of a lost technological past. There were no more transoceanic ships, no airplanes.

Were there?

Of course not, man, he thought.

He remembered the last scenes of chaos that had been televised before he'd snatched Hannah from her school and making their way to the meeting site. The Flense had appeared in all parts of the globe seemingly simultaneously and spread quickly, leaving no time for governments to respond. Armies tried to mobilize, but they were all in disarray. Civilization fell in a matter of hours, returning to a state hundreds, if not thousands, of years in the past.

So, what possible reason would these people need with these maps, if they couldn't get to the places they depicted?

On the wall was a whiteboard with yet another map taped onto it. He stood up and walked over to look at it, puzzling over the codes:

$$AM — 3 + 6 \ (+1?)$$
$$AF — 4 + 4$$
$$JM — 2 + 2 \ (+1?)$$
$$JF — 1 + 1$$

Below them were two extra lines, written in the same hand:

1 MALE INFANT
13 STILL INSIDE

He stared at these last lines for several seconds, then his eyes flicked up to the circle. It intersected a river and was labeled with the number 8.

Recognition stole over him. This was a map of the location of the dam, their bunker. *Bunker Eight*. And the codes were an inventory of the people inside— or, rather, those that had been inside *plus* those that still were. AM and AF stood for adult male and female, respectively. JM and JF were juveniles. It was the mention of the one male infant, Jorge, that had provided him the key to decipher it.

He hurried back to the desk and checked the top map again, quickly adding up the numbers in the column.

"Seventeen," he whispered, and thought back to the scene at the gate last night. He remembered seeing at least a dozen people, though he couldn't recall exactly how many more. The age and gender breakdown was certainly in line with what was on the paper.

"Bunker Seven," he muttered. "Those people last night were from Bunker Seven."

He quickly thumbed through the stack again, looking for Bunker Two. It was marked along a branch of the same river as Eight, about a hundred miles north of the Canadian border. "Three adults," he whispered. "Two male, one female. And no juveniles."

Was that all the survivors? Were the three still here on base?

The map on the wall proved that Cheever and Wainwright knew about Bunker Eight. But had they known already? Or had Bren told them? The numbers were evidence that she had shared at least that information. They added up too perfectly.

Just as he had guessed, she was taking them to the dam.

With his heart pounding against his ribs, he checked the maps one last time. Notations printed beneath the key in the corner — B1 through B10 — corresponded to each of the ten bunkers that he and the other survivors had always known existed.

It seemed, however, that the exact locations of several wasn't known, just the general vicinity. Four were in North America, whereas the other six were spread out between Europe, Asia, Australia, and Africa.

There was no Bunker Twelve.

Nor, for that matter, was there an eleventh.

CHAPTER

THE SOUND OF SHOUTING ROUSED EDDIE FROM HIS
thoughts. He dropped the maps back onto the desk, stood
up, and went over to the window and nudged the blind away
enough to peek outside.

A vehicle had pulled up to the gate and was waiting to
get into the compound. Someone had gotten out and stood
in the glare of the headlights shouting something. Several
men gathered inside the wire with their rifles trained on the
newcomer. They shouted back.

The standoff continued for another minute or so before
Colonel Wainwright appeared, jogging across the quad and
trying to button up his shirt.

Eddie watched as he spoke with the people at the gate
for a moment, then relayed instructions to the men around
him. Two guards exited the compound inspect the vehicle.
They ordered the man who'd gotten out to kneel down on
the ground with his hands on his head. A third ran toward
the barracks. Another remained where he was, his rifle
trained on the vehicle.

Captain Cheever arrived a couple minutes later, marching
straight up to the colonel. They conferred with the driver,
who was then allowed to get back onto his feet again.

Eddie watched this play out with a vague sense of dread. He'd first thought the vehicle was Bren returning. But that didn't appear to be the case.

A guard who'd headed off toward the barracks soon reappeared with several more men, all armed. They surrounded a trio of women who appeared to have been roused from their sleep and were still in their nightclothes.

Alarm filled Eddie when he recognized Kari, Susan, and Hannah. His daughter broke away from the others, burst through the guard, and ran for the gate.

"Stop!" one of the men shouted and raised his rifle.

Without thinking, Eddie smashed the window. Screaming for his daughter, he leapt from the office, landing lightly on the tarmac ten feet below, his legs already coiling to run.

The guards swiveled and fired toward him. Eddie felt a sharp sting on his arm, but he ignored it and kept running.

Hannah changed course, veering in his direction. He yelled at her to stop, but she didn't. The guards fired another round.

"Stop shooting!" Captain Cheever screamed at the men. He ran at them, his hands raised. "Stop shooting, goddamn it!"

Eddie swept Hannah up in his arms in midstride. There was one more gunshot, followed by Cheever screaming again at everyone to hold their fire.

By then, Susan and Kari had broken from the group. They ran toward the gate.

"Eddie!" came a shout from the vicinity of the new vehicle. Eddie stopped and turned. A figure stepped out and into the light. The colonel ordered him to stay put, but he didn't. "Eddie!"

"It's them, Daddy," Hannah said. She pushed herself out of his arms. Numb with surprise, he set her down as he stared. "It's Danny."

"Danny?"

"And he brought Finn and Bix!"

"Open the gate!" Finn shouted. "Goddamn it, open the fucking gate!"

Eddie's nostrils flared. He smelled blood, and not just his own. He saw Finn rush over to the fence and kneel down. Someone was lying on the ground.

"Open up!" Finn screamed. "Danny's been shot! Oh my god, please! He's dying!"

CHAPTER 38

"HE'S DEAD," CAPTAIN CHEEVER QUIETLY SAID. "YOUR friend is dead."

He shut the door, and gave Eddie and Hannah a grim look. After a moment, he sat down on the stool with a sigh.

Hannah lowered her face into her hands and silently cried. Eddie glared at the man and didn't say anything. He was shaking, too, though it was more in anger than anguish.

He didn't feel the cuts he'd incurred breaking through the window. In fact, they'd already started to scab over. And while the shot he'd taken to the arm, now bandaged, still hurt, the pain was a distant thing, faraway and unimportant.

He had refused the medic's painkillers, who seemed to think Eddie was mad for doing so. But he didn't want to be impaired in any way. He wanted to be involved. Except he'd been ordered to remain in the infirmary under armed guard.

"I want to see Wainwright."

"The colonel's busy, as you can imagine," Cheever said.

"I demand to speak to him now!"

"I'm sorry, but that just isn't possible." He shook his head and managed to look genuinely sorry. "We think it was a stray bullet."

"It wasn't a stray, dammit! Bring Wainwright," Eddie said, speaking through his teeth. "Those men, the guards, they were shooting at me, not toward the gate. There's no way in hell a stray bullet could've hit Danny."

Captain Cheever raised his hands. "What do you want me to say? We're investigating."

Eddie wasn't absolutely certain that Cheever was innocent, but he knew the man hadn't been the one to shoot Danny. He'd been facing the other direction, trying to get the guards to stop. Wainwright had been the closest. He had to have been the one who fired the fatal shot. Nevertheless, Eddie had to struggle to keep himself from reaching out and choking Cheever. He needed to lash out at someone in his grief.

The captain turned to Hannah, concern on his face. "Perhaps we should be having this conversation in private."

Eddie shook his head.

"Listen," the captain said, lowering his voice, "maybe you think you saw something. There was a lot of chaos. Tensions were high. It was a surprise to us all when you crashed out of that window, so of course people were going to react. That's how they're trained. They thought you were . . . infected."

"I was screaming my daughter's name. And stop deflecting the issue."

"Your friend getting shot was an accident. That's all it was."

"*This* was an accident," Eddie said, lifting his bandaged arm. "What was done to our friend was not. He was murdered in cold blood. Ask the two boys who arrived with him, Finn and Bix. I'm sure they saw everything."

"Well, they are being interrogated right now."

"By who?"

Captain Cheever pursed his lips. "The colonel."

Eddie jumped up, but Cheever waved him back. "He's not alone. There are others with him. Nothing will happen to your boys."

"Has Harrison Blakeley been told that his son is here?"

"We haven't told anyone yet, though everyone on base probably knows by now what happened. Word travels fast in this place. But the colonel needs to conduct his interview without interference. Once he's done—"

Eddie grabbed the captain and raised him up into the air. "The colonel is the problem! I'm telling you, you can't trust him."

"I've known the man for years," Cheever cried. Panic and surprise filled his eyes. "He's an honorable man!"

"Why would he order his men to get my daughter out of bed? Why have heavily armed men escort her to the gate? What kind of danger does a little girl pose?"

"Your man, Danny, he insisted on seeing you. He refused to come inside until you came out. He asked for you by name, but nobody knew where you were. You were missing, and none of the guards said you had left. The colonel fetched your daughter instead. Let me go!"

"That makes no sense! The next obvious choice would have been one of the other adults in my group," Eddie growled. He threw the man back onto the stool. "Not her!"

Cheever shrugged. "I don't know what to say. Maybe that's how you would've done—"

"Ever since we came here, you and the colonel have evaded our questions. My people have been disappearing and all you've done is give us lies! You told us that Danny left on his own."

"He did."

"Did you actually see him leave? Did he *tell* you he was leaving?"

"Private Ramsay was on duty that night."

"Ramsay is mixed up in this, too!"

Cheever's eyes widened. "Listen, maybe your guy went out looking for those two boys. Maybe that's why—"

"And he'll never be able to tell us because your colonel killed him!"

"And I'm telling you Colonel Wainwright would not have shot him! Please wait until our investigation is completed before throwing around accusations!"

"Who told you Jonathan and Nami died in your infirmary?"

"What?" Cheever blinked in confusion. "The medic. Why?"

"And who buried them?"

"Private Vinnie used to be on the burial detail. Ramsay is pulling the extra duty until we find someone else."

"Ramsay again! It sure seems like he's at the center of everything, don't you think? Wasn't it Ramsay who left Jonah and Vinnie behind in the desert?"

"So?"

"So what if I told you that I happen to know Jonah is alive?"

The captain shrugged. "I don't know how you would, but even if it were true, that doesn't mean anyone lied. The search team never found any bodies, just a lot of blood and a dead motorcycle. It isn't that great of a leap to conclude that they were both dead."

"Did you know that Ramsay sabotaged the bike intending for the men to die?"

Cheever opened his mouth, but nothing came out.

"Did you know that more than half of the graves in your cemetery are empty?" Eddie asked.

Cheever didn't answer. He stared at Eddie as if the man had lost his mind. "Why would you even say a thing like that?" he finally asked.

"Dig them up if you don't believe me."

"This is ridic—"

"Tell me this, Captain: Why are there so many? Since we've been here, I've seen five graves being dug."

"This is a tough world. People die. Only the strong survive for very long."

Whether Captain Cheever intended to parrot the colonel's words from earlier in the day, Eddie didn't know. "A lot of *apparent* deaths," he growled, "but very few in reality."

Cheever shook his head. "I don't—"

"Do you oversee the burials?"

"Some of them, yes. But as base commander, Wainwright is responsible for the census. Unless he specifically asks me to, he manages those details."

"The body count. How convenient."

"What are you implying?"

"I'd be willing to bet that Wainwright and Ramsay are somehow mixed up in this together. What are they doing with the missing people?"

"What missing people?" Cheever asked, clearly at the end of his patience.

Eddie bent down over the captain. "You listen to me. People here are mixed up in something crooked, and I think your colonel is at the center of it. I think he executed Danny at the gate because he knew something. And as long as those boys, Finnian Bolles and Bixby Blakeley, are in that man's presence, they're in danger, too."

For the first time, Captain Cheever looked uncertain. He pushed himself off the stool, still warily eying Eddie. "Sit tight," he said. "I'll be back."

"I'm coming with you."

"You're being held for trespassing and destruction of property. Or did you forget about that?"

Eddie laughed. "Held?"

Cheever stepped over to him. "We still have rules here. They're the only things that keep this place from descending into anarchy."

"Rules," Eddie spat in disgust.

"Look, Mister Mancuso, I give you my word that I will check out your accusations. But I can't just go barging in. This needs to be handled . . . judiciously. Because if you're wrong—"

"I'm not."

Cheever sighed. "All right, if you're *right*, then your presence will only make my job that much harder, don't you think?"

"At least let Bix's father know his son has returned."

"Fine. Just give me some time to investigate."

Cheever pulled the door open and stepped out into the hallway. He instructed the guard to keep an eye on them. "Make sure they stay put. I'm going to see the colonel."

The guard nodded. He was a young kid by the name of Kenny Benneder, a private not much past his seventeenth birthday and eager to please. He nodded and settled in with his rifle on his knees, determined not to let his commanding officer down. But he was tired from all the excitement and his eyelids felt heavy, so he was glad when another guard arrived to relieve him a few minutes later.

"Take ten, boy. Get some fresh air," Private Ramsay told him. "I'll cover for you."

* * *

Captain Cheever did not head straight down to confront Wainwright. There were a few things he needed to check first, a couple people he needed to speak with before doing so. He didn't want to walk in on the interrogation unprepared.

He shook his head with regret, knowing deep in his heart that no matter what Wainwright said, it was not going to end well. A lot of what Eddie had told him confirmed suspicions he'd held for a while.

The old man had been a friend since Cheever was assigned to the depot as a first lieutenant straight out of OCS, a year or so before the Flense. Wainwright had taken him under his wing.

Within six months, the colonel promoted him to captain and made him his executive officer, even though that role typically fell to someone with the rank of major. They had developed a special bond. Lyle Wainwright had always treated him like a son.

Which is why Eddie's accusations shook him to the core, especially his claims about the empty graves. How he could possibly know something like that was beyond Cheever, but it certainly warranted checking into.

However, he planned on visiting the cemetery last before attending to the colonel. What he expected to accomplish there in the graveyard he didn't know. Maybe he just needed to set his mind at ease. He had a theory to test that might indicate whether the graves were fake or not.

Along the way, he picked up a piece of steel rebar. His thinking was that freshly disturbed ground would be sandy and loose. The rod would push easily into it when inserted. If it stopped prematurely, hit undisturbed clay, then that would be a sign that the grave was shallow and therefore fake. Lazy men, men who worried more about appearances, wouldn't bother putting forth the effort to dig a full, deep grave.

The cemetery was a small marked-off area in the northeast corner of the base. It had been established there in the early days, right after the Flense began to spread and there were a lot of casualties. Not all of the bodies had been infected and required putting down. Some victims had succumbed at the hands and teeth of the diseased. Some simply couldn't bear to live in such a world anymore.

The rest were collateral damage.

There actually was an old cemetery outside, but after the fall, it was easier and safer to dig the graves inside the wire. Now it was filled with close to seven hundred graves, some containing multiple bodies.

They were all marked with sandstone chips the same color as the desert floor. Each new grave was dug next to the previous one, continuing the row until it reached the end before starting a new one.

Five graves had been dug since the arrival of the people on the bus. Of that, Eddie was correct. One was a woman who had been a resident since soon after the Flense. She was old then and only got older. A few weeks ago she refused to get out of bed; the day before yesterday, she'd passed from malnutrition and kidney failure. She was one of the rarest of all the survivors— a victim of old age.

He was able to push the metal rod into the soft clay and sand of her grave all the way up to his hand, burying close to three feet of iron.

The rod refused to go more than about a foot into the next grave over. It behaved exactly the same in the next three.

"Goddamn it," he whispered. He spied another piece of rebar between mounds and realized that Eddie must have used the same trick. He picked it up and hurled both rods into the darkness, where they clattered over the rocky ground. *Sonofabitch!*"

He flexed his sore fingers, checked that his sidearm was loaded, then headed off to find the colonel.

CHAPTER
39

CORPORAL LAWTON SAT WATCH ON THE STEPS OUTSIDE of the administrative building's front door. He jumped to his feet when the captain approached and saluted. "Sir!"

"At ease, Corporal." He gestured inside and asked, "Why are you standing out here? Aren't you supposed to be inside?"

"Colonel didn't want me coming in."

"Why not?"

"I guess because of the broken door. Said he needed privacy."

Cheever frowned.

"If you're going in," the corporal said, "could you take this?" He pointed to a box filled with wrapped sandwiches and bottles of water. "He told me to go see if I could rustle up some grub in the mess hall, but that was twenty minutes ago."

"He hasn't been out to check on you?"

"No, sir."

Cheever glanced nervously at the door. "Sure, no problem." He used his key to unlock it. "Stay out here, please. Don't let anyone else in. Understood?"

"Yes, sir. Um, sir?"

Cheever hesitated.

"Is it true what they're saying?"

"About what, Corporal?"

Lawton stepped closer and whispered, "That those people have a cure."

Cheever gave the soldier a surprised look. "I-I don't know anything about that."

He let Lawton hold the door open for him, then waited for it to click shut behind him and lock before setting the box down on the floor again.

Stepping away from the door, he removed a silencer from his pocket and screwed it onto his revolver. Thus assembled, he slipped the weapon into the back of his waistband and pulled his coat down over it. He wasn't sure how he'd spin the colonel's death just yet. The camp would swallow whatever story he gave them, but only if the scene had been properly staged.

He picked up the food box again, squared his shoulders and headed down the hall.

The drone of voices grew louder. Yellow light poured through a hole in the duct taped window, illuminating the fine desert dust that never seemed to settle out of the air.

As he stood outside the door and leaned down to eavesdrop on the conversation inside, Cheever worried why the old man would want to conduct the interview alone and in private, without witnesses.

What are those boys telling him?

Bad things, things a man would die before copping to.

The door abruptly opened, and a young boy stepped out and ran into Cheever, nearly forcing him to drop the food. The kid backed up again, his eyes wide with surprise.

"Grant!" the colonel exclaimed, seeing him there. "How long have you been standing out there in the hallway?"

"Just, uh . . . ." He held up the box.

"Ah, good, Lawton found some food. Bring it in! Set it there— No, not on the desk. Over there." He pointed at the filing cabinet along the side wall. "Boys, this is Captain Grantham Cheever, my right-hand man."

Cheever eyed the old man carefully, studied his body language, the sweat beading up on the paper thin skin of his forehead.

What have they told him?

He was surprised to see a black man seated at the worn wooden chair beside the filing cabinet, his arms wrapped about a young boy perched on his lap. Both stared in his general direction, but did not make eye contact. *They're the blind ones.*

The boy who'd nearly groined him followed him in. He started digging through the food box as soon as Cheever set it down.

The other two, both teenagers, stood over by the map of the bunker that the colonel had hung on the wall two nights before.

Their bunker, he thought. *The dam.*

"I was just about to tell these boys about our rescue plan," Colonel Wainwright said. "They have quite the story of their own, which you should hear."

Cheever tried to look interested. He didn't want his friend to sense his true feelings, that he already knew. "Couldn't be any more incredible than the story I just heard," he carefully replied.

Wainwright shook his head. His thumb and fingers worried the pistol on his own hip, a nervous habit he'd developed since all the killing he'd done in the early days of the outbreak.

Cheever had seen the man pull and fire his revolver well over a thousand times, rarely missing a shot. He was deadly with the thing. In fact, Wainwright had always joked that the pistol was a natural extension of his own body, like the fist is an extension of the arm. He probably slept with it in his cot.

"How are our friends?" the taller of the two teenagers asked. His eyes were red, and he looked exhausted. He wore an ill-fitting Nebraska State sweatshirt and baggy sweatpants, and for a moment Cheever couldn't figure out why they looked wrong on him, but then he realized that they were meant for a girl to wear. The lettering was pink. "How's Danny?" he asked. "And Eddie?"

"You are . . . ?"

"Finn Bolles."

Cheever nodded. "Well, Mister Bolles, Mister Mancuso is lucky. He sustained a surface wound on his arm. He also has a number of scratches on his arms and neck from—" He pointed at the mangled blinds in the window. "The medic is attending to him still."

"And Danny?"

Cheever hesitated, then shook his head. "We couldn't save him. I'm sorry."

The shorter of the older boys slammed his palm on the wall. He also wore a set of sweats meant for a girl, and Cheever wondered if they'd salvaged their clothes from a coed college dormitory room. He knew firsthand that most of the department stores and private homes had been raided in the years since the outbreak, emptied of just about anything useful. And since most of the survivors had been men, women's clothing would be easier to find.

"Bix," Finn warned.

But the other boy pointed at the captain. "Danny was right not to trust you!"

"Me?" Cheever replied, startled.

"Bix," Finn repeated. "Let's not—"

"You shot him in cold blood!"

"Son," the colonel calmly said, "I can assure you that Captain Cheever did not shoot your man. He was nowhere near the gate."

Captain Cheever turned a cold eye to Bix. "Why would I shoot him?"

"So he wouldn't talk about—"

"Enough!" the colonel snapped. "Everyone just calm down. Let's get back on track."

Bix dropped into a chair and covered his face. The taller boy went over and tried to console him. Despite the dazed look on this boy's face, Cheever noticed something else, a sharpness. The kid's brain, whether he was aware of it or not, was busily trying to fit all the pieces together.

Wainwright pulled Cheever to the side and spoke quietly to him. "This Danny fella that was killed, this didn't happen to be the same one who left in the middle of the night a few days ago, was it?"

Cheever tore his eyes away from Bix to face the old man. "Yeah."

"You told me he left on his own."

Cheever nodded. "He did."

"So, why would these boys say that's not what happened."

Cheever's throat felt as dry as the desert. "What are they saying happened?"

"That he was taken from here, that he was beaten for information about the bunker. That he was then sold — him and two others, apparently — to some roamers up north. Cheever, you didn't—"

"Sounds like a story to me," the captain quietly replied. He turned his cold gaze toward the boys.

Wainwright gripped Cheever's arm, forcing the younger man to look at him. "They said they were made to cage fight infecteds."

"Did they say who allegedly did all this to them?"

The colonel stared at Cheever for a moment, frowning.

"It's all true," the blind man said, speaking up for the first time. He didn't move from his chair, but he'd swiveled his head toward them, tracking their location by their voices. "I was sold to the same people, too. Me and my two boys. I don't know what this couple meant to do with us, but they went on and on about saving people. And Wraiths."

"Grant," Wainwright whispered, pulling Cheever out of the room and into the hallway, "I thought you said the girl volunteered information about the bunker."

"She did."

The colonel studied his protégé's face for a moment, then said, "You told me we were done with those whack jobs. They were supposed to stay on their side of the river."

The captain didn't answer.

"Grant," the colonel said, shaking him harder, "you gave me your word you'd deal with those people. But—"

He stopped and looked down in surprise at the gun pressed into his gut.

"Grant?"

"I'm sorry, Lyle," Cheever said. "I really am." And he squeezed the trigger.

* * *

Eddie heard the muffled gunshot from clear outside the building, and he was up the front steps within seconds, moving past a surprised Corporal Lawton before the guard even knew Eddie was there. "What the—" the young man cried, and fell senseless to the ground from shock. Later, he would swear he'd seen a Wraith.

"I'll take this," Eddie said, relieving the kid of his rifle.

The wood of the door splintered between the locking bolt and the hinges, but it took a second kick and a blast from the gun before a hole opened up wide enough for Eddie to fit through.

Light spilled into the darkened hallway from the office, illuminating the colonel as he lay on the floor clutching his side.

Eddie covered the distance in a flash, but he was already too late to catch the killer. He stepped past the fallen man into the office, where a shocked Finn and Bix stood pressed against the wall.

Bix pointed at the window, and Eddie flung back the blinds just as a gunshot echoed in the night. Wood chips separated from the frame, spraying into the room. Everyone ducked.

He pointed the gun out, not caring where the bullet went, and fired off a round. Another shot tore a hole through the blinds and shattered the glass on a framed certificate hanging on the wall.

"You need to stop him!" the colonel cried weakly from the hallway.

"Why?"

"Because he'll destroy the camp."

Finn crawled across the floor. "Listen, Eddie, this isn't our fight. Let's just get the rest of our people and get the hell out of this place."

More gunshots rang out, followed by several people shouting. By the time Eddie made it back to the window, Cheever was gone.

"We can't," Eddie told Finn. "Not yet. Bren's gone with the bus back to the bunker."

Finn's mouth dropped open. He spun around to face the colonel. "Why didn't you tell us?"

"I was . . . about to. She accompanied a rescue team to bring . . . the rest of the survivors back here."

"Who put the team together?" Eddie demanded, spinning around. "Was it Cheever?"

"Yes," Colonel Wainwright said, gasping for air. He'd pulled himself halfway back into the room and now lay against the door frame. Fresh blood spurted out when he pulled his hand away from his wound. "Jesus, I can't believe he shot me, after all I've done for him."

Eddie stared at the man, confusion on his face. "Are you saying you didn't know?"

The colonel coughed and shook his head.

"I . . . suspected. The disappearances . . . . Happened before."

"Who shot Danny?"

"Sergeant Bolton. He fired the last shot."

"Is he involved?"

The colonel nodded.

"Where is he?"

"Relieved of duty. Sent . . . to quarters. Dammit, I should've seen it sooner."

"Will Cheever try to take over the base?" Finn asked. The last thing he wanted was to get in the middle of a gunfight.

"That or run."

The sound of an engine reached their ears, followed by several others starting up. Finn ran to the window, ignoring Eddie's cries to get away. "Looks like they've chosen to run. They're at the gate on motorcycles!"

People were shouting now. A gunshot rang out, and Finn ducked instinctively.

"This place is freaking insane!" Bix cried. He started crawling across the floor to get to the door.

"Make yourself useful, Bix," Eddie told him. "Put your hand on the colonel's wound. We need him!"

"Why?

"Just do it!"

"Let me," Byron offered, slipping off the chair. "Someone needs to find the medic, and I doubt I'd be of much help there."

"No . . . medic," Wainwright panted, his voice fading to little more than a whisper. "They're all . . . Cheever's men."

"Get Hannah," Finn yelled. "She learned a lot from Doc Cavanaugh when—"

Eddie bolted for the door. "I left her at the infirmary!"

Finn shouted at Eddie to come back, but the man was already out of the building before he could cross the room.

There were more gunshots outside, then a crash that sounded like metal being torn.

"That'll be the front gate," Byron quietly said. He sat in the doorway pressing his palm on the colonel's abdomen. Wainwright was still conscious, but only just.

The building shook from an explosion. The lights dimmed.

"What the hell?" Finn shouted.

"You have to . . . go after them," Wainwright said. His skin had gone as white as paper.

"No way in hell we're doing that," Bix cried.

"We're leaving," Finn said, standing up. He ducked as several more gunshots rang out. "But not for him. We need to get back to the bunker and find Bren."

He turned to gather up the maps he'd seen on the desk. "We're taking these with us, Colonel," he said.

But the commander didn't argue. He lay on the floor, his eyes open and glassy, staring at nothing.

CHAPTER

40

MORE EXPLOSIONS ROCKED THE NIGHT, SENDING everyone to the floor as dust sifted down from the light fixtures. Objects fell off of tables and shelves. But the explosions weren't bombs, and the last gunshots had faded into the night twenty minutes earlier. Cheever and his men had fled.

Finn finished rolling the maps. He'd instructed Bix to look for more information on the bunkers. As they gathered up loose papers, more of their people arrived.

The hallway outside was crowded by people seeking answers. Many of them were from Bunker Seven. Most of the long term denizens had either fled to the other end of the compound to avoid the explosions at the gate and the gunfire at the armory, or gone to fight the fires.

"I'm not finding much more about the bunkers," Harrison Blakeley said. He and Susan had gone through the papers in the filing cabinet, heeding Finn's orders as willingly as if he'd been leading them forever. Finn didn't have time to reflect on this, he just accepted it.

Upon seeing his son, Harrison paused only long enough to give Bix a quick hug, then asked Finn what needed doing.

While they searched, Finn explained as best as he could what he knew. Eddie filled in the rest, arriving with Hannah not five minutes after he left. She had fled the infirmary upon hearing the first shots of gunfire, leaving Ramsay alone where Eddie had tied him to a bed using patient restraints. It likely saved her life, as the building was soon raided by armed men rescuing him. The structure was now burning to the ground.

"Think Cheever knows about Bunker Twelve?" Bix asked.

"I don't know," Finn replied. "I don't care."

"But if he does, then—"

"We're not thinking about that, Bix! We're going after Bren!"

Finn stepped out into the hallway and shouted for quiet. "Captain Cheever and his people are on the run," he said. "If there are others outside the fence sympathetic to his cause, he'll likely return. You need to prepare to defend yourselves."

"Take us with you!"

"I can't, not where I'm going. This is your home now. Stay and defend it. Protect those too weak or too small to fend for themselves."

"We have no one to lead us!"

Finn turned to Harry Rollins. "I think you should stay."

"I'm no leader."

"Neither am I, and yet here we are. Anyway, you know it's even riskier going back, and I can't do that to your family."

He gestured to where Byron was sitting with his two sons. "They'll need your help, too, especially Jerry. And Charlie's a good kid."

"You'll come back once you find Bren?"

"Yes. Straight back, I promise."

"Then Bunker Twelve?"

Finn nodded, but he was doubtful. Judging from the maps and the papers they'd found, there was simply no proof of a twelfth bunker. Not even a mention.

"Finn! Hey!"

He turned to see Kari pushing her way through the crowd. "I got us another ride, some weapons, and food. Oh, and guess what else?"

She stepped aside, pulling the person behind her forward.

Hannah shrieked and pushed Finn away. "Oh my god! Jonah, you're alive!"

* * *

"Absolutely not!" Finn said. "I can't let you leave Hannah—"

"It's not your choice, Finn," Eddie told him. "I'm coming with you. So is Hannah."

"It's too dangerous!"

"Bren is Hannah's best friend. And someone has to keep an eye on Jonah."

"Why can't he stay here with the other children?" Bix asked.

Jonah scowled at him. "Don't start with me, Blackeye. After what I've been through—"

"We've all been through a lot," Finn said, cutting him off. He turned to Jonah. "You do know where we're going, right? Seth Abramson's not going to be happy to see either of us."

"The feeling's mutual, Bolles. Besides, who else is going to make sure you stay out of trouble?"

"Why you sonofabitch!" Bix cried. "I ought to . . . ."

Finn pushed away from the two. He grabbed Eddie and pulled him to the side where Kari, Harrison, and Susan were finishing loading up the last of the weapons and food in the van. It didn't look like very much, but they would hopefully only be gone a day and a half.

"Listen, Eddie," he said, "don't get me wrong. I could sure use your help, but I don't know what's going to happen out there. We might run into Cheever and his men. They're armed and trained. And then there are the Wraiths."

"You think staying here is safe?"

Finn gestured at the gate, where several people were working to repair the damage that Cheever and his men had done while fleeing. A half dozen others stood outside, watching the desert landscape in the flickering light of the burning buildings. "Once things settle down here, it will be."

"No place is safe, Finn," Eddie said. "I think you should know that by now." He shook his head and gave the boy's arm a squeeze. "There are no guarantees. Safety comes from having your friends and family around you. Not from isolating yourself."

Kari walked over and slapped a set of desert camouflage into his arms. "Better put these on," she said. "That is, unless you plan on attending a sorority pajama party anytime soon."

"Hey! What about me?" Bix said, trailing at her heels. He pointed at the Delta Delta Delta on his sweatshirt.

"You're definitely not pretty enough to be wearing that," Kari said, and threw him a set.

"Loading's nearly finished," Harrison said. "We're ready to go."

Finn nodded, then watched the man step over to his son. The two talked in low voices, and Finn felt his heart tighten. It was rare to see the two express their feelings to each other, but he knew that it didn't mean they didn't love or worry about each other. Their bond, while invisible, was palpable.

It made him miss his own father all the more, despite the acrimony that had long existed between them. Only in the final days of his father's life had Finn begun to understand that their own bond had been just as strong.

"Is Harry around?" he called over to Kari. He stripped down to his underwear and pulled on the camos. He didn't care anymore that others could see his skinny legs— except they didn't seem so skinny anymore.

"Woo woo!" Hannah said, appearing around the back of the truck. "Sexy!"

Finn felt his face grow red. He gave her an embarrassed smile and said she was going to get him in trouble with her father.

"Harry and Fran took the kids around to the family residences," Kari answered. She shooed Hannah away.

"I wanted to say goodbye."

"He knows."

"He should be up here, with the guards, directing them."

"Don't worry about them," Kari advised. "They'll figure it out. And with Fran at his side, they'll do okay. She's a good, strong woman."

"I just worry that since they're the newcomers here—"

"They'll be okay. It's us you should be worried about."

"Why?"

"Look at us, just a bunch of misfits." She smiled and handed him a rifle and a couple extra magazines. "By the way, have you ever fired one of these?"

"No."

"Then you're in the back of the pickup with the rest of the virgins."

"I'm not a—"

"*Firearms* virgin, Finn." She shook her head at him. "Firearms. I'll be giving a lesson on loading, sighting, firing, and clearing jams. And safety," she added, directing the muzzle of his down to the ground.

Bix joined him as Kari walked away. "I knew you were a virgin."

"Would you knock it off, perv!"

"Just saying." He shouldered his own rifle and walked away. "In case you're wondering, I get to sit in front. With the non-virgins."

CHAPTER 41

THEY WERE ON THE ROAD BEFORE DAYBREAK, A caravan of two vehicles— the truck they got from the base and the van Finn and Bix had arrived in.

Jonah knew of a place where they could refuel along the way, which was good as the gas tank on the van was close to empty.

There were six of them in the pickup: Finn, Susan, Eddie, Hannah, and Kari in the bed while Jonah drove. Harrison and Bix shared the van.

"We should have loaded the supplies in the truck and sat in the van instead," Finn groused. "Bad planning."

They'd all taken to wrapping bits of clothing around their faces, covering everything but their eyes to protect them against the sun, wind, and dust. Even so, he felt like he'd inhaled a lungful of grit.

Along the way, Kari taught them what they needed to know about using their weapons. She explained that they were Colt M4 carbines, military grade, which were in such abundance on the base that they didn't feel bad about taking a few from the armory, along with sufficient ammunition that Finn felt like they might actually stand a chance in a gun battle.

He sincerely hoped it wouldn't come down to that. On the other hand, he was eager to get out and try his aim once they stopped to refuel.

The ride was bumpy. Jonah kept up a bruising pace, hoping to cut the two-hour drive in half and make up some of the time they'd lost. But it meant that the people in the back were getting thrown around.

After the lesson, Eddie made Hannah climb through the sliding window and buckle herself into the passenger seat, despite her complaints.

Behind them, the van fishtailed through every sand drift and gravel bar. Harrison was at the wheel, which left Bix to sit back with his feet on the dash and laugh and point at them until his father told him to behave.

Jonah slowed at a junction and turned onto it, yelling back that the fuel truck was a mile or so ahead.

Halfway in, they passed a downed motorcycle. Sand had already begun to drift over it. The adjacent rock outcropping was stained darkly with blood. Bits of tattered clothing were caught up in the weeds, rippling as they passed.

At last they arrived at the fuel truck. Jonah skidded to a stop in the shade with the van pulling up right behind them. The air reeked with the smell of gasoline.

"Those bastards," Susan swore, bending down to touch the ground. It was still damp. "They emptied the tank."

Jonah confirmed it, holding up the dangling hose. "They probably figured somebody'd come after them."

"Sonofabitch!" Bix cried. "Now what?"

"We carry on," Finn said firmly. He turned to Jonah. "How much gas is in the truck?"

"We're good. We left with a full tank."

"Okay, we'll all just have to fit then. Three across in the cab, five in the bed. Leave the van here."

"And the supplies?" Harrison asked. "Where do we put them?"

"On the floor, on our laps," Finn said. He walked over to the van and opened it up. "We sit on some of it, the rest we tie what we can onto the roof. We just need to make it to the bunker."

"That's a good seven hours," Jonah said. "We might not have enough gas."

"Well, what do you want me to say?" Finn cried.

"We go back and—"

"No! That'll put us another three or four hours behind. Besides, we may not need to go all the way there. Bren and the rescue team might be heading back now. We could meet up with them an hour down the road for all we know."

"And how are we going to tie supplies to the roof? We have no rope."

Finn unsheathed his knife and walked back over to the van. He pulled the passenger side seatbelt out as far as he could and sawed it off at their attachments. "I think these'll work," he said, throwing it at Jonah.

Eddie pulled him aside while the team transferred the supplies. "You realize Cheever might be heading to Eight, too, right? At least some of them are likely to support him."

"Or not," Finn said.

"They came this far."

"I don't want to talk about it, Eddie. We save our people. If we meet Cheever along the way, we'll deal with that then."

* * *

The drive was miserable. The sun baked down on them, and the heat and dust rendered their thirst unquenchable. Jonah, Susan, and Eddie took turns driving. The men tried to make Hannah and the women sit inside the cab. Susan went, but Kari flatly refused, insisting instead that she needed to be in back "if and when the shit hits the fan."

All this talk made Hannah argue that she should be in back, too. But Eddie would have none of it. "And stop swearing," he told her.

"I was just saying what Kari said."

"What *Miss Mueller* said. And it's no excuse."

"Daddy!"

"I mean it."

For Finn, the hardest part of the ride was knowing that Cheever and his men were somewhere up ahead of them. There were traces of their passage— tire tracks in the sand; a single Wraith, freshly shot in the forehead and left for the vultures in the middle of the road; a downed power pole blocking the way, the wood newly chopped. More and more he had to accept that they were heading straight for the bunker. And that meant a confrontation was inevitable.

The group arrived at the gorge around three in the afternoon and caught their first glimpse of the dam forty minutes later. Eddie was driving. He slowed their approach.

"There's the bus," Hannah cried. "I can see the bus!"

"Shh!" her father warned.

She sat in the passenger seat with Bix between her and Eddie. Bix's head had been keeping rhythm with the road's bumps as he dozed off. But it popped up when Hannah yelled and he cried out, "Banana cream pie!"

Finn twisted to take a look, but they'd gone around a turn in the road by then and the dam was out of sight.

"Everyone be on the lookout for Wraiths," Kari said.

"Anything moves gets a bullet in the head," Susan added, and they all nodded.

They pulled over at the last curve but remained hidden from the dam behind a line of trees. Eddie shut the engine off. "Good timing, too," he said. "We're running close to empty."

"There's still fuel in the refueling tanks below," Jonah said, pointing to a small building visible a few hundred yards beyond the dam. "Only way to empty them would be to pump them out or burn them, and it doesn't look like either has happened."

"That how you gassed up the bus?"

He nodded. "By mouth."

"Great."

They piled onto the road and stretched their bruised and aching muscles. Finn and Jonah walked ahead to see what they might find. Nothing moved. After a few minutes, they returned to the group.

"Think they're inside?" Kari asked.

Finn shook his head. "What worries me is that the bus is still here. If they arrived two days ago, why haven't they left yet?"

"Don't read anything into it, Finn," Eddie said. "Stay focused. It means they're still here."

"Anyone see any motorcycles? Any other vehicles?"

"No, but that doesn't mean anything. They might be somewhere else out of sight. We have to assume Cheever's here."

"Maybe they took the cutoff road and are heading for the ranch instead."

"Everything seems so quiet," Hannah said. "Maybe it's empty. They could already be gone."

"You heard Eddie. Don't jump to conclusions," Susan warned. "Remember that it's supposed to look empty. That's why nobody ever came by when we were inside."

"A few did in the beginning," Jonah quietly said. "I remember seeing them in the monitors."

Everyone looked at him. Nobody said anything. They'd all seen people in the beginning, both infected and not. They'd all watched the former attack the latter and done nothing but sit in mute horror, too afraid to open the doors.

"What's the plan?" Finn asked.

"You're in charge of this little escapade," Jonah said. Finn couldn't tell if he was being patronizing or not.

"The cave?"

"We could try," Harrison said, "but I doubt Seth Abramson would have let an hour go by without sealing the door to Level Ten. He moved pretty quickly to seal off levels after the attacks he staged."

"He tried to make it look like my father did it," Hannah said, her face growing red with resentment.

Eddie shook his head. "Honey, don't."

"And then he blamed Jonah."

Jonah placed a hand on her arm. "It's okay, Hannah. Let's just focus on what we need to do now, which is find Bren and rescue the rest."

"Then what, Mister Know-it-all?" Bix griped. He grabbed a rock and chucked it into the gorge below them. "They didn't want to leave last time. What makes you think they'll want to now?"

"The base," Finn replied quickly. He gave Jonah a hard look, who returned it. "Tell them there's a community with more people, fresh grown food, sunshine."

"You think Seth will give up what he's got now for fresh vegetables, especially if Bren's in there with him? Did you forget how he accused your father of building a kingdom inside the dam."

"If memory serves, you made the same accusation," Bix replied. "So did your father!"

"Bixby Michael!" Mister Blakeley said. "Enough."

"But—"

"Dammit, Bix!" Finn snapped. "You, too, Jonah. Both of you just shut the hell up for a second?"

Everyone stared at each other before Finn spoke again. He didn't apologize for swearing, though he could see he'd hurt his friend's feelings. *If Harper were here—*

But he's not here, so shut up. SHUT UP!

"There are three possible ways in," he said, forcing himself to breathe slow and deep. "The front door—"

"Which is probably locked," Susan said.

"The back door on Level Six."

"Blocked."

"And the cave to Level Ten."

"Also blocked. Probably."

"If they got the monitors fixed, then they'll have eyes on the front and back doors. The cave is our best bet of getting inside without being seen."

"Dad just said it'd be blocked," Bix grumbled. "Jeez, don't you listen?"

Finn ignored him. "We've got Eddie. He tore his way through it once before, he can do it again."

"I'm not so sure about that, Finn," Eddie piped up. "That was when I—"

"You can still do it."

"I was going to say, it was a highly emotional time. I'm not sure I could summon the same strength."

"We'll just have to see, won't we?"

He shouldered his rifle and stepped away from the edge. The rest of the group exchanged worried glances before following him.

They made their way through the trees to a point directly above where they guessed the hidden opening for the gate was, then descended. Finn led with Eddie and Kari bringing up the rear.

They all strained their senses for signs of Wraiths. But it seemed the ones that had attacked them nearly a week before were gone. Jonah theorized that they had probably been the ones that attacked the bus. They'd been scattered or killed since then.

"And I think they followed that guy from Bunker Two," he finished.

Finn didn't say it out loud, but if that were true, then his brother may have been one of them. He gave a shiver and stepped out onto the gravel path leading to the hidden cave opening.

They found the gate wired shut, but it had clearly been meant to foil Wraiths, not people. Eddie unwound the wire and pulled the gate open.

"Anyone remember to bring a flashlight?" Bix said.

Jonah pulled the cell phone out with a smirk. "Always prepared."

"You're no boy scout," Bix grumbled.

"Okay, Jonah, you lead," Eddie said. "I'll bring up the rear. Everyone take hold of the person in front of you. Keep your rifles at the ready. If you encounter anything, only those at the front fire. Those in back, retreat. Kari, you follow Jonah, since you have the most experience with a gun."

"Hey, I know how to shoot," Bix argued.

"Back here with me," Harrison said.

"This party sucks," Bix remarked.

Jonah grinned and pushed past him. "Sucks even more when your folks chaperone."

CHAPTER 42

THE HEAVY STEEL PLATE DOOR AT THE BOTTOM OF THE tunnel had been seated back into place, but not reattached. Instead, Seth had blocked it with objects he'd cannibalized from other parts of the dam complex— wooden crates, heavy equipment, furniture. He'd wedged it all tightly between the door and the metal railing of the walkway, making it impossible to push the door away.

After several minutes of trying, Eddie reported that he'd only managed to move the pile an inch or two. Jonah suggested he try sliding the door to the side. With his help, the two men were able to clear a space big enough for Hannah to climb through. She began moving what she could away.

An hour later, they regrouped on the catwalk above the sump pumps and made their way over to the chamber's inner door.

"At this rate, we should hit the stairwell sometime around next week," Bix said.

Finn pulled him aside while the rest went to check out the door. "You've been in a sour mood since we arrived back here," he said. "What's going on?"

"Look at him," Bix said, nodding in Jonah's direction. "The guy's like a bad case of jock itch. Just when you think you've gotten rid of him, *bam!* He's back with a vengeance."

"That's not really it, is it?"

Bix was quiet for a moment. "It's this damn place. I thought we'd left it behind for good. I mean, it's bad out there, but I'd still take it over being back inside here."

"Last time I checked, nobody's trying to cage match us with Wraiths in here."

There was a loud grinding noise from the direction of the door, then the sound of crumbling cement. With a grunt of effort, Eddie pulled the door open. "We're in," he panted, and dropped the piece of metal piping he'd used as a lever.

Finn clapped Bix on the back. "Let's get Bren and leave."

It felt strange to walk those halls again. Like Bix, Finn had thought he'd never return, never have to hear the familiar echoes and the low throb of the turbines. But here he was, back where he'd spent the last three years of his life, the one place that had kept him safe and alive . . . .

And killed his father.

They made their way to the end of the hall and stopped by the door to the stairwell. With some trepidation, Finn typed in his old code, expecting it not to work. But the light turned green and the latch released. He pulled the door open and listened for any sign that someone might be above them. All was quiet save for the seashell rush of air swirling through the ten-story shaft.

"You know," Bix whispered at Finn. His voice shook as they ascended. "You always talk about your brother like he was some kind of hero."

"He was. Everyone liked him."

"It just got me thinking."

"Drop it, Bix."

"No, I mean, you're always comparing yourself to him and—"

"I said drop it."

They lapsed into silence at the landing, hastily checking inside. But there were no sounds of people. They repeated the quick checks at the next two landings.

They skipped Levels Six and Five, which Seth Abramson had sealed off, as well as Level Four, which, other than the storage of heavy equipment and other nonconsumable items, had served no real function for them during their stay. Instead, they hurried up to the quarters on Level Three, impatient to find the others.

Eddie held back, a frown on his face. When asked what was wrong, he commented that the air smelled stale, rotten.

They opened every door that wasn't already open, but it quickly became evident that the old rooms were no longer being used. Everything useful had been removed, leaving only garbage behind.

"They might have consolidated upstairs," Finn said. "Closer to the kitchen. We'll find them. I know we will."

He could see the doubt and concern growing on the other's faces.

They proceeded to check the remaining rooms on the level and eventually arrived at the door of Sato and Asuka Fujimura. Finn remembered thinking that the couple would never leave the bunker.

"I was thinking about what Byron said about Harper," Bix said.

"Seriously, let it go, Bix."

"Don't you think it's strange he never mentioned you to anyone in his bunker? Or your dad? I mean, you talked to us about Harper all the time."

"I haven't given it much thought," Finn lied. He tried the door, found it locked, and punched in his code.

"I'm just saying."

"Harper made the best of the moment he was in, Bix. He never dwelled on things he couldn't control."

"Break it up, lovebirds," Jonah said, stepping out of the room across the hall. "Let's check upstairs and get the hell out of here. This place is giving me the creeps."

"Yeah, well, you give me the creeps," Bix replied.

Jonah rolled his eyes and hurried away.

"Why do you always have to antagonize everyone?" Finn asked.

"Because I care, bro. Sometimes I think I care too much."

"You never know when to stop."

Finn pushed the door open, then reeled back, gagging. He slammed the door shut before Bix could get a glimpse inside. But the smell was enough to tell what happened. Finn had caught a glimpse of the couple laying arm-in-arm on their mats. He'd seen no blood, no signs of trauma. They appeared to have been dead at least a week.

They checked the top two levels in silence, but found them empty as well. The kitchen had been ransacked, and most of the food was gone. The game room was left as they'd remembered it.

"They didn't take the homemade Monopoly board I made," Bix said, picking up the box. "Sammy Largent loves this game." He tossed it back onto the table.

"We still haven't checked the power plant," Finn said. He turned to head for the stairs.

"They're not going to be down there," Jonah said.

"You don't know that!"

"Why would they go there? Why would they take everything and go there, Finn?"

"We still need to check!"

"It's a waste of time! God, you are just like your father! You know that?"

"Don't you dare talk—"

"Stop!" Eddie shouted. "That's enough out of you boys." He turned to Jonah. "Finn's right. We have to check."

"We should be on the road, going after them."

"Where?" Finn challenged, pulling out of Eddie's grip. "Tell me, where did they go? Huh?"

"I don't know! But how is checking in the power plant going to help? They are not there!"

"If you're so worried about time, then why don't you use your mouth for something useful. Go pump some fuel out of the tanks for the truck."

Jonah glared at him for a moment, then pushed through the group and headed for the stairs.

"Uh oh, you've hurt his feelings," Bix mocked.

"You really are a jerk sometimes, Bix," Hannah said, shoving him into the wall before going after Jonah.

"Stop, Hannah!" Eddie said. "Jonah! We stick together. Now, we're going to check Level Four. As a group."

"There is nothing there."

"We go and we check it off our list, Jonah. Then we head down to the power plant. If we still don't find them, then we put our heads together and come up with a plan. But until then, let's finish the search."

Once more, they entered the stairwell, this time heading down. They exited at Level Four and stepped out into the hallway.

Almost immediately, Eddie raised a hand to stop them. He had a troubled look on his face, and he raised his nose into the air and took a sniff.

"What is it?"

"Feel that?" He raised a hand to his cheek. "A breeze. There's a breeze. And . . . ."

"What?"

"Nothing." But the furrows on his brow deepened.

They ran the length of the hallway toward the front door. Rounding the curve, they could see that it was slightly open. It didn't seem to have been forced.

Eddie arrived ahead of them and pulled it wide. His rifle was up, ready to shoot anything that might come through. But nothing did.

"Oh my god!" Hannah screamed, seeing the scene. She tried to run out, but Harrison Blakeley stopped her.

Bodies littered the ramp outside, at least a half dozen. Blood was everywhere. Bags and boxes of supplies, some of it food, sat in heaps, as if it had been readied to move. Everything, including the concrete walls, was riddled with bullet holes.

Strewn throughout the killing field were the motorcycles.

"It's Cheever," Eddie said, quickly turning over the closest body. He waved a swarm of flies away. "Shot in the head. Couldn't have been more than a few hours ago. Rigor hasn't set in yet."

"We must have just missed them," Jonah said.

"Anyone see Bren?" Finn cried. He ran from body to body, turning them over.

"They're people from the base," Susan said. "Cheever's men."

"Not all of them. I recognize this woman as one who left the base with Bren," Jonah said, turning over another body.

"Um, guys," Harrison said, grimly motioning them to the body of a man he stood over. "It's Dominic Green."

"And here's Chip Darby."

"Jesus," Eddie said. He ran a hand over his scalp. "It was a massacre. What the hell happened here?"

Finn shoved past him and ran for the bus at the top of the ramp. He screamed Bren's name.

"Wait!" Eddie shouted after him. "Let me."

He boarded the bus. But after quickly checking it front to back, he reappeared shaking his head. "They're not here. It's empty."

"No Bren or Seth or Kaleagh. No Largents or Caprios, either. That's at least nine missing. Where are they?"

"Plus at least a dozen more from the base unaccounted for."

"How could they have done this?" Kari asked. "There were no firearms in the bunker."

"Could they have taken the guns away from Cheever's men?"

"Disarmed them? And then done this? With only two casualties?"

"We are talking about Seth Abramson. I wouldn't put this past him."

"I don't see Ramsay's body," Eddie said. "I can smell him, so I know he was here."

"He did this? Why?"

"He didn't like Cheever," Jonah replied. "He might've killed the man to discourage anyone from the base seeking revenge."

"If it was him, then he wasn't alone," Bix announced. He stood at the doors and swung them away from the walls. "They left us a message."

The words had been scrawled across the scratched and faded surface in blood.

Eddie read them each aloud: *"Salvation . . . or damnation?"*

"Daddy?" Hannah asked. "What does it mean?"

"It means I know where they were taken," Finn said. "And why."

CHAPTER
43

"HORSES," FINN CONFIRMED. HE POINTED AT THE telltale pile of manure on the ground. There were several more within view.

"Maybe a half dozen, by the look of it," Susan noted. "But why didn't they take the bus?"

"Because it's dead," Jonah said. He pulled his head out from under the hood, where he was trying to figure out why it wouldn't start. "Battery's got juice, but the engine isn't cranking. By the smell, my guess is the motor overheated and seized."

"Even if it did work, Adrian wouldn't have taken it," Finn said. "He was anti-vehicle."

"Motorcycles are dead, too," Harrison said. "They pulled the wires."

"Not all of them." Eddie wheeled one of the bikes up the ramp. He straddled it and gave the starter a kick. It roared to life and ran for a moment before he switched it off again. "They must've been in a hurry. With a little luck we may be able to repair the others."

"Still doesn't explain why he didn't take them," Susan noted. "He couldn't have had enough horses for everyone to ride."

"What I don't understand," Eddie said, wiping the grease from his hands onto his pants, "is why he'd take our people."

"Revenge," Bix said.

Finn nodded. "For what we did to them back at the ranch. We destroyed his operation, exposed his lies. He took our people so Bix and I would follow him back there."

"But it'd be crawling with Wraiths by now," Bix pointed out.

"Exactly."

Understanding swept over Bix's face. "We've turned the place into one giant killing cage. He means to lure us in!"

Finn nodded.

"Then how do we stop him?" Susan asked. "Sun's going down. If we leave now, we'll be caught out on the road after dark."

"And if we leave in the morning, we may not catch them at all," Eddie said.

"They've got a solid head start on us," Finn acknowledged. "We still have to fuel up the truck. But he's also on horseback, which means they'll be taking the long way around. They'll be camping somewhere along the way tonight."

"Yeah, with everything booby trapped," Bix reminded him.

"Which is why we wait till morning."

"They'll be at the ranch by noon. There's no way we can catch him."

"We won't have to. We're going to cut him off before he does."

"How?"

"The footbridge." He pointed at the functioning motorbike. "And we're taking that thing across with us."

* * *

"You're freaking nuts. No, not nuts, you're insane—"

"In the membrane. I know." Finn smiled grimly at his friend. "But he's got Bren, not to mention Mia and Samuel Largent."

He remembered the flower drawing that Mia had colored for him, the one he'd stuck to the ceiling above his sleeping mat all those months ago. He'd lost it back at the ranch, along with the rest of his stuff.

His eyes drifted upward at the empty spot, and he felt his anger grow.

There had been little argument from the group, as daylight swiftly left the sky and shadows quickly spread over the land. There had been no time.

Jonah and Eddie worked together to draw fuel from the storage tanks down below and refill the truck. Harrison and Susan struggled with the motorbikes, but were unable to get any of the others to run. The rest of the group collected and repacked supplies in preparation for the next day's rescue.

Then they sealed themselves inside the bunker.

Finn could feel the darkness pressing against the walls of the dam, prying its fingers against the front door. He shivered. It was going to be a long night, and sleep was likely not in the cards.

Only after the rush to prepare and protect themselves did the others try to argue Finn out of his plan. But no one proposed a feasible alternative. Jonah was the exception. He said Finn's strategy was the only one with a reasonable chance of working. "They know we're coming. They'll be expecting us behind them, not ahead."

"Well, if you love the plan so much," Bix said, "then you can go with Finn. I'll happily give up my spot. I mean, have you seen this bridge? I literally peed my pants crossing it the first time."

Jonah could have jumped on the comment with a snide remark, but he didn't.

"Won't work with anyone else," Finn said. "Adrian wants the two of us. If he sees Jonah, he'll get suspicious and we lose the element of surprise."

There was a lot of grumbling about how difficult it would be to follow along out of sight until the right moment. Finn reminded them that Jonah had binoculars.

But the truth was, he didn't want any of them involved at all, including Bix, who was needed to get the bike across. Once on the other side, he planned to ditch him. Jonah would never let his guard down long enough to let himself be fooled in that way.

He intended to meet Adrian alone and negotiate for everyone's release. He would give himself up in exchange.

"Okay, so we stop the rat bastard on the road. Then what?"

"We hold him until the rest of you arrive in the pickup. Once we have him surrounded, he won't have any choice. He'll have to give up."

"You know I love you, Finn," Bix said, "and your theory about the Flense was brilliant. But that is about the lamest plan I've ever heard."

"It'll work," Jonah quietly said.

Finn couldn't explain it, but for some reason he suspected Jonah knew what he was planning.

They ate what they could — not because they were hungry, but because there was nothing else to do — then they settled in for the night in the game room. But Finn was restless and slipped out to return to the room he had shared for three years with his father.

Bix found him there a little later.

"Look at it this way, Finn. By this time tomorrow, it'll all be over. We'll have Bren back. And the rest. We'll take them to the camp. Then we'll find Twelve and screw the Flense."

Finn leaned back onto the worn and dirty cardboard and sighed unhappily. He wished he had his friend's confidence. Or even the ability to fake it. "You know, it's just been nothing but one disaster after another since we left here."

"The disaster started long before that, bro. None of this is your fault."

Except it was, it always was. After all, he had failed to stop Eddie from getting burnt in the boiler room. He hadn't noticed the missing food. He had pushed for them to leave. He had promised them they'd find Bunker Twelve.

For three years, their little group of thirty-one had remained safe. Then, in the space of two weeks, they had lost ten. If things turned bad tomorrow, they'd lose more.

He looked over at Bix, intending to disagree with his friend, but he was already, impossibly, asleep.

CHAPTER

THE TRAIL OF HORSE DROPPINGS MADE IT CLEAR THAT they were on Adrian's heels, not that there was any doubt in Finn's mind which way the madman had gone and where he was headed. Even stopping to double-check the manure's freshness, which Bix argued that Jonah should be an expert at, "since no one knows caca like Jonah knows caca," it took them just under two hours to reach the cutoff road leading to the cable bridge.

Adrian had made his camp at the junction. His fire was out and the ashes on top were cold, but the embers were still hot underneath. The ground showed evidence that a lot of people and horses had spent the night there.

Scouting the site, Kari nearly stumbled into a snare, but Eddie stopped her in time. He showed the group the tripwire and traced it back to a claymore mine buried just underneath the forest litter. They didn't know if it was meant for them or if it had been accidently missed in the morning's haste to leave.

Harrison carefully disconnected the trigger from the battery and spooled the wires around the mine, then slipped it into his pack. "No sense to leaving it behind," he said.

They also found another of the plastic boxes identical to the one Jennifer had given to Finn right before he and Bix escaped the ranch. A walkie-talkie was wired to it. Bix reached out to pick it up. This time it was Finn who stopped him. "Leave it alone." Worry creased his brow as he stood and peered into the woods around them. "I don't like it."

"But it might come in handy."

"We already have one and we don't know how it works or what it does. We don't need another."

They gathered as a group at the end of the bridge and looked out over the canyon. Jonah whistled in awe. The sound echoed back at them, sounding like the cry of an eagle. "Go ahead, Blakeley," he said, shaking his head. He gave them a wry smile. "I'll take the road. Meet you guys on the other side."

"Invitation's still open," Bix replied. He walked about ten feet out and stared for a moment straight down to the river far below before returning. Finn knew what he was looking for, but he didn't want to know if it was still down there.

"No thanks," Jonah said.

"Scared?"

"Never, but I'm not crazy, neither."

"It's stable," Finn said. "It'll hold."

"You sure about that? Maybe it'll hold you two weasels but that bike's got to run at least two-fifty. Which is more than the two of you put together. Soaking wet."

"Funny. Ha ha."

He clapped Bix on the back. "Just kidding. I'd probably piss myself, too."

"Ain't no shame in that."

"You two better get a move on," Harrison said. He handed Bix his pack and rifle. "There's extra ammo in there. Be careful. And remember what we talked about."

Bix nodded.

"I love you, son."

Bix blushed. But when Hannah stepped forward with a hug and whispered that she did, too, the blush deepened so much that Finn feared he might faint from oxygen overload.

Eddie wheeled the bike to the edge of the bridge. "How exactly were you planning on doing this?" he asked. "The base plates are barely wide enough to walk on. You'll either have to straddle the bike going across, or—"

"No way!" Bix said. "No freaking way anyone's riding the thing across."

"Then one of you will have to get in the front and pull on the handlebars and steer while the other pushes from behind."

"Then that's what it'll have to be," Finn said. He stepped forward and took hold of the handlebars. Bix didn't argue. He'd rather not have to walk backwards across the damn gorge.

Moving slowly and steadily, they made their way out over the canyon.

After fifteen minutes, they'd gone about a quarter of the way across. Finn straightened up to ease the cramp in his back. He waved the group on. They hesitated a moment longer, then turned and melted into the forest.

The sound of the truck engine reached their ears, then was gone.

"How are you hold up?" Bix asked.

They were still in shadow, as the sun hadn't yet breached the tree line, but they wouldn't be for long. Already, sweat dotted Bix's forehead.

"Not as bad as I thought it would be." He'd been so focused on keeping both his feet and the front tire on the narrow track that he'd stopped seeing the river far below.

"You need to rest, let me know."

"No, let's keep going."

"You see anything down there?"

"No. You?"

"Nope."

They continued on for another ten minutes. The cables seemed to creak all the more from the added weight, but the bridge didn't swing as much as it had the last time. It helped that there was no wind.

"What'd your father tell you?"

"When?"

"Back there. He said to remember what he told you."

Bix was quiet for a while. Finally, he said, "He thought my mom would be proud of me."

"She would."

He sighed. "You know, in the past, I wouldn't have taken it as a compliment. My dad and I were always the kids in the family and we liked it that way. Two peas in a pod is what she always said. And I always just thought that she was a total— Well, that she was always too stiff. It used to piss her off how little we took seriously. 'You'll never grow up, just like your dad.' That's why she left."

"Sorry."

"She was ashamed of us."

"Well, she—"

Finn's foot slipped off the side of the grate and he dropped to his knees. His rifle twisted on its strap, knocking him on the side of the head. The bike began to tip.

Bix struggled to keep it upright, throwing a hand out to the cable rail beside him and grunting from the effort. Finn scrambled back to his feet and righted it. For a moment, neither boy moved. They just stood there and panted, their faces white from the near-miss.

"Here's a suggestion," Bix said. "Don't do that."

"Yeah, I think until we reach the other side, less talking the better."

The bike probably wouldn't have fallen. The gaps between the support wires woven between the base and hand cables were small enough that the machine likely would have snagged on one. But even so, there would have been no way they'd be able to pull it back up onto the bridge if it had. They simply lacked the strength and leverage.

They reached what they thought was the halfway point, and each took a moment to rest and get some water.

"Want to switch places?" Bix joked.

Finn rolled his eyes.

"Just thought I'd ask, you know, to be fair."

"No, but when this is all done, you owe me."

"Name it. How about a nice busty Norwegian fully schooled in giving full body massages. And when I say full, I mean *full.*"

Finn snorted. "I think maybe that's your fantasy."

"Her name would be Helga. Helga Björgund . . . lund . . . son. That sounds Scandinavian, right?"

"Helga? You got something for Vikings?"

"Hell yeah.

Finn laughed. The bike started to shake, making him stop.

"Ready, bro?"

"Yeah."

Another twenty minutes passed. Finn's arms were shaking badly by then, and Bix didn't look so great either.

"You know you don't look so great," Bix panted.

"I was just thinking the same thing about you."

"How far do you think we've come?"

"Why don't you look?"

"I'm not looking anywhere but at my feet. And I refuse to see anything else but those damn metal grates."

Finn exhaled in exasperation. "Okay, stop." He planted himself, then looked up past Bix's shoulders. "About three-quarters of the— Oh, shit!"

"What?"

"Nothing," Finn said. "Don't look. Don't look! Just hurry!"

"What?" Bix whispered.

Finn tugged on the handlebars. He stepped back, no longer obsessing that his feet were planted exactly right in the center of the grate. His eyes weren't focused on the front tire anymore, they were glued to the other end of the cable bridge.

"How far?" Bix asked. His voice shook with terror.

"They're on the bridge."

CHAPTER 45

"LEAVE THE BIKE!" FINN SCREAMED AT BIX. "WE'RE not going to make it like this!"

"No!" Bix yelled back. "Keep going! We're almost there."

"Those things are almost half way across, Bix. We have to go! NOW!"

"Just forty more feet, Finn. You can do it. Come on, I know you can." He let go.

"What are you doing?"

"Keep going! Save Bren." He stepped away from the bike. "See? You got this."

Finn wobbled. "No! Push!"

Bix spun around, pulling the rifle to the front of his body and chambering a round. He kneeled as he took aim. "Go, Finn. I'll buy us some time."

"There are too many! They're coming too fast!"

"Go, dammit!"

Finn pulled hard on the motorbike and nearly fell off the platform again. He whimpered in fear, but kept going. A single shot rang out. Out of the corner of his eye, Finn saw something tumble off of the railing. It crumpled to the platform fifty yards away and rolled off.

"Are you going?" Bix cried.

"Yes!"

Bix aimed again and fired another round.

He missed! Oh my god, he missed!

Three rapid blasts followed, rippling through the canyon. In the distance, a figure jolted. It staggered forward, then seemed to recover. But it was soon overtaken by two more Wraiths right behind it and trampled into the metal.

How much further? How much further?

Finn could feel the angle steepen behind him, so he knew he was getting close. But the slope also made it harder to pull the heavy bike. His feet kept sliding. His hands kept slipping. The cramp in his back was beyond painful. It burned, sending spikes of pain into his neck.

The Wraiths had reached the halfway point. There was no way Bix would be able to stop them in time, not with bullets.

"Let's go!" Finn screamed. "Bix! I'm dropping the bike!"

"No!" Bix yelled back. "Don't you dare! It's the only way you'll be able to cut Adrian off!"

He fired off another three rounds, then set the rifle onto the grate at his feet.

Finn pulled harder on the handlebars, drawing the bike six more inches toward the edge. He watched as Bix pulled off his backpack, yanked the zipper open, and reached inside.

"What are you doing?" Finn yelled.

Bix didn't answer. His arms started to whirl.

The claymore! He's got the claymore!

Bix set the mine on the bridge, picked up his rifle and shot dead the closest Wraith before shouldering his pack and jogging back. "Go!" he shouted at Finn. "Go! Get off the damn bridge!"

With dawning horror, he realized what Bix was planning. And he knew what would happen when the mine exploded. "There's not enough wire, Bix!"

"I know! Go!"

The last ten feet were excruciating. The angle was almost too steep, and Finn's arms almost too exhausted that he nearly gave up. But the bridge supports suddenly appeared at his sides, and when he looked down, there was solid ground beneath his feet.

He dumped the bike and his pack and tried to raise the rifle to his shoulder. His arms shook so badly that he couldn't aim. He feared he'd hit Bix instead.

The Wraiths had reached the mine. Their movements threatened to knock it over the side. One kicked it and it spun along the grate before coming to a stop. It started to tilt off.

Bix was kneeling, trying to attach the wire to the battery and not paying attention.

"Hurry! Bix, they're—"

The mine exploded in a white flash. Finn threw the rifle away from him as he ran back out onto the bridge. The cables trembled and held. White smoke rolled toward the spot where Bix had been crouching, engulfing the Wraiths that had already passed the bomb. Bix was back on his feet, running, waving at him and screaming to get off the bridge.

Finn started to back up. He could feel the bridge shaking beneath him from Bix's pounding feet. Bix stumbled, sprawled and nearly fell off. But he was back up, grabbing the rail.

The bridge trembled as cables began to snap. Bix flailed for a moment. A half second later, a loud *TWANG!* tore the air. The bridge tilted to the side, throwing him back against the rail. He spun around. "Get off!"

"BIX!"

There was another loud, metallic snap. Finn jumped and landed hard.

By the time he spun around, the bridge was gone, and so was Bix.

CHAPTER

46

"BIX!"

Finn grabbed the unbroken safety cable and leaned as far over the side as he possibly could. The frayed and twisted remains of the bridge disappeared out of sight beneath him.

"Bix?"

A ball of white smoke, tinged red, hovered over the canyon like a bleeding apparition. It immediately started to dissipate and drift away.

Far below, scattered along both banks of the river, were the bodies of a dozen Wraiths. Finn searched for Bix among them, but he couldn't tell any of the mangled forms apart as they were all wearing the same desert camos.

He sucked in a sharp breath. These weren't just random Wraiths. This is where the rest of Cheever's men had gone. Adrian had infected them.

On the opposite side of the canyon, the other half of the bridge hung in a knot against the rock face. Wraiths still fell from it, their bodies crashing from one outcropping to the next until they slammed to the ground. None of them moved after that.

"Bix!"

"Well now, I have to say I did *not* expect that."

Finn spun around and came face to face with the business end of a rifle that looked all-too familiar.

"Ingenious way to escape them things. Not very smart for your buddy, I'm afraid."

Finn's eyes flicked to the spot where he'd thrown his rifle, but it was gone. A pistol rested in a holster against the man's hip.

"Come on now, boy," the man said. "I don't want you to hurt yourself, so why don't you step away from the edge. Slowly."

"Who are you?" Finn demanded.

"Shucks, shame on me for not formally introducing myself. Where are my manners?" He tipped his head slightly. "Name's Ramsay. Wayne Ramsay. And you are the young Finn Bolles, if I'm not mistaken. Somehow, I expected . . . more."

Finn stared at the man without replying.

"Sorry about your friend. Heroic thing he did for you. Such a waste."

Rage filled Finn.

"Come on now, boy. Let's go. I know someone who will be delighted to see you after all this time. Time does make the heart grow fonder, don't it?"

"If you've hurt her—"

"Oh, I ain't talking about that pretty little girl of yours. Bren, is it? Short for Brenda? Or is it Brendina?"

Finn's eyes narrowed. He flicked his gaze past Ramsay and into the woods behind him.

"Don't worry. She ain't here. It's just you and me. The good reverend — you remember him, right? — he's gone ahead. The rest of the party'll be coming along soon enough."

"How did you know we'd come this way?"

"Didn't, to be honest. But we needed to make sure no one tried to cut us off at the pass." He snickered at the joke. "May I call you Finnegan? Or is it Finnster?"

Finn tried to suppress his growing rage. He wasn't sure he'd be able to keep his cool. "You're one of Cheever's men, from the camp, aren't you? You're the one who arranged the deals with Adrian and Jennifer. You sold my friends to be turned into Wraiths."

"They begged to be saved, boy. They said, 'Save us, please! Save us!' Who am I to deny them that?"

"Liar!"

Ramsay gave him a fake frown. "You saying you don't believe in salvation? Then I guess there's no hope for your lovely Bren. Or anyone else, for that matter." He barked out a laugh that echoed across the canyon. "Of course it's a lie, boy! Everyone knows it! Everyone but that damned reverend and his sister!"

Sister? Jennifer was his sister!

"Your girl, now, I bet she begs good."

"You're sick."

He dismissed the insult with a shrug.

"Why did you kill Cheever?"

The man's smile faltered. "The captain? He couldn't lead himself out of a paper bag. Shame, though, that he had to go that way. He'd have made a good infected, like the rest of them."

"Why?" Finn gestured at the canyon. "Why infect all this people?"

Ramsay dug into his pocket with his free hand and pulled out a walkie-talkie. It looked just like the one they'd seen back in the camp. "Had to make sure you didn't escape back over the bridge. Amazing piece of technology, this thing. One press of the button puts them to sleep. Another wakes them up. No idea how it works, though."

Cold realization flowed through Finn. The Wraiths were never meant to reach them on the bridge. Bix had died for nothing, just as Ramsay had implied.

"Sure glad to see you brought a bike across. Either super brave or super stupid, but riding sure beats walking any day."

He waved the gun, urging Finn to his feet. Finn didn't move. "Come on, boy, get your sorry ass up. Don't make me hurt you."

"You won't. Adrian won't let you."

"Accidents happen. And if you're dead, he won't need pretty little Bren anymore. Be a shame to infect her, turn her into such a horrible, frightening thing. Of course, I could just let you watch first. The rev won't care. He can have her after I've had—"

"Bastard!" Finn leapt, but the man backhanded him across the face as easily as if he were swatting a fly. Finn went reeling into the dirt.

"Stop sniveling and stand up!"

Finn screamed in rage. He grabbed a fistful of dirt and threw it into the man's face. Ramsay backed away, spitting dust and coughing. He swiped at his eyes, swearing.

Finn tried to pounce, but the man was still too quick. He had the rifle up and pointed at his chest. Fury filled his bloodshot eyes. "Do that again and—"

"You're a sick man," Finn screamed. His voice echoed through the canyon. "If there is salvation, you'll never get it."

Ramsey spun the gun around in the air and raised it over his head, as if he meant to smash the butt against Finn's teeth.

Finn didn't move. "Go ahead," he growled. "Do it!"

They stared at each other for a moment, then the fury evaporated from Ramsay's face, replaced instead with a cold, hard, emotionless stare.

"Won't mess up that pretty face of yours before your girl gets a chance to see you."

He stepped back, chuckling. Then he sidled over to the edge of the gorge to check below. He kept the rifle pointed at Finn the whole time, his finger on the trigger and his eye on Finn's face, trying to judge if Finn might try to charge him again.

"Just need to make sure this Bix fellow— What the hell kind of name is that anyway? Bix? Sounds like the sound a bird makes when it's puking. *Bix! Biiix!*"

He laughed at Finn's rage.

"Just need to make sure that he's, you know, really dead before we leave."

Finn got to his feet.

"Uh uh! Stay right there." He raised the gun, seating it into the crook of his arm, then grabbed an anchor post for support and leaned over.

Finn stepped forward. He didn't care at that moment if he got shot. He couldn't let the man live. He took a step just as the shot rang out.

The man's head disappeared in a cloud of red. And when it cleared a moment later, half of his face was gone. He tilted further out over the side, as if it might help him see better, then he let go of the cable and fell.

A moment later, the muzzle of a rifle appeared over the edge. "You just going to stand there?" Bix panted. "Or are you going to give me a hand up?"

CHAPTER

47

THEY FOUND RAMSAY'S RUCKSACK JUST INSIDE THE LINE of trees. It was filled with food, water, and ammunition, although the rounds fit the pistol and so were essentially useless to them. They also found two more claymore mines.

There was no second motorbike in sight, however. He had crossed the cable bridge on foot and evidently planned to walk up to the main road.

"Junction's just a couple miles," Finn said, digging through the other pockets. He was still shaking badly and could barely speak.

"You're welcome, by the way. Climbing those damn metal cables was a pain in the ass."

"You think I'm going to thank you for that?" Finn snapped. "If you ever do something like that again, I'll—"

"You said that the last time, too, you know. Anyway it worked."

"I thought you were dead!"

"What else was I going to do?" Bix asked.

"I told you! Forget the bike! That's what I said. Run, I said! But no, you had to explode the freaking bomb and get yourself killed!"

"I didn't kill myself! And if I hadn't done that, those Wraiths would have been on us in seconds!"

"Actually not! That guy had this thing to control them. But now it's gone."

"I didn't know that!"

"If you had just listened to me," Finn panted, "if you had just run, then we both would have made it to the edge in time."

"And we'd have no motorcycle. And that asshole would be alive!"

"Gaaah!"

"I'll take that as a thank you and say you're welcome."

Finn didn't answer.

"Look, we've got the advantage now, bro. Adrian's not expecting to meet up with that guy until he gets to the junction, which means he'll be totally unprepared for us when we take him sooner. We've got the jump on him!"

He reached up to pry Finn's hands off of his shirt. "We got this, man."

Finn pushed himself away. "No, we don't! The plan never had a chance. The only reason we've gotten this far is because we got lucky. If that idiot hadn't stuck his head out for you to shoot—"

"I'd have blown it off after I reached the top. Come on, man, stop dwelling on what-ifs. Bren needs you. We all need you."

"I'm just going to get everyone killed. Everything I do is wrong. I'm not Harper!"

Bix punched Finn in the face, though not hard enough to knock him off his feet. "I've had it up to here hearing about Harper! You're not him! You're you. You make your own decisions."

"And look at all the people who've died—"

"Look at the ones you've saved!"

"Like who?"

"Byron and his sons. Plus who knows how many more. And it was you who figured out I'm immune!"

"That was just a guess! Jonathan and Danny and Nami are dead. Dominic, Chip—"

"You can't save everyone, Finn. Come on. Enough self-pity. We need to hurry before we lose our advantage."

He stood up and walked back over to the motorcycle and righted it. He wheeled it over, then switched his backpack to the front and got on.

"Let's go, Finn. And no slobbering on my shirt, either. I just got it and who knows when I'll be able to wash it again. I ain't going out in public with snot on my shoulder."

Finn snorted. "God, you're such an asshole."

"Yeah, well this asshole is driving, so you got shotgun. Literally."

He handed over their only remaining rifle, then leaned forward so Finn could get on behind him. "Just warn me if you plan on shooting anything, preferably things that are not part of either one of us."

They reached the end of the access road within minutes and turned onto the highway heading east.

All sorts of emotions were swirling through Finn. Aside from the shock and relief of what had happened back there at the bridge, he was embarrassed at his breakdown. He was supposed to be the stronger of the two. Bix was the more immature — he'd even said so himself — and yet when they were under pressure, Bix had been the one to think clearly. It was obviously a side of his friend he'd never known existed.

"Your dad was right, Bix," he said. "Your mom would be proud of you."

They rode for another half hour, discussing how best to take Adrian by surprise, and in such a way that didn't jeopardize the others.

"How many do you think he's got helping him?" Bix asked.

"Can't be many, I imagine. There were at least a dozen, dozen and a half, Wraiths back there. He'd need just enough men to be able to manage our nine— the Largents, Caprios, and Abramsons. I'm assuming he didn't turn them, since all the bodies I saw wore camouflage."

Bix didn't reply.

"So, maybe three others besides himself?"

"That's what I'm thinking. We only have the one rifle, so we can't pick them all off very easily, not before they take hostages and threaten to kill someone."

Finn was silent. He hadn't wanted to kill anyone, not unless he had to. It now looked like he'd have no choice.

Get it through your thick head that this is a different world, Finn.

It also made him realize that he hadn't even stopped to consider what Bix might be going through right now. After all, he'd just murdered a man.

Will I be able to kill, when the time comes?

Bix pulled over the side of the road. They'd just come to the top of a rise, and they could see the road stretching on for a good ten or fifteen miles ahead. It was the same road they'd traveled on after fleeing the ranch, but Finn didn't recognize any of the scenery. He'd been too hyped up to take notice.

"I've been thinking," Bix said. "Our only hope is to separate them. It's the only way it'll work."

"You have a plan?"

Bix nodded. "But we only got one shot at this. And it means both of us doing more killing."

CHAPTER

FINN SAT IN THE SHADOW OF AN OLD HIGHWAY SIGN and watched the group approach through the scope of the M4. His heart was racing and he felt lightheaded. He squinted against the glare off the road to see if he could spot Bren among the figures, but they were still a long ways off, little more than a blur against the gray-white of the horizon. The shimmering made them appear like a cluster of phantoms. He couldn't even distinguish the horses among them.

To his left was a rise. He couldn't see Bix in his hiding spot at the top, but he could feel him watching the procession through the binoculars they'd found in Ramsay's backpack. He hoped his friend was right, that when it started to go down, the reverend would react in the way they hoped he would. If not, then someone was likely to get seriously hurt, maybe even killed. And there was no backup plan.

He lowered his gaze to the rifle by his side. Ammo was not an issue, it was the accuracy of his aim. He'd had very little practice. In fact, he had had only the one chance to shoot the thing, and that was shortly after they left the base yesterday morning.

Kari had shown him how to sight properly, how to breathe and then hold the air inside, how to squeeze rather than pull on the trigger. His shots had been surprisingly accurate, and she'd been impressed, but that was when he was shooting at a rusty tin can from fifty paces, not at a living, breathing, walking human being. Not when other lives were at stake. Not when there was the possibility of shooting someone else instead by accident.

"You can do it," Bix had told him. "Go for the big man first. Shoot his horse out from under him if you have to."

"I'm not going to shoot a horse!"

"If it's a choice between the horse and Bren?"

Finn had stared at his friend for a moment, wondering when he'd turned into Jonah— cold and calculating, heartless. But then he realized Bix was right and the judgment passed.

The exchange still left him with an unsettling afterimage, a negative impression of Bix, like from one of those old time photographic films. There was definitely a dark, practical side to the boy, a side that the happy-go-lucky part of him masked.

"Can't we just hold them till the rest of the group catches up?"

"We have to hit them hard," Bix had said, speaking as if he were some kind of genius military strategist. "And this is the perfect spot."

Finn had no basis to challenge him, nor any reason to believe his plan wouldn't work. So he'd had to accept it. He had to admit it was no worse than his own plan, though he still didn't like the idea of shooting anyone."

"The first thing we need to do is get them separated. Then we pick them off one-by-one."

337

"Why am I the one doing the shooting?"

"Because I'm doing the separating."

The dark, shimmering spots finally resolved themselves into distinct people and horses. With a sinking feeling, Finn saw that there was also a large vehicle in the group. Before long, he knew that it was one of those military trucks. Bren and the rest of the survivors must be hidden inside.

"So much for not trusting automobiles," he muttered to himself.

They were still a quarter mile away when he could see them clearly enough to count the riders. There appeared to be three, one in front of the truck, two behind. They were moving at a fairly rapid clip, the riders pushing the horses in a fast trot.

Three riders— Adrian, Luke, and Billy, he thought, though he couldn't be sure. He didn't know if either of the boys had survived the Wraiths or the fire back at the ranch.

Three riders, plus one man driving the truck. Four shots, four bullets. And four pieces of his soul stolen away.

Bix has done more than his part. He killed Ramsay. He took your place in the cage and fought — and killed — Nami.

Nami was already gone.

He's done more than you have. What have you done, besides kill Jennifer? It's your turn.

He rotated the scope further down the road and thought he saw a sparkle, a reflection of light perhaps off a windshield way off in the distance. Was it the pickup truck?

He glanced again at the ridge. Could Bix see the second vehicle further off with the binoculars? He wiped sweat from his forehead and tried to work the kink out of his neck. Soon the horses would be directly in front of his hiding place. Then it was do or die time.

Moving carefully, in case the riders were scanning for movement, he settled down into the hollow beneath the sign and angled the rifle toward the nearest part of the road in front of him. He used a rock as a base. *Breathe, hold, sight, squeeze*, he thought. *Don't rush it.*

Now he could hear the clip-clop of the horse's hooves on the road and the whine of the truck's engine. The riders shifted positions, rotating, always in motion.

It still appeared to be just the three men. Finn's job was to take out Adrian. But he now realized he should first shoot the horseman — or horse*men* — guarding the back of the truck.

He nudged the scope to see the front rider's face. It wasn't Adrian. In fact, it wasn't anyone he recognized. The other two riders were on the other side of the truck, and the glare off the windshield prevented him from seeing the driver.

A hundred and fifty yards away, he heard the sudden buzz of a small engine, and a motorcycle appeared. It raced up the road ahead of them, clearly intending to scout the other side.

"Shit," Finn muttered. They hadn't expected someone on a motorbike. So, now there were four riders *and* the driver. And they didn't know who or what was in the back of the truck.

"Do it, Bix," he whispered to himself, as if his friend could somehow hear him. *"Take him out."*

The biker disappeared over the other side of the ridge as the caravan came to a stop below. The truck's brakes squealed; gears were shifted into neutral. The horses stamped their hooves restlessly.

Finn counted the seconds, but all he heard was the wind. A minute later, the rider reappeared and zoomed back down the road. "All clear!" he shouted.

"Dammit, Bix! What happened?"

A new horse rider appeared at the front. It was Luke. He gave a shrill whistle and waved them up the road. The horses clopped and pulled away. The truck revved its engine. The gears shifted. Then came the bang of a single gunshot.

Just one.

"What the hell?" Finn said, almost forgetting not to shout. "Who the hell is shooting?"

The sound of it rolled across the land, causing Luke to hold up a hand.

He turned and rode around to the back, yelling. The other two horse riders appeared. They separated from each other, moving to opposite sides of the road, and raced up the ridge with pistols in their hands.

Finn waited. Then came the muffled explosion of the claymore.

The truck driver shouted out his window. Luke went over to the motorcycle rider. "You said it was clear!"

"It was!"

Luke pulled a gun from his hip and aimed it at the man. "Did you check—"

A second explosion came, closer and louder this time. The horse reared back and nearly threw Luke off. But he had pulled the trigger. The motorcycle rider toppled off and lay still on the road. A woman's scream rose from inside the truck's canvas covering.

"Turn around!" Luke screamed at the truck driver. "Go back!"

Finn watched, then remembered what he was supposed to be doing. He lowered his cheek to the stock of the rifle and sighted. *Breathe, hold, sight, squeeze.*

Luke was perfectly outlined against the truck's canvas, but Finn couldn't shoot him. If he missed, or if the bullet passed through Luke's body, it might hit someone inside. He shifted the site to his left.

The driver's head came into view in the scope. He centered the crosshairs. The man was trying desperately to shift into reverse. He leaned forward just as Finn squeezed.

The rifle jumped against his shoulder, knocking the breath from his chest. Luke's horse jumped and he spun around, searching for the origin of the shot. He disappeared around the other side.

Finn focused on the inside of the cab. The driver was still alive, still trying to shift into reverse. After giving up, he decided to simply turn the truck around. Finn sighted again, but the driver disappeared in a flash of sunlight reflecting off the glass.

Shoot, Finn. Do it! Just shoot!

But he couldn't see. He was shooting blind!

Squeeze the trigger!

But if I miss, I'll hit someone in the back!

SHOOT!

Finn sighted onto the center of the driver's side of the windshield and prayed he didn't miss. He didn't bother with the breathing and the holding. He squeezed the trigger and felt the rifle jump again, only this time he remembered to pull it tight against his shoulder first. The truck kept turning.

Finn tried again to see inside the cab, but there was too much glare. The truck completed its rotation, and the cab was out of sight.

341

But now Luke was fully exposed. Finn swiveled the rifle toward him. Luke kicked his horse into a run, circling the truck again, shouting at the driver. People inside the truck were screaming. Finn tried not to be distracted by them.

The truck kept turning. It was coming back around again. Finn sighted the scope around the front as it came into view once more, and he saw the driver slumped over the steering wheel.

Luke reached the door and tried to get it open. His horse tripped and fell from underneath him. Luke clung to the doorframe as the poor animal was pulled beneath the tires. It screamed in pain and fear. The truck rolled over its flailing legs, snapping the bones.

Finn put it out of its misery with his third shot.

The truck came to a stop, stalling as it couldn't roll over the carcass. Luke immediately jumped off the running board and sprinted to the back.

"Come on," Finn growled. "Where's Adrian?" He was shaking from the adrenaline. He'd just shot and killed a man. But shooting the horse had been worse. "Show me that rat bastard Adrian!"

In the new quiet, Finn heard the stumbling gait of hooves at the ridgeline, and he swiveled the rifle there. A horse appeared. Its side was wet with blood. The rider was gone. Bix had succeeded. Now there was only Luke.

And Adrian. Where the hell is he? Is he in the back of the truck?

Finn lifted his head to look to the horizon. The glint from before was still there, a little more pronounced. He thought he could see a cloud of dust rising up behind it, but they were still too far away.

"Give it up, Reverend!" Bix shouted from his hiding place. "Four of your men are dead. In just a few minutes, you're going to be surrounded!"

A figure appeared around the other side of the truck. Finn thought it might be Adrian, but it wasn't. It was Luke again. He held someone tight against his chest. "Go ahead and shoot," he cried up at the hill. "But you better not miss!"

"No!" Bren shrieked. "Please no!"

CHAPTER 49

LUKE WAITED. "YEAH, I DIDN'T THINK SO. COME OUT and let's talk."

"Oh, I'm good right here," Bix yelled back.

"Why don't you tell the reverend to come out," Finn called from his hiding spot. "We'll talk with him."

Luke spun around and tried to locate him in the trees. He didn't seem to realize that Finn was a lot closer. "No, you talk to me. Father Adrian is . . . a little busy right now."

"Tell Luke to let her go, Reverend!" Finn shouted. "Take me instead. Leave everyone else."

Luke's eyes turned to the sign. He smiled. "I see you hiding there."

"Stay cool, Finn!" Bix yelled. "It's all of us or nothing!"

"Bix!"

"Stay right where you are, Finn!"

Luke laughed at their disagreement and pulled Bren tighter against him. She struggled and let out a soft cry. She couldn't do much, as her hands were bound behind her back.

"If you hurt her," Finn shouted, "so help me God, I'll—"

"What?" Luke snapped. "God don't help sinners."

"Look up the road," Bix said. "Our friends are going to be here in less than five minutes. You'll be surrounded. There's no way you'll get out of this alive once they arrive."

"Then we all die. Y'all got till the count of five to come out, unarmed. Or else I put a bullet in this pretty little lady's brain."

"Wait—"

"One two, buckle my shoe!" Luke shouted in rapid succession. "THREE FOUR CLOSE THE FUCKING DOOR! I swear, I will shoot her!"

"No! Okay! Stop!" Finn stood up and stepped to the side of the highway sign. He held his hands up to show that he didn't have a gun. "I'm unarmed. Don't hurt her!"

"Finn!" Bren yelled. "No!"

"Tell the other one to come out, too!"

"I'm here," Bix said, appearing at the top of the hill. He was fully exposed in the sunlight, silhouetted against the sky. But from that distance, Luke had little chance of hitting him, especially with Bren struggling beneath him. Finn was the easier target. "Stay cool, Finn."

"Hands up where I can see them!"

Bix raised his hands. "Where's the reverend? We talk to him only!"

"You talk to me!" Luke shouted back.

"Why are you doing this?" Finn asked again. "What did we ever do to you?"

Bix started to descend the hill. Luke raised the pistol and screamed at him to stay right where he was. "Don't come any closer. Y'hear?"

He began to drag Bren toward the back of the truck, keeping her between him and the boys. The motorcycle rider on the road was beginning to stir. Finn realized that Luke had shot him only with a stun gun.

Why shoot him at all?

"Get up!" Luke grunted at him.

But the man just groaned and didn't move.

"Useless piece of sh—" He kicked the man again, then whipped the pistol around and shot him.

A small spray of red appeared in the air. The figure jerked and grabbed his leg. Bren screamed, but it was drowned out by a louder cry of anguish from the back of the truck. A body fell out and onto the road, hitting the hot pavement with a sickening crunch.

"Why are you doing this?" Finn yelled, as Luke holstered the gun and replaced it with a knife.

The fallen person struggled upright, still keening. Finn saw that it was Maria Caprio, and with a sickening feeling in his stomach, he knew before Luke cut her bindings that the motorcycle rider in the helmet was her husband, Vincenti.

It sickened him to realize that Luke had sent one of their own ahead to scout ahead, perhaps suspecting an ambush. Whether luck or intuition, Bix hadn't set off the claymore to kill him.

But now Vincenti lay on the road writhing in agony and cursing.

Luke pulled Maria up by her hair, separating her from her husband, and ordered her to start walking toward the approaching pickup truck. "Make sure they stop! I don't want them to get any closer."

"No! I won't!"

Another shot rang out, and Vincenti screamed again and clutched at his other leg.

346

"Oh no!" Maria shrieked. But Luke pushed her brutally away.

The pickup truck was clearly visible now in the distance.

Luke watched her limp up the road before turning and pushing Bren toward Finn.

"The good Lord don't tolerate unrepentant sinners, boy," he said.

He came to a stop about thirty feet away. Bren was shaking terribly beneath his arm, which he'd wrapped tight around her throat.

"And you, my boy, are about as unrepentant as they come. That's what the reverend says."

"He has a twisted idea of what those things mean," Finn spat.

He had taken the opportunity of Luke's distraction with the Caprios to grab the rifle. He now had it sighted on Luke's head. But he was shaking and unsure he could even pull the trigger.

"Why doesn't he come out and tell me that himself?" Finn asked, his voice rising. "Or is he a coward?"

The muscles in Luke's arm rippled as his grip on Bren's neck tightened, choking her. She tried to struggle, but he jammed the pistol hard into her side. "That's better, honey," he said into her ear when she stopped fighting.

"Let her go," Finn said. He tried to keep his voice steady. He had to do something soon, or else Bren would die anyway. She was turning blue. And the pickup truck had stopped too far away to be of any help. It was up to him. But what could he do? "Take me instead. It's me you want."

"Yes, it is." Luke jerked his head to the side. "Drop the gun before you hurt someone. Start walking. To the truck."

"Leave her here."

"No, I don't think so." He brought the pistol up to her neck. "Drop it or I'll put a bullet in her."

"Then you'll die, too."

The smile on Luke's face twitched. But at least the color was returning to Bren's face. He started to back away. "Let's go."

Finn followed, keeping the rifle trained on Luke's head. "Tell Adrian to come out!"

They were getting closer to the back corner of the truck. Finn knew he'd have to act soon. If he didn't—

Gunfire erupted to Finn's left, somewhere near the top of the hill. He almost turned to look. Luke did, however, jerking the pistol in the direction of the ongoing shots. It was all the distraction Finn needed.

At the same time, as if sensing that it was her only chance to escape, Bren ducked out from under his arm. Luke spun back, opening his mouth to yell, but Finn had already centered the site of the rifle on his temple.

The bullet entered the man's head just above the left eye. He stood for a moment with his mouth agape, then he fell.

But so did Bren.

CHAPTER
50

THE GUNFIRE ON THE RIDGE ABRUPTLY STOPPED. FINN barely noticed. He fell to his knees beside Bren, calling her name and pulling at her body, rolling her onto her back to find the bullet wound. There were cuts all over her arms and face, but he couldn't find the one that had sent her down.

"*Fihhhn...?*" she whispered.

Her eyes fluttered open, but her gaze was unfocused. A heartbeat passed before it cleared. Then she was in his arms, sobbing. He clutched her to him, realizing she'd only fainted.

But then he was pushing her away, getting to his feet.

Adrian! his mind screamed. He'd somehow gotten ahead of them. That was the gunfire! But who was he shooting at?

Bren pulled him back. She wouldn't let him go. She scratched at his arms and legs and sobbed.

"I have to finish this!" he said, and stripped her hands from him. He ran back to the rifle and picked it up. "It's over, Reverend!" he yelled, and aimed at the ridgeline. Bix was gone. Finn angled for the back of the truck. "Or do you want to die, too?"

He swung around, backpedaling on the tarmac so he could see inside the canvas covering. But Bix was already there, standing on the bumper and leaning in. He turned and yelled at Finn not to shoot. "He's not here."

Finn froze. "But—"

"How about pointing that thing somewhere else, Ace?"

"Whuh— Where is he?" Finn spun around and scanned their surroundings. Next he checked underneath the truck. "Where is he? Where did he go?"

Bren grabbed his arm. "He's not here, Finn. He never was."

"What?" He swiveled the rifle to the ridgeline again, expecting to see the man and several others coming over it. "I heard gunshots."

"That was me, Finn," Bix said.

"How?"

"First things first. Let's get the others untied and Mister Caprio's legs bandaged up." He whistled at the retreating figure of Maria in the distance and waved her back. The pickup had reached her by then. They stopped to bring her back.

Finn turned back to Bren. He couldn't believe it was over so easily. She was still alive. They were all still alive.

She hugged him tight again, then bent down to attend to Mister Caprio.

The road beneath him was wet with his blood. The pool spread, looking too big. But Finn knew it could've been worse. He also knew he'd survive. He might not walk again. Or, if he did, it would be with a limp. But he'd live. He had those things inside his body, fixing him.

Bren tore a strip from his tattered shirt and began to bind one of the wounds.

Bix appeared out of the back of the truck again, Mister Largent by his side rubbing his wrists. Finn's eyes widened. "Are Sammy and Mia—"

"Fine," Mister Largent said, his voice a croak. "They're all fine. Scared, but unhurt."

Together with the men from the pickup, they managed to lift Mister Caprio into the bed of the army truck and out of the sun. They gave him water from one of the packs.

"They made me scout ahead," he said, his face white with pain. "I'm sorry. They said they would kill Maria if I didn't."

Finn stood back and watched as everyone greeted each other. There were tears of relief and hugging. Only the elder Abramsons held back.

Seth glared accusingly at Finn. He refused to lift a finger to help. Kaleagh Abramson stared into the corner, as if deeply ashamed. Finn was too angry at Seth to feel bad for her.

Bix stood off to the side, explaining to his father and Jonah how he'd used a small fire to set off one of the pistol rounds at the beginning, then a handful after he'd emerged from his hiding place.

"It was Finn who took out the driver, though. I don't think I could have made that shot myself."

Finn did not feel heroic at all. He didn't feel relieved. He didn't even feel lucky. Instead, he just felt restless, like there was unfinished business. And he felt like they were all sitting ducks in the middle of the road.

Kari and Harrison Blakeley returned in the pickup truck from the other side of the hill and declared that it was, indeed, clear. They'd found the bodies of the two dead horsemen and one dead horse. The claymores had done a job on them, but from their description, Finn knew that one of them had been Billy.

He pulled Bix away. "Why wasn't Adrian here?"

"He must've chickened out."

"The man in charge?" Bren said. "He left us before we even left the bunker. They told us he was going to get ready for when you arrived."

"That doesn't make any sense," Finn said. "All of this, this charade, it was done to lure me and Bix back to his ranch. He was using you as bait. He wanted to sacrifice us all. Why wouldn't he be here to make sure it worked?"

"Because he screwed up," Bix said. "He didn't expect us to win. We did. End of story."

Finn scanned the landscape, looking for any sign of the man.

"The guy can wait forever, for all I care," Bix said. "We've got better things to do."

Finn turned to the others, looking for answers. "This doesn't feel finished."

"It is. You got Bren back."

"But—"

"Can't you just be happy it's over?" Seth spat. He jumped out of the back of the truck and approached Finn. "It's over."

Finn stared at him for a moment before realizing that it really was. He let out a breath, which seemed to deflate him, and he crumpled to the road. Bren came to him and held him.

The others dragged the bodies off the road, then took stock of their supplies. A small argument broke out between them, as they discussed the merits of returning to the dam versus going to the army base.

Finn ignored them. He didn't care anymore where they went. Harper was gone, and Bren was safe. He was done making decisions. He just wanted to crawl into a hole.

"Back off, Seth!" Eddie's shout snapped Finn out of his thoughts. He looked up and saw Missus Abramson cowering beneath her husband's glare. "Let her have her say."

"She's got nothing to say! Kaleagh, get back on the truck. Sit down and shut up!"

"No," she screamed, and slapped her husband across the face. "How could you not tell him?"

"So he can drag us all through hell again? That's what started this, remember?"

"Tell who what?" Eddie demanded. "Kaleagh?"

"Keep your mouth shut," Seth growled.

"Mom?"

The woman pushed herself away from Seth. "How could you? I'm so ashamed."

"We are going back to the dam and nowhere else!"

Harrison and Jonah stepped forward and grabbed an arm each. Together, they pulled Seth away from her. "Let her speak."

Finn stood up and walked over to her. "What is it?" he asked. "What is he not saying?"

"We have to keep going," she said, sobbing. "You can't go back."

"Keep going where?"

"Stop it!" Seth shouted.

"He deserves to know, Seth!"

"Know what?" Finn asked.

"That man you call the reverend," Missus Abramson said. "He didn't care if you got Bren back. He knew you'd have to go after him anyway."

"Why?"

"You bitch! You'll get us all killed!" Seth roared. "Is it worth it?"

Finn stepped closer to Missus Abramson. "Why do I have to keep going after him?"

"Because he has your brother."

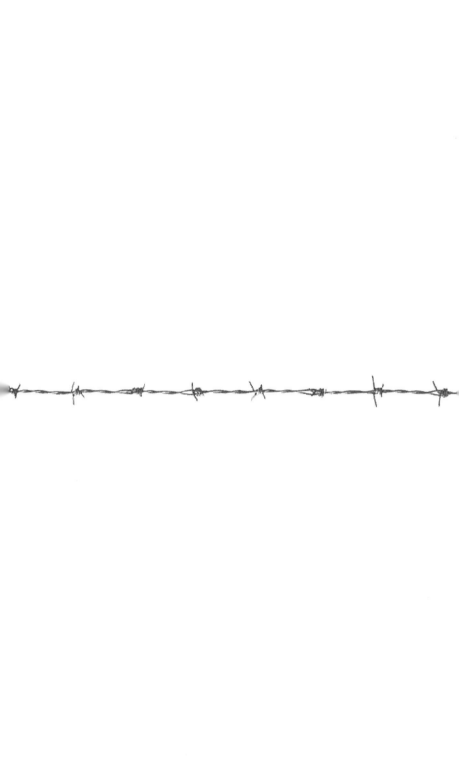

If you like post-apocalyptic and dystopian worlds, check out
S.W. Tanpepper's epic cyberpunk series GAMELAND

Golgotha (prequel)
The Series:
Episode One: *Deep Into the Game*
Episode Two: *Failsafe*
Episode Three: *Deadman's Switch*
Episode Four: *Sunder the Hollow Ones*
Episode Five: *Prometheus Wept*
Episode Six: *Kingdom of Players*
Episode Seven: *Tag, You're Dead*
Episode Eight: *Jacker's Code*
Velveteen
Infected: Hacked Files from the GAMELAND Archive
Signs of Life (Jessie's Game Book One)
A Dark and Sure Descent
Dead Reckoning (Jessie's Game Book Two)

AVAILABLE IN DIGITAL AND PRINT
eBooks 1 and 2 are free!

http://www.tanpepperwrites.com/gameland

SAUL TANPEPPER is the creator of the acclaimed cyberpunk dystopian series, GAMELAND. A former army medic and PhD scientist, he now writes full time in several speculative fiction genres, including horror, apocalyptic, science fiction and paranormal. A frequent world traveler, his works are heavily influenced by these experiences and his background as a biotechnology entrepreneur. He currently resides in California's Silicon Valley with his wife of more than twenty years and his two children. He is the author of the story collections *Insomnia: Paranormal Tales, Science Fiction, & Horror* and *Shorting the Undead: a Menagerie of Macabre Mini-Fiction.*

To receive updates, subscribe to Saul's e-newsletter, *Tanpepper Tidings*

https://tinyletter.com/SWTanpepper

For more information about this and his other titles, visit www.tanpepperwrites.com

Made in the USA
Middletown, DE
11 January 2021

31352523R00217